Coyle and

Book one: Curse of Shadows

By

Robert Adauto III

Edited by Amanda Bidnall

This is a work of fiction. All of the characters, organizations and events portrayed in this novel are either products of the author's imagination or are used fictionally.

The story takes place in historical San Francisco, 1892. For the purposes of the story, I have added fantasy and engineering elements which would be out of place in the real world given the time period.

CHAPTER 1

Military vault Archangel

Clark's Point

San Francisco, April 1892

"The best laid plans of mice and men often go awry," quoted Drake as he stuffed a wad of chew into his lip.

"What's that?" asked Gerrick, leaning down. His eight-foot, heavily-muscled frame was built like a freight train. Most ogrek were hairless, covered in tribal tattoos, and faithful to their employers, making them easy second in commands for special missions.

"Mail Pouch chewing tobacco," Drake said. "It's out of West Virginia. Want some?"

"Not that." Gerrick waved his hand. "What was it you said?"

"Ah, that." Drake folded the paper pouch and stuffed it into his pocket. "That was Robert Burns, a Scottish poet. Talking about things going wrong. It popped into my head just now, but it seems apropos."

Gerrick squinted at Drake.

"It means appropriate given the situation," Drake said while he chewed.

"Like something might go wrong?"

Drake nodded his head and spit a line of tobacco juice.

"Let's hope not. Tonight's not the night for things going wrong," Gerrick said.

"Amen to that."

There were twenty-four mercenaries in all, each of them armed with a bowie knife, carbine rifles and the combat skills to use them with efficiency. But no amount of muscle, armor, or weapons could prevent fate from dropping in. And it always did, unannounced and uninvited. But, as with all mercenaries, when there was a risk, there was a reward—and their pay tonight was more than enough to drive a man or ogrek to the edge of the abyss.

Their job was simple: break into a secret military storage warehouse, secure a very dangerous asset and get her out to the next objective.

Very simple. But not easy.

Drake was the perfect man for the job. He was one to plan very carefully and prepare for everything. He was given free rein to choose who, and how many, to take on this mission. The suggested number was ten, but he opted for twenty-four. Twice the number of the guards. He still felt as if he needed more.

Rain gushed from the night sky and drenched the mercenaries as they hid among abandoned storehouses and studied the scene with a careful eye. Their target warehouse was just ahead, a faded blue shadow through the torrential downpour. There were two sentries posted at the wrought-iron gate, but the rest were invisible. This was typical for a high-priority, top-secret installation. If a dozen guards were plainly seen on a regular basis, everyone would know it was a high-priority, top-secret installation. Best to pretend it was merely private property owned by the United States government. No trespassing. Move along.

Drake had received word that the veteran warehouse guards had been given a week off and replaced with fresh-faced, knock-kneed twigs, making them much easier to take down. After scouting the guard's locations, Drake nodded. Gerrick gave the signal, and they advanced as a single unit: swift, silent and deadly.

They met and overpowered every guard before anyone could raise an alarm. One by one, their limp bodies were tossed over the railing into the frigid waters of the San Francisco Bay with slit throats. Within moments, the mercenaries arrived at the gate and used forged keys to gain entry. The iron gates swung wide, and the men poured inside like water through a levee.

An automaton sentry waited just outside the main entrance, shielded from the rain by a canvas tarp. It was a simple, human-shaped mechanical apparatus with one purpose: to either grant access inside, or sound an alarm that would bring half of the US Army upon them. It swiveled to life and turned its small, circular head toward the group. A line of small bulbs on its head served as eyes. Its stainless-steel body pockmarked from exposure to the sun and briny ocean air. Three thin, multi-jointed arms hovered over various switches and buttons on a lighted control panel.

"Access key?" a mechanical male voice asked politely through a small rectangular speaker.

"Archangel," Drake said. He spat a line of brown chew before he wiped his face with the back of his glove. Twenty-five years of chasing Comanche through the scrub and sun had made his skin leathery and worn. His time in the desert had also worn away his patience. He sighed and glared at the machine.

There were a series of mechanical clicks and taps before it replied, "Access granted."

Its thin metal hand pulled a switch, and the armed men filed through the armor-plated double doors. A string of electric lights flicked on, and Drake glanced at a similar automaton sentry on the inside. Its shiny dome was powered off. He'd been assured the indoor sentry would not be an issue. He blinked and let his eyes adjust to the new light.

The warehouse was wide and tall and filled with endless rows of stacked wooden crates of all sizes. Most of the crates bore the symbol of the Templars painted in black. An occasional stray rat scampered through the man-made terrain, and by all appearances, it looked just like any other waterfront warehouse at Clark's Point. But many of these warehouses were secretly owned by the government, and this particular one was especially "under the black"; so top secret most of the generals of the US had no knowledge of what lay therein.

Gerrick tapped the black symbol on one of the crates. "A dagger with a snake wrapped around it. Interesting."

Drake grunted. "Templars of the Unseen Path. A bunch of righteous characters trying to keep evil away."

"Why are the symbols crossed out?"

"These Templar jokers started something they couldn't control, so the government took over."

"*Archangel* was the passcode. Is that her code name as well?" Gerrick asked. The two had worked numerous jobs together, and Drake was patient enough for Gerrick's incessant curiosity.

"No, that was the name of the program they were running. Project Archangel," Drake explained. "Ever read *Frankenstein* by Mary Shelley?"

"I-I don't read," Gerrick said. He quickly added, "Not my thing."

"Well, it's about a scientist who made a monster, and this here warehouse is full of monsters made by scientists."

"And you think this asset we're picking up will help us?" Gerrick asked, wiping rainwater off his bald head.

"Pretty sure we're not asking," Drake said. He studied a blueprint for a few moments. "This one is the most dangerous of the bunch, so we'll need to be careful."

Drake gazed at the various paths lining the paper and shook the water off his Stetson before making a decision.

"She's down on the left here," he said, and the men followed him deeper through the winding maze of crates and barrels. There was a heavy metallic *snap!* and they paused.

"Front door locked?" Gerrick asked.

"Astute," was all Drake said, and spit his chew. He scratched at the grayed stubble on his jaw and kept walking.

"Will we need a password to get out? Or will the first one work?" Gerrick asked. His voice was a tad higher than normal as he looked behind him.

"We'll be fine," Drake said. "Let's get to the target and get the hell out of here."

They finally arrived at rows of boxes, each separated by heavy wooden beams embedded with curious, glowing orange gems. Gerrick drew close and squinted.

"Don't touch anything," Drake hissed.

"What are they?"

"Aurorium. Harmless to us but a formidable hindrance to what's inside these boxes. Kind of like barbed wire on a cattle fence. Except this stuff keeps these creatures weak enough that they won't cause anyone trouble," Drake said.

They gazed down the long corridor of iron boxes separated by glowing orange dots. Each box rose in height to their shoulders and was wide as an arm span with a padlocked hatch for access. Drake covered his nose and mouth. The odor of bodily excretions, mixed with a strange musk, flooded the air.

Whispers and guttural voices, low growls and snuffling echoed through the cavernous space as they arrived at a cage marked *Fang-0120*. Gerrick and the others stared at the dark slits of the cages, expecting inhuman claws to reach out at them. The hardened mercenaries kept a wary eye out and their rifles ready.

"Are those slits for air?" Gerrick asked, rubbing his nose.

"No, they're for administering pain compliance," Drake said. With a grunt, he dropped his pack and pulled out a white metal rod with an aurorium tip. He twisted the rod and pulled it out to its full length.

"Here, take this." Drake handed the rod to Gerrick. "Shove it in there."

Gerrick glanced at Drake before jabbing the glowing end inside. A piercing shriek made him jump back. The ogrek shot toward Drake with something close to stark terror.

"She sounds like a woman," Gerrick said. "Not a vampire."

"And what are vampires supposed to sound like?" Drake squinted at Gerrick before he turned to the cage and rapped his knuckles against it.

"You awake now? Good. Allow me an introduction. My name is Drake and I'm in charge of this little operation." He thumbed towards the ogrek. "And this here's Gerrick. You are …?"

There was a rush of panicked breathing before a weak answer came back.

"Fang."

"Pleasure to meet you, Fang." He tipped his hat. "The boys and I have heard so much about you. Now, I have some questions. Have you heard of *The Curse of Shadows*?"

"Yes," Fang whispered in pain.

"You sure?"

"Positive." Her British accent was clipped yet somehow attractive given the situation. Gerrick squinted through the narrow opening but there was nothing to see but inky darkness.

"Well, a couple of guys stole it. Maybe you know their names. Trevin and Moreci?"

"I know them," she hissed.

"I was tasked with finding this book, and I think you might have an interest in finding them. But just so we're absolutely sure, can you tell me what the book is all about?" he asked.

There was a long pause before she responded. "It's a very old, very rare book created in the nether-realm. It curses people into monsters. They tried to use something similar on me, but… it didn't work properly."

"Sounds about right," Drake said. He looked around. "Then let's get this association between us straightened out. You work for us, and we don't kill you, understand? If you hop out of place, we will kill you. If you try to change our plans, we will kill you. If you look at Gerrick's neck the wrong way, we will kill you."

Gerrick frowned and rubbed his neck.

Drake pulled out an aurorium bullet and turned the glowing end in front of her.

"See this? Forty-five-caliber aurorium shell. Pretty sure this'll put a good-sized dent in you. And they gave us a few between the twenty-four of us. Are we clear?"

"Crystal."

"And the matter's settled. Gentlemen," he said, and pointed to a corner. "We'll need those iron rods to move her cage out." Four heavily muscled men moved to obey.

Drake and Gerrick stepped away as the men tugged the cage out into the open space. The space around them awakened with grunts and snarls as the men dragged iron across concrete.

Gerrick shot a look at Drake. "This is all real, isn't it? These are real vampires?"

"Not all of them," Drake said. "There's more preternatural beings here than just vampires. Hell, if you want just vampires, go to the Sierra Madre del Sur, Mexico. Vampires up to your damn eyeballs. Up here? Well, they want a little of this and that. The US military's a finicky bunch."

"How old is she?" Gerrick rubbed his neck again.

"She looks young. Maybe early twenties?" Drake squinted at the lights. "But, of course, she's a vampire, and I hear she's been around a few hundred years."

"So what's going to happen to her afterward?" Gerrick asked.

"We don't care," Drake said, directing the men to the lift points. "I'm supposed to hand the book and her over to the buyer, and after that, it's up to them. Maybe they'll make her into a house pet or something. Who knows?"

The men eased the cage out when a sudden, violent jolt from inside made them drop it. The others readied their weapons at the growing unrest around them. Drake shouted and got them back to on task. With wary glances, they moved closer as the vampire within growled low and deep.

"How are we supposed to control her?" Gerrick asked, staring at the iron box.

"She's kept feral until needed. Molded by the best technicians, scientists and psychologists. See this?" Drake pulled out a small wind-up music box. He turned the crank, and a soft melody chimed. The change in behavior was instant, and the malicious sounds turned to soft, comforting whispers.

"She likes music?"

"*Music hath charms to soothe the savage beast.*" Drake winked. "William Congreve. Curious, isn't it? That's all she is. Another beast that God gave man to dominate. And a woman, at that. All of these, every one of them, raised and created to be weapons of war and covert operations. Now, this one here is quite the clever one and supposedly the most dangerous of them all, but she'll do just fine with us in control." He pointed to the orange gem at the end of the rod. "The aurorium is about the only thing that can kill her. Who knew the rarest of minerals, with the same energy properties as a bolt of lightning, would be deadly to vampires and her ilk. Here, give me that."

He pulled the rod out of Gerrick's hands and shoved it into the cage until her screams were long and bloodcurdling.

"See? Just a beast, tamed under the thumb of God's superior creation." Drake tapped his chest. "Let's go."

The murmurings from the other cages grew into growls and shouts. The men ignored the unnatural clamor. Some of the creatures stretched out, trying to grasp at them as they journeyed down the rows. Some hands were massive and covered with coarse hair. Others were unnaturally thin with open sores and rotting skin. Still others had thick, scaly flesh and webbed hands.

The mercenaries carried their prize through the maze with haste and assumed confidence. Some of the men tried to glimpse their captured prey, hoping to see what a real vampire looked like—not knowing they would witness a vampire's fury before the night was over.

"Ain't nobody here seen one of these?" Drake asked the men who peered into the dark cage. No one responded. "There's an old wives' tale that says if you spot a vampire that means it's been hunting you." He laughed. "But tonight, we're the hunters. We got this, *comprende*?" Drake nodded, and a few responded with nods of their own, though their nervous eyes told otherwise.

Arrived at the doors, the sentry automaton blinked on and swiveled its head around to face them.

"Access key?" it asked.

"Archangel," Drake said with a huff.

"Password not recognized," it said. "Should we try again, or should I activate the alarm?"

"I said the password is *Archangel*," Drake repeated.

"Password is not recognized," the metal sentry repeated. "Should we try again, or would activating the alarm be a suitable alternative? You have fifty-five seconds to decide before the defaulted alarm is raised."

"I said the password is *Archangel*, you metal twit!"

"You have fifty seconds to try again."

"If you don't get this right, we'll have the First Infantry on our asses," Gerrick added.

Drake rubbed his face hard and took his hat off to wipe the sweat from his brow.

"There's only so much incompetence I'm going to tolerate," Drake sighed. "That's the damn password."

"Obviously it isn't," said Fang. "Good thing I know what it is."

Everyone shared a glance as slim hands slipped out and casually rested through the opening. Thin scars lay in haphazard streaks across fair skin. Her fingernails appeared normal, though dirty and chipped. Not the eagle's claws he was told to watch for. Drake squinted into the cage. He pulled the strap of his carbine closer.

"You have thirty seconds to try again," the sentry said as roars and howling echoed through the cavernous building.

"You don't appear to be feral," he said to Fang.

"And you don't appear to know how to properly break someone out," she said. A heart-shaped face materialized within inches of the opening. A face too beautiful to be kept in an iron cage. Eyes the color of glowing embers shifted and studied the group, one by one until they settled on Drake. Her expression was demure, coy, curious. A playful smile crept across her full, pink lips.

Ice slinked down Drake's back.

"You're stuck in a top-secret military weapons cache surrounded by… *monsters*, and you didn't know there were two passwords. You didn't think this one through, did you?" Fang's eyebrows scrunched together as she pouted.

"Why the hell would I listen to you?"

"Do you know how many men are in an army regiment?" she asked. "A thousand or more against twenty-four of you. Sounds reasonable," she said. "And me? Well, they'll just put me back in my corner until it's time to play."

Drake shot a look around, hands clenching at his sides. He pulled out his handgun and pulled the hammer back.

"What if I stick the barrel of my Colt in your pretty little nose and threaten you with a face full of aurorium?" He raised the weapon at her.

"It won't change the fact the Army is coming." She shook her head and gazed steadily at his sweat-lined face.

He pulled the gun away. "What do you want?" he hissed.

"The music box." She held out her hand.

Drake studied her smiling, kind face. "I give you the music box, and you let us out. I may as well trust a rattlesnake."

"You have fifteen seconds to try again," the mechanical voice echoed.

"Uh oh." She pouted.

Drake cursed, and slammed the music box into her waiting palm. "There! Now you have it. Open the damned door, or we're all dead!"

"You have five seconds to try again."

"No need to tremble, little boy," she teased. "*Abyss*," she said.

"You have… gained egress," the sentry said, and the huge doors unlocked and pulled open. Fang pulled the toy inside, and the soothing music played from the small confinement as the men shoved the cart outside into the downpour.

"I ain't sure if this was worth the gold," Drake said.

Through the sheets of rain, the chimes of the music box played along with the soft whispers of the vampire. Those near glanced at each other as she whispered with a kind, loving voice. A stark contrast to the stories of her brutality. Or maybe those stories weren't true?

"Let's go, gentlemen," Drake said. "We got a book to find." He wiped his face and took his hat off. Steam rose from his matted hair.

Gerrick side-eyed him. "We're almost done, Drake. We'll get a beer at Maggie's after this."

But Drake ignored the consolation. His bloodshot eyes stared at the cage for far too long. He wiped his head again and leaned close to the cage.

"Shut up in there," he said. "Who are you talking to, anyway?"

Fang ignored him and giggled the way girls do when they're whispering their secrets.

"I'm warning you!" he roared.

Her voice hushed, as if scolded. But, before long, more giggles spilled out.

"Are there two of them in there?" Gerrick asked.

"*Stop!*" he shouted. "Stop the damned the cart!" The men held fast as he grabbed the aurorium rod and shoved it inside. Horrid screams erupted as he struck the vampire again and again. Violence filled the air and some of the men shrank back, including the tall ogrek. Drake finished and yanked the rod out, baring his teeth.

"You all done? Because I'll keep this up until your little imaginary friend is dead!" he growled.

The cage rocked with a bang, and the men jumped. Grumbling from within turned into cursing, turned into fists smashing against the iron hatch. Knots boiled across the metal with horrible speed.

Drake stepped in and slammed the rod inside.

She roared.

Rifles were pointed at the cage, some trembling, and all waited for the inevitable command to open fire. Drake's arm jerked violently, and the rod was yanked out of his grip. The mercenaries froze. Loud moans and sobs echoed out from within and the mercenaries eyed each other.

Gerrick turned to Drake. "Do you think—" He stopped when the iron cage erupted with violence.

Metal groaned under the strength of the vampire. Weapons were readied, and the men repositioned for more accuracy. Lightening creased the sky as great drops of rain fell.

"Do… do we have another aurorium rod?" Gerrick asked as he stepped back.

Drake shook his head.

Screeching metal pierced the air as the iron door wrenched open and the men's eyes shifting between Drake and the emerging threat.

A tall woman unfolded herself and stepped out, arching her back and rolling her shoulders, ignoring the rifles pointed at her. Lightening flashed across the sky, highlighting her features. Tangled, short hair the color of midnight lay pasted across an attractive, lean face. Skin-tight, black leathers clung to her slender frame, far too slender to have punched her way out of an iron cage. With her eyes shut, she tilted her face up as cold rain tapped against her pale skin. Taking a deep breath, she stood there for a moment mumbling to herself, lost in thought it. Finally, she turned to the men and opened her eyes, the glow of fiery vengeance emanating from under her brow. Her sharp gaze counted the armed men in rapid succession. There was a great sense of a dangerous predator amidst them, one they wouldn't escape from.

She lowered her pointed chin, locking eyes with Drake as a plume of frozen air rose from her smiling lips.

"You know what they say," Fang said. "If you spot a vampire…"

Drake's skin froze.

***

If there was anything at all Fang was good at, it was spreading chaos. Using her training meant violence, either by blade, firearms, bare hands or sharp teeth. She never asked to be made into who she was, but in times like this, she was thankful to be an indomitable force. When she was in her element, as she was now, time slowed like molasses compared to her speed.

Rifle bores flashed in the dark, filling the air with sizzling lead. Her quick eyes tracked the bullets trajectory and made small adjustments to the initial salvo and dodged out of the way. It would become a problem when more weapons were fired at once, but right now there was complete pandemonium as men uttered their last before the angel of death collected their souls.

Five mercenaries fell before she felt the sting of a carbine. Sharp claws dug into their soft flesh and she ripped open a throat before he could scream. A bullet tore into her shoulder blade and she somersaulted through the air, twisting her body through the storm of bullets. Her feet hit the deck, landing between two thugs. With terrible strength she grabbed their heads and slammed them together, splashing

her with their bone, brains and blood. That one moment cost her;
bullets tore through the flesh of her back and legs. With a grunt she
back flipped and picked up the iron door to shield her from the fiery
spray of the rifles. Open, bloodied wounds along her skin sealed shut
when a bright burst of aurorium exploded inches away from her face.
Even though she squeezed her eyes shut and held her breath, the
noxious cloud of vapor flashed-burned her skin like scalding water.

She spun, and launched the iron door into a cluster of men.
Limbs and meaty chunks flew in different directions. Bullets zipped
past her as she leapt into another group, tearing throats, shattering
bones and disemboweling men too slow to move. An orange-tipped
bullet split the air and she lunged, but not in time. White-hot metal
raked across the back of her leg. She cried out. The searing pain
threatening to cripple her, but she had to keep moving, had to make
them miss, had to kill them before they killed her. This was her hour of
escape, and failure was not an option. She grabbed two by the throat
and leapt into the sea. Under the temporary safety of the freezing
water, she squeezed their throats with her vice-like grip. They
shuddered until they were still.

There were ten mercenaries left.

Bullets sizzled through the freezing currents. She pulled herself behind a piling and gathered her bearings. Shredded from the elbow down, her left arm repaired itself. Bone grew and strengthened, new skin stretched, pulling itself back together until the wounds were a distant memory. The aurorium scratch on the back of her leg would take much longer to heal. She glanced down at the scars on the back of her hands and let the other wounds mend.

The chill of the water brought back the past she fought so hard to forget. She stared out at the expanse of the sea stretching into darkness. The shape of her sister loomed in the distance as memories flashed back to their fateful voyage through the North Atlantic. The seas were much more violent then. Over two-hundred years had passed and this one memory would never leave her alone.

She squeezed her eyes shut and gritted her teeth. Shaking away her haunted past, she concentrated on the task on hand. Trevin and Moreci had forced her into the mold of a trained monster, covered her body in aurorium scars, and made her the way they wanted her to be.

Not anymore.

She squinted toward the surface, where Drake and his men were waiting. With fists clenched, she swam back to the foot of the pier to finish the job. A diversion was necessary. Make them look one way, attack from behind. She had done this a thousand times. Simple.

With powerful blows, she split the pilings and tore them apart one by one. The pier fell to pieces, cutting off the men's escape to land. Unless they were very strong, very fast swimmers, they were trapped.

The rainstorm yielded to a drizzle as she glided through the water and popped up underneath the pier, listening to the chaos: feet losing purchase, men falling down, weapons skidding into the water. Others shot blindly into the sea. Two of them spoke, the ogrek and the leader, Drake of their withering, incompetent operation.

"Where's she at?" Gerrick asked.

"We lost fourteen men in less than half a minute. Money be damned!" Drake shouted.

Walls of plaster, thick wood cracked apart, and electric lights exploded as the warehouse collapsed into the rolling sea. Flames spread through what was left. The roars and screeches of the caged beasts were deafening.

Such a perfect diversion.

Fang leapt from the sea and picked Drake's men off one by one, attacking from different points. Their guns fired wildly at the empty air and rolling waves. Pent-up fury rushed through her veins, and their screams were stifled as they sank into the dark water. She leapt once more out of the water, landing on the ogrek's shoulders. His wide muscles tensed, but not to fight. He was confused, terrified.

Useless.

Her sharpened teeth sank into his neck, and blood gushed from the pierced skin. Warm tingles washed over her skin, and her eyes glazed over as crimson rivulets streaked down her chin. She drank what her body had been craving for years. Weakness and fatigue evaporated as delicious warmth flooded her muscles and bones.

The hollow shell of Gerrick crumpled to the floor. A wide smear of blood covered her mouth from ear to ear, dripping onto her chest. Drake squinted through the smoke and flames, watching the shape of the vampire advance.

He pointed his forty-five-caliber revolver. The aurorium bullet burned bright inside the barrel, her warning signal.

"You think you can cover fifteen yards in a hurry?" he asked.

She tilted her head.

"I don't miss, neither," he added.

"I'm pretty certain you missed a few times." She wiped her mouth.

He cocked the hammer back.

She blurred.

His finger squeezed, but she was next to him, bending his elbow. His ear disappeared in a burst of hot, orange flame.

He cried out, and his knees slammed into the planks, the gun clattering to the side.

"One of your mistakes was not carrying enough aurorium," she said, picking splinters from her knuckles. "The handlers always carried aurorium-embedded pendants, knuckle-dusters, neck collars and other tools. Kept me on my toes. Compliant. Fearful. Orderly. But, that was from experience. They got tired of losing men."

She flexed her fingers, rolled her neck and squinted at the puddle of mess kneeling before her. Flames from the warehouse glinted off his dripping, bloody face. Wet planks shimmered orange and gold beneath her feet. The pitiful cries of beasts had long since subsided.

"Aww, your lips are quivering," she teased. "And you made a mess in your pants. I thought you were a professional."

"Ears are ringin'," he groaned.

"Indeed. Now. Tell me, who hired you?" she asked.

He grimaced. "Damn ear's gone. Can't think straight."

She had no pity for him. His heart rate had increased with stress, but it indicated he wasn't lying. He was a hired gun with limited knowledge of his employer. Amateur.

"What are your leads on Trevin and Moreci?"

"Trevin's in his whorehouses just a few blocks from here. No one's seen Moreci." His breaths came in ragged gasps, and he kept his eyes shut. Pain compliance always worked. She had had years of it.

"And what are they going to do with the book?"

"Why would I know?" he spat.

She used her Reach. The slightest vibrations echoed from his conscience. Loathsome memories lapped against her own conscience, and she recognized the abhorrent emotional scarring on his soul, part and parcel of a murderer. And he wasn't just a murderer of men.

"You don't like women, do you?"

He moaned.

"I can't read minds, but there is something I feel in my spirit, if I have one, and I just know that I know that I know."

He mumbled and shook his head. "I don't... I don't understand."

"You've murdered women, haven't you?" She studied him: heart slamming against his bony ribs, breathing irregular, tremors in his eyes. A guilt-ridden mask lay deeper than the creases in his pockmarked face.

"You've murdered little girls—haven't you?" Her tone chilled to ice.

Their eyes met. The sneer of his lips and the prideful gleam in his eye gave her all the answer she needed. She had seen faces like his. Arrogant. Cocky. Disturbing.

"What's it like to be you?" he asked.

"Like what?"

"All alone."

She didn't answer.

"That's what I thought. You know, the world is full of people trying to live their life the best way they can. And then there's you. All alone without a care for anyone or anything. Admit it. No one wants you. That's why they keep you locked up." He winced and squeezed his blood-covered hand into a fist.

"I don't need anyone," she growled.

"Like hell you don't. I can see it in your damn yellow eyes. The only thing that could make it worse is if you weren't fully vampire, and I'm willing to bet you aren't. I know they pumped those chemicals into you. Made you strong. Agile. Quick as a rattler. Probably stuck some wolf fangs in your mouth. But they couldn't do anything about that deep hole inside you that everyone's born with. Hell, even a coyote needs a pack. You think you're the exception?"

"I don't want to be wanted or needed, because I don't need anyone." Her cheeks grew hot.

"You keep telling yourself that. I know you're hardly killable, but face it. Someday you're going to die, and ain't nobody coming to your funeral. Hell, you'll end up under a lump of dirt without so much as a stick or two to mark the occasion."

Her heart thrummed. She flexed her hands, freezing drops of rain melting against the heat of her face.

"I'll help you out. I got another aurorium shell in that forty-five Colt. Why don't you do yourself a favor? Put it between those fangs in your mouth—"

She snapped his head around, and his body folded.

She walked away with a gnawing pressure flooding her chest. She raised a fist up to her mouth, squeezed her blurry eyes, and sat at the edge of the pier, legs dangling over. The ocean rose and fell beneath her in perfect rhythmic beats. She stared at nothing. The rain returned.

"What's it like to be you?"

Her mind grappled with his challenge. What was the answer? Was it different than his assessment? She turned her head and eyed the handgun lying near his body. It took too long to turn away.

She pulled one knee up and rested her chin against the shredded leather and stared at the water. The last time she had looked out over the rolling ocean, she'd been searching for her little sister. Her throat had grown hoarse from her calls, to the point of bleeding. She cried out to God, to the sea, to anyone listening. But nothing and no one brought Embeth back.

A lump broke through the surface and her bleary gaze focused on the corpses drifting along with the swell of the ocean. All of them floating on crimson clouds until they were collected by ships or swallowed in the depths of the sea.

What if Embeth had been floating like that? And for how long? Did someone collect her remains? Or was she still—out there?

Her mind wrestled with the fact that these men in the ocean were dead because of her. Just like Embeth.

She took a deep breath, held out her open hands, tilted her head back and squeezed her eyes shut against her bitter reality. Frozen air rushed over her skin. Her palms filled with water, daring her fingers to endure another moment. It was difficult to smile—and honestly, what was there to smile about?

The rain filled her palms. She made a fist, squeezed the water out and opened them again. But it wasn't water she was looking at. She was squeezing out the blood she had spilled over the years. It filled her palms before she squeezed it out again. Open and close. Death after death. Curse after curse. And if she'd killed her sister, then that's what she was.

A monster.

A killer no one believed existed. A whisper in the dark no one suspected. She was covered with transgressions that came along with the curse, stains on her conscience that would never wash away.

Without another thought, she stood and picked up Drake's gun. The aurorium bullet inside pricked her skin. She clicked the cylinder into place and sat at the edge.

"What's it like to be you?"

A lot of things and nothing good, she should have said. She was fast, but not with answers.

The gun was heavier than it seemed. She was out of the iron cage, but still a prisoner. She wanted out, and this bullet was the closest thing she had right now. No more guilt. No more gnawing emptiness. Her finger rested against the trigger. The slightest squeeze would be all she needed. She took a deep, cleansing breath. Her last.

"What are you doing?"

She turned and stared at the little girl sitting next to her. She wiped her eyes and blinked.

"Embeth?"

CHAPTER 2

Embeth wore her favorite dark green dress with the extra frills. She was almost an exact replica of the vampire, though her dark hair was longer, brushed back over her small ears. Her dark brown eyes were round, mousy, always curious. Her thin legs dangled over the edge of the planks. Not a drop of water on her. Fang looked at her sister and couldn't decide if this was a hallucination or—

"What's that?" she asked Fang, pointing at the floating corpses.

"Don't look down there. Embeth, I... I thought you would never want to see me again." Fang slid the gun away, unsure if she was going mad.

Again.

"Why wouldn't I want to see you again? You're my big sister."

Fang wiped her eyes. "I just thought... Never mind. I'm glad you're with me."

They smiled and embraced. Embeth's little body was warm, and her hair smelled like apples and summer flowers. They kissed each other on the cheek and held each other. It was so different than the last time they were together. If Fang was tumbling into madness, then this was the best kind.

Embeth wrapped her arms around her neck and whispered, "If you ever think for one moment that you're alone, I'll pinch you on the neck."

"Do your worst."

Embeth squinted, trying her best to appear mean and gave her skin a twist, and Fang laughed and kissed her again. She eased away, wiping her eyes.

"What's wrong?" Embeth asked.

"It's nothing," she said and looked away.

"What were you doing with that?"

Fang looked at the gun she'd tossed to the side.

"I was just thinking. You know when you can't find the right answer and, and you just..." She stammered and shook her head.

"Just what?"

"Nothing. I'm just tired, I guess." They kicked their feet at the edge of the pier and were quiet for a time. The fire roared behind, its warmth comforting them. Fang's shoulders dropped, and her muscles eased.

"I guess a bad man stole a book, huh?" Embeth piped up.

Fang glanced at the little girl and looked into her dark eyes. "How did you know that?"

"I just know stuff."

"You just know stuff." Fang cracked a smile.

"Mm-hm." Embeth shrugged.

The pressure in Fang's chest washed away, and the knots of tension were replaced by a warm sensation and something she didn't recognize. She liked it.

"So what are you going to do about it?"

Fang blinked and looked out at the pinpricks of light traveling along the streets. Men were awake, and the military would be there soon.

"I don't know what I should do about it, if anything."

"What if the bad person wants to hurt people with the book?"

"I guess I hadn't thought of that."

"What if you got it back?"

"And why in the world would I want to help people? Nobody cares for me, nobody wants me."

"Because that's what good people do." The purity of her smile brushed away the darkness. "They help people even when they're not liked by others."

"Embeth, I'm… I'm not that person. Not even close. Don't you remember what happened? Don't you know who I am?" She wiped tears away from her hot cheeks.

"I know who you are." She smiled and pressed her head into Fang's shoulder. Her small gesture sending rolling waves of warmth through Fang's tortured, cold soul.

They stared out at the sky as the swells rolled underneath their feet. The only useful skills Fang had were her cunning and ruthlessness. Kill or be killed. Helping people was something else entirely. People were meant to be taken advantage of, played with, fed upon.

"What if you did it for me?"

Fang nodded. "I would do anything, anything for you."

"Then you need to find the book and stop the bad people from using it."

"Embeth, I don't even know where it is. I don't know who the bad guy—"

"Moreci."

"Right… Moreci." She frowned at Embeth. "I don't know where he is. I don't know a lot of things, I guess."

"I guess you need help, then."

"I don't know anyone who would help me."

"Probably someone smart. Smarter than you." Embeth squinted, and a wide grin stretched across her face.

"Embeth, I told you. I don't know anyone."

"You're smart too. Clever. I think you could make someone want to help you. In a nice way, of course."

Fang rubbed her face. Of course, Embeth was right. She was always right. But, how was all this going to happen? She was on a burning pier near a city full of men who would probably kill her on sight. And this was not in her scope of practice. Seducing? Yes. Asking for help, no.

She shook her head. "And how do you think all of this is going to come about?" But she flinched when she saw that Embeth was gone. She jumped to her feet and looked around, but the dead were the only things on the pier.

"Embeth?" She caught herself before she could scream. *"Embeth?"*

Fang was alone again. Only this time the feeling wasn't a certainty. And it was good to have her sister again. Even if she still wasn't sure if she were a spirit or—

The last remaining walls and pieces of the warehouse fell into the ocean. Lights gathered in bunches on the shore, and tiny points of light dotted the bay.

Embeth was right. Fang would need help. But who would trust a monster like her? She dove into the water and swam. Bitter cold shocked her senses. The currents pushed her away, but she adjusted course, her modified sight cutting through the darkness as she swam towards a familiar landmark. Her mind formulating a new plan.

She would need a detective, a very good detective. The two of them could work together to find the book. Embeth said Moreci had it, but Fang didn't know where he was. Trevin, however, was close by. She would talk to Trevin tonight, find out what he knew and then kill him. His life was filled with a desire for violence. She would bring it to him.

***

Seventy-five yards away, a hidden agent sat under heavy tarps and stared through a pair of powerfully modified binoculars to see through the dark. A notepad full of scribbles rested on his lap next to a worn hipflask.

A voice buzzed into his earpiece. "Status report."

"Yes sir," the agent said. "The warehouse is destroyed, and agent Fang has disappeared into the waters."

"Then her retrieval was a failure?"

"Completely, sir."

"Perfect. Status of Drake and his crew?"

"Gutted, sir."

"Ah, more good news. I adore when my plans come together."

"Um, yes, sir."

"And Fang is heading to…?"

"Best guess would be to a weapons cache, then to find change of clothes and then off to find Trevin."

"But I didn't hire you for best guesses, did I?"

"Sir. No, sir."

"I thought not. I'll let you go so you can follow her, then."

"Thank you, sir."

"Oh, and be sure to contact me when Trevin is dead."

"Of course, sir." The radio crackled once and was silent. The agent gathered his belongings and set about his work.

***

Fang pulled herself onto the riprap and lay still. Her eyes searched the buildings for prying eyes. The pouring rain concealed her shape, but she could never be too sure. Her body was frozen against the rocks, just another shadow among the shadows. She waited less than three minutes before pulling herself up and slipping across the street.

Throughout the city, the military kept hideouts with caches of supplies, and the nearest was a block away. She slipped through a window, peeled out of her wet clothes, and strapped herself into a fresh suit of reinforced leathers. A pair of daggers in her sheaths, stocked utility belt, and a thick night-cloak to keep off the rain, and she was hunting on the street in less than two minutes.

The closer she drew towards the main city, the louder it became. And instead of a few men walking the streets near the docks, there were droves. Trevin's old haunts were nearby, in the defunct streets of the Barbary Coast, the term most San Franciscans used to describe an area known for its wild debauchery. She blended in with the other riffraff. Forgotten miners, drunk sailors and prostitutes of all ages scuttled through saloons and parlors. No one batted an eye at the dark-cloaked woman who walked beside them as she searched for Trevin with her mind.

Her Reach sought the most disturbing conscience among the disturbed. Not an easy task given the surroundings, but she knew she would find him. His was a rotting carcass amidst blocks of refuse, and his pungent soul finally effused.

He was a block ahead, directly in front of her. She leaned against a wall and watched. The sounds of clinking glass and bawdry songs slinked out from the saloon doors as they opened. The shape of him was unmistakable, as was his trademark white, three-piece suit. A slim woman clung to his side. Fang noticed the woman's head turning this way and that, gathering as many details of the street as she could. Just like Fang would do. So, Trevin had an assassin guarding him. Fang wasn't put off by his bodyguard. The woman was merely a window Fang would smash to get to the real target.

The pair walked away nonchalantly through the crowds. Fang followed, her eyes boring into the back of his head, heart swimming in adrenaline, fingers flexing. Her daggers were merely inches away, resting in sheaths on her belt. Fang drew a sharp breath as she slowly gained ground on the pair. Each step assuring their deaths. Fang was in her element and for once, under no duress of orders from men with aurorium.

The pair ducked into a dilapidated brick building, one of his whorehouses. She arrived at the entrance and was met with a sea of drunk sailors leaving after spending their hard earned money. She paused, glanced inside and caught Trevin's companion gliding up the stairs. Someone grabbed her bottom.

"Oi! I'll take this one here, mates," a sailor laughed and elbowed the others.

She turned. Her Reach whispered his crimes of rape. She smiled and nodded to the corner. The men cheered as she led him into the dark alley. Before he could say another word, she snapped his neck and stuffed his corpse into a trash bin.

She walked the length of the building and waited. Her enhanced hearing picked out the muffled screams from a prostitute's room on the third floor. Her fingertips dug into the brick and mortar and she shimmied up to the curtained window like a spider. A groan caught her attention and she peered down. A drunk woman teetered in the alley and stared at Fang a moment. Fang returned the stare. The drunk raised her bottle in a salute and sauntered off. Fang peered back through the window.

Trevin was leaning over the woman and pointed his stubby finger at her. His warnings became urgent when he pulled out a knife. Fang waited until his back was turned before she exploded through the glass, baring fangs and daggers. Like a pouncing tiger, she soared through the room—when the air changed. It was as though she'd jumped into a vat of molasses. Her heart skipped. Adrenaline flooded her veins, but not to fight—to run.

Aurorium.

Trevin turned, held a thick arm out and swatted Fang aside, sending her into the wall. The daggers clattered across the room. The shock on his face was what she had hoped for, but the shock on hers was what made him frown.

"Fang?" he said, gripping his knife. "What in the world are you doing here?"

Terror coursed through her body as she crawled away from him. Her strength evaporated, lungs spasmed. A high-pitched screech dug into her ears, and her vision blurred.

"Oh. You must not have known about my aurorium-infused blood?" He grabbed a handful of her hair and yanked her face close to his. "You're a mess. Bleeding out from your eyes is never a good sign of health, is it?"

His words were muddled and strange to her. The aurorium's effect was devastating. Her stomach turned into knots, blood ran through her like boiling water. She raised a weak hand, as if that would do anything.

"My dear, poor vampire," he taunted. "Such a lovely experiment. Don't you know how perfect we created you? How wonderfully crafted you are? Holy water, crosses, silver, sunlight. All the typical contrivances most vampires fear and loathe have no effect on you, do they? But Moreci and I were given a special defense just in case."

He picked her up and threw her across the room. Wood shattered as she crashed into a cabinet. She could barely breathe. He picked her up again, wincing as he held her throat and pushed his face close to hers. Waves of searing pain pummeled every inch of her body.

"The aurorium. That has an effect, doesn't it? Someone smarter than us felt a blood transfusion was necessary in case a situation like this ever turned up. And it looks like it's paying off."

He threw her into the wall. Lath and plaster shattered, and Fang flopped on the bed. Stinging needles dug into her body, nerves, bones. And, just for a moment, she wanted so much to be back in the small cell again, sleeping peacefully with her dreams of Embeth.

"We gave you a home and a purpose. Better than the life you were living in the asylum, wasn't it? I'm sure your parents would have been proud of you. But they disowned you, didn't they?"

He picked her up over his head and slammed her into another wall. Every inch of her body was on fire, and her breaths came in ragged gasps.

This was what dying felt like.

She was torn between the promise of sweet relief and the bitterness of not keeping her promise to Embeth.

"Your lungs will collapse any moment, followed by the imminent snapping of your spine as your back spasms. Terrible price to pay for a night out, Fang."

He grabbed her hair and pulled her face up.

"What were you thinking?" he asked. He looked deep in her drooping, bleeding eyes. "Did you think you'd be free? Be able to kill us anytime you want?"

"What's happening?" a woman asked.

"Veiul," he answered, looking toward the open door. "Look who showed up."

Fang's eyes floated through the room until she found a familiar face—not a vampire, but some other kind of preternatural. One that could shift her appearance.

"Ah! We haven't worked together in years," Veiul said, and her face shifted until she resembled Fang. "You do look familiar…" Veiul's face melted and shifted again into that of another woman. "What are you doing out of your cage?"

"She tried to assassinate me," Trevin said. "Can you imagine the audacity?"

Veiul's face and voice, shifted back into Fang's. "Ah, well... um... I may be strong and pretty, but I'm not too smart, am I?" She tapped her head and crossed her eyes, laughing with Trevin.

"And she just found out about my aurorium," he said, and finally noticed the blood on the floor. "Oh! Goodness, look at this mess. Fang, you're bleeding all over the place. All over my shoes! And the poor woman's new carpet!"

"Are you going to take her head?" Veiul asked, squinting at Fang.

"Yes. Of course."

"You have quite the collection, don't you?"

"Over forty-five." He looked at the ceiling and rubbed his pudgy, clean-shaven jaw. "And hers will fit nicely in my collection of conquests. But let her suffer for now. We'll go to Maggie's first and get a drink. Then we can find a glass jar."

Veiul looked at the prostitute. "And what about her?"

Trevin turned. "Leave her alone. What's she going to do? Tell everyone there's a vampire in her room?"

He turned to the prostitute. "Hear that, love? Don't do anything here until I get back, and I'll pay you handsomely." The woman nodded.

"Well, then," Trevin said. "That's settled. Fang, good seeing you again." His smile was vulgar. "And I can't wait to see you on my shelf." He stepped carefully through the debris and out of the room. His footsteps echoed down the hall before Veiul turned her sneer to Fang. The two stared at each other, a mirror image of two assassins. Only one was dying.

"Let's make this interesting," Veiul said. She plunged her dagger into the other woman three times and grinned. She yanked out the blade and held it under Fang's nose.

"Smell this banquet." Thick blood dripped off the blade and onto Fang's chest. "I want you to hunger and have a hope of survival before you die."

Veiul slammed the dagger into Fang's heart and curled her lip. "That's for leaving me in Peking." She ripped the dagger out and glared as she closed the door to the room.

The wound in Fang's heart was barely healing itself. Waves of agony crashed over her, and she tried to sit up but that slid further down instead.

A whimper drew her attention, and she looked at the other woman. A trail of red flowed from the prostitutes wounds. Adrenaline rushed through Fang's veins, instinct beckoning her to feed. But the woman was innocent. And Fang never touched the innocent. Unless...

She used her Reach and touched the dying woman's conscience. Traces of a single murder lingered on her dark soul. Someone close to her, a male, older relative. She killed him without remorse.

Guilty.

Fang concentrated on the rise and fall of the dying woman's chest as she crawled across the debris.

CHAPTER 3

Hunter's Point

San Francisco police and detective training grounds

Six months later

> *Let no evil this day soil my thoughts, words, hands.*
>
> *Amen.*

Coyle finished praying and looked down at her hands. Could they accomplish what she wanted—these insignificant hands that sought her own selfish ways?

She raised her head and closed her eyes. Took a deep breath through her nose. The kind the doctors taught her. She exhaled through her mouth. *Time to focus.*

Settled?

She squinted up at the bright sun, arched her back and rearranged her shoulder-length light brown hair into a tight bun. A few of the men looked her way, appreciating the shape of her. She was fair-skinned, graceful, petite and seemingly coy though her demeanor held a sense of boldness and tenacity. Not a trace of make-up lined her strong, yet charming face and she didn't need a speck of it to attract men. She wore no smile across her thin lips and the shadow of a bruise lined her thin nose and into the corner of her hazel-green eyes. Her gaze shifted from the leer of the men back to the cloudless sky. The sun's rays alighting on the bare necks of the academy trainees as they awaited their fates. All of them fiddled with their notebooks or clothes or hats, nervous before their test for detective. She wished she had brought her pipe, regardless of the looks she usually received. She liked her pipe. Other ladies liked… whatever tickled their fancy. To each their own.

A few dirigibles—bloated constructs filled with gas and propelled by small steam engines—floated through the blue sky. Their colors varied depending on their use: Silver and blue for passengers, gray for the US Navy, white for cargo, dark gray with red glass cabins for private use. They all followed their predetermined paths, traveling to their destinations as safely as possible. She had never ridden on one and preferred staying close to the ground. If people were meant to be in the air, God would have given them wings.

She inhaled the chilled, June air and regretted it. The reek of nearby slaughterhouses and Chinese shrimping boats resting in the sun made her pull her hand to her nose. She couldn't wait until this was over. Both the stench and her nerves were driving her mad. Nearby church bells rang out two o'clock. She had been on the grounds since five that morning.

Chatter about the latest body found in a Chicago-area brothel perked her ears. She took a step closer their group and inspected her fingernails as they described the crime scene: hands tied to the bedposts, a vertical incision from the neck to the lower abdomen. Vital organs had been removed, set aside and carefully dissected. The latest victim of the Ripper.

A cold tingling sensation grew in her belly. She could envision the scene all too well, and if she didn't take this detective spot, the bodies would keep piling up. Every corpse the Ripper left behind was a testament to the promise he'd made to her.

An unoiled door snapped everyone's attention to a wide gate yawning open. A frumpy applicant limped out, holding his elbow. His expression was sour under bunches of straw-colored hair. Smears of dirt ran along one side of his uniform. A pair of men followed. The tall one, built like a scarecrow, was marking a stack of papers in his hand.

"Maybe next year, eh, Constable Marston?" The tall man chuckled and pushed thin-wired frames up his bent nose. He glanced down at his papers and mumbled something the students couldn't hear.

He shared a word with a colleague and tapped his pencil against the papers before calling out, "Constable Sherlyn Coyle, front and center!"

"Here, sir!" she said, her skin tingling, throat dry and knees wobbling.

This is it.

She dabbed her forehead with a kerchief, took a deep breath and let it out through parched lips. She smoothed away the wrinkles of her uniform dress and walked to the tall man, Master Detective Meys, with a lively step. Someone bumped into her and mumbled an apology. She didn't bother to respond.

She stepped up to the master detective and cleared her throat.

Was that too loud?

He ignored her arrival, burying his nose in the stack of papers. She stood at attention, the best she could without looking like she was wracked with nerves.

"Well, then," Meys said. "Constable Coyle?" His tone was condescending, abrupt.

"Yes, sir," she answered. Sweat dripped down her back. Her eyes were riveted in his direction.

"You ready?"

"I am, sir."

He forced a half smile.

She swallowed.

"Gentlemen, let me introduce Constable Sherlyn Coyle. She has slight bruising across her nose, the result of her recent tussle with some of the local gang. She has no problem using her fists when provoked. You may have noticed the lack of trousers on this one," Meys said. "Hopefully, you also noticed this constable chose to wear perfume and not cologne this morning. Part and parcel of her feminine charm, we assume. Though she may want to reconsider her choice of *eau de toilette* because she's still not married."

Coughs and chuckles peppered the air. She stared past the men toward the jagged edges of the growing city skyline. San Francisco, the "Golden Gate City." Were the gleaming opportunities designed specifically for men in this city? It certainly seemed like it. This morning she hoped to change that. But she was very aware of the heat in her cheeks. And, of course, everyone was looking at her.

"Constable Coyle," Meys continued, "is the first woman to enter the San Francisco Academy of Investigation, an establishment that has produced the bravest, finest law enforcement detectives our city has to offer. This institution serves our communities faithfully and produces tactical-minded men who work with strength, endurance, and a reverent duty to protect and serve. Constable Coyle has decided to ignore her state of being: her God-given duty to bear children and the gift of providing a home for a husband."

There were more than a few sneers and shakes of heads. Coyle kept her chin up while sweat trickled down the back of her neck. She did see the irony of it all, though: her desire to pass this test and work alongside men who wouldn't appreciate her skill or hard work. They would only ever see a dress.

"It is against our code of ethics to allow a woman to join our estimable ranks. However, she hired an attorney who found a loophole in our policies, and the courts folded in her favor," he said.

Hisses and grunts tumbled from behind bushy beards and mustaches. She glanced to the side and caught the master detective's smirk. He was a showman, and she was the show. She slowly balled her hands into fists and relaxed them. She couldn't, however, act on her base impulses. She had to apply her energy and attention to the matter at hand: the detective position.

And not the urge to land her fist on his beak.

"Each of you is here because you completed your studies and passed the necessary written examinations to participate in the final scenarios, which, if completed successfully, lead to the promotion of detective. All of you are competing for that title, but there are only three positions to fill, and so far Constable Mueller has taken the first. That leaves..." He eyed Coyle.

She cleared her throat. "Two, sir."

"She knows her math, gentlemen," Meys said. He waited for the laughs to fade before he turned to her. "And how old are you, Constable Coyle?"

What part does my age play in all this?

"Twenty-two, sir."

"A bit old, yet still within the range of a good marriage if you change your mind." He turned back to his audience.

"Two more positions available." His voice dropped as he gazed at the field of men. "I don't need to tell you how embarrassing it would be if *she* were to take a position from one of you fine gentlemen, do I?"

Quiet hostility had grown warmer than the sun. Coyle found herself staring at her boots.

"Let's begin," he said, and he rested his thin fingers on her shoulder. "Constable Coyle, let's step inside the test arena, and I shall brief you on your scenario."

She turned on her heels and followed, her palms damp, her logical mind questioning.

Do you enjoy being in the spotlight of humiliation? Because this may be your future.

With a vacant gaze, she stared ahead as they walked through the wide gates and into an area populated by building facades and play-actors waiting for their cue to begin the scenario. She looked around at the large, open-air, eight-sided structure. A grandstand full of judges sat on uncomfortable-looking benches. The men squinted at her, and she couldn't decide if it was from the sun or out of spite. They would be responsible for deciding her future. She smiled at them, knowing it wouldn't work. She wasn't here to change the world for femininity; she needed to be a detective for her own reasons. But they didn't have to know that. They *couldn't* know that.

She put her mind to work and scanned the new surroundings.

On the east end, behind her, fifteen judges sat on raised benches. Eight wore beards, five wore mustaches, two were clean-shaven. Twelve were aged well past fifty, the rest were younger than thirty. A pair spoke to each other. She wasn't close, but she could read lips.

An older gentleman said, "What on earth is she trying to do here? Show up our boys?"

The other answered, "James, sometimes a girl wants to try something out of her league. I mean, do you really think she'll solve this case?"

The older gentleman replied, "Well, I'm sure she meant well."

Coyle looked away and cursed under her breath.

To the north was a fake storefront: "James and Son's Sundry." Three men tried to look busy. One wore an expensive suit with worn, heavy boots. He was not an actor but a constable. Probably another judge.

To the west was an open space with a cluster of six male actors huddling, waiting, staring at her. To the south stood a fake hotel with an open window on the second story. A heavy man smoking an expensive cigar fingered the curtains—a constable supervisor, by the look of his jowls. She was being watched from all angles.

"As you know," Meys said, "these scenarios are based on real events. With the assistance of Dawn Industries, we have procured gnomish technology, which reproduces the crime scene. I'd love to go into the mechanics with you, but I wouldn't want to lose you with big words. Thanks to the generosity of the gnomish people, Dawn Industries created a special camera called a World Image Reconstruction Evaluator, or WIRE. The camera records a crime scene in every detail and allows investigators to enter the past as if it were the present. You will only enter what the camera recorded, which was taken within minutes of the crime. Using this technology, you will walk through the boundaries and be transported into the crime scene to investigate the given scenario. You will have a set time of half an hour while the judges and scorekeepers watch from their places. You may interact with the test as you would with a real crime scene. Any questions?"

"Yes, sir. Is this scenario based on a crime we, uh, the trainees would have knowledge about?" she asked, glancing at the short, brightly colored haired gnomes standing on ladders and platforms near tripods.

He stopped and turned. "Actually, it is based on an unsolvable crime that has stumped our best for the past six months."

Her throat went dry.

"Here we are, Constable Coyle," Meys said. "I will give you a brief synopsis of your scenario. I will explain what details you need to know, and I will not repeat myself, are we clear?"

"Yes, sir," she said. She flexed her hands and listened as if her future depended on it. This was everything she wanted, the proverbial open door, and all she needed to do was follow through. Easier said than done, of course.

God, help me.

Meys looked down at his papers and checked his notes. His words tumbled out with quiet haste, his mouth barely opening. He stopped and looked at her with a smile.

She blinked.

"I'm sorry, I couldn't hear the scenario. You were mumbling. Could you—"

"I do not... repeat... myself. Good luck, Constable," he said with a forced smile. "Scenario begins now! Turn on the WIRE projector." He walked toward the viewing podium. Chuckling peppered the air. Coyle's face went flush with heat, and she took a step

after the dolt but stopped herself. Complaining was no use. She looked

for help amongst the judges. Steely eyes from the men glared back at

her. No help from the gallery, either. She was alone.

Just like always.

She turned to the bustle of activity behind her as the actors

regrouped and prepared for the scenario. Gnomes on platforms pulled

switches and activated the large cameras. Projectors hummed to life.

Bright, silvery light transformed the plain wooden structure into a two-

story pub. Colors were fuzzy, distorted. But after a few moments, the

image was complete: a saloon named Maggie's, located near the

docks. She was familiar with the backwater pub and its crooked

patrons from her patrols. The wood appeared old and worn. Shadow

and light fell into their respective places.

She sighed and walked toward the pub. As soon as she stepped

across into the shadow, the air changed. The bright afternoon sun

evaporated in the WIRE projection, and the light and shadows were

replaced with a dark, chilly night. She shivered and looked behind her.

The dark line of night separated her from the reality of bright sunshine.

It was a bit disorientating, but she wasn't here to investigate technology. She stepped closer to the pub and reached into a pocket for her pad and pencil— where were they? Did she drop them? She stopped and looked behind. Nothing but footsteps lay in the dirt. Were they on her dresser? She distinctly remembered placing them in her pocket this morning. Then she remembered and cursed under her breath.

Someone bumped into me. A pickpocket. Who would do such a thing?

She chewed the inside of her cheek and blinked. Someone cleared their throat, and she looked up at the waiting judges. She was already under immense pressure from all sides. How would she be able to think clearly and rationally? She clenched her fist and let out a loud sigh.

The men turned at the noise, but she ignored them. When her eyes spotted what lay on the wooden porch, fear and apprehension stole her breath. It wasn't too late to turn tail and leave. But she knew this was her opportunity, and she wasn't going to throw it away.

A severed head lay in a pool of blood on the porch. The shock of the mess was striking. Ugly. *Gory.*

She swallowed to protect her composure and her eyes looked down. Her foot tapped the wooden slats. They felt and sounded real. Looking around brought a surreal sensation. The air smelled like oil from lanterns, dust from the rafters, and the pungent odor of gobs of blood. Pulling out a handkerchief, she pressed it up to her mouth and nose, doing her best to ward off the crushing odor.

A headless, obese body, dressed in a three-piece white suit and lying face down, blocked the entrance. He appeared to have fallen trying to exit the pub's door. Small chunks of flesh and congealed blood covered the white coat's collar and shoulders. She looked at the doorframe and found blood spatter, most of it dried, but some streaks still carried a dull chocolate-red sheen. Her eyes wandered over the seemingly random patterns, the disarray of the essential fluids of life.

She stepped inside the pub and sought answers to a single obvious riddle. How had this happened? Yes, he'd lost his head, but *how*? More than likely from a long sword or a swift stroke of an axe. But why couldn't anyone else figure this out? Why was this unsolvable? This was her test to see if she belonged with them or not.

Long, bloody flecks marked the interior walls adjoining the doorway on the left and right sides, but not above. She looked along the lower portions of the walls but found nothing useful.

She turned aside to interview the crowd. "Did anyone see anything?" she asked, searching the faces for a response. The judges outside listened through speakers and watched her work as though the walls didn't exist.

"There were a lot of people, but I saw what happened," a younger man answered.

"Thank you. Let's step over here, and I'll take your statement." She reached into her pocket for the notepad and let out a quiet curse. There would be no note-taking today. "Can you tell me your name, please?"

"John Smith," he said.

"And what did you see, Mr. Smith?"

"The bloke was sitting at a table inside there," he said.

"Can you show me?" she asked.

He pointed at the table. A chair lay on the floor. "As I said, he was sitting right there, having a drink by himself, when he made a noise."

"By himself? Are you sure of that?" She nodded to another drink opposite where the dead man had sat.

"Uh, pretty sure he was by himself," he said. He shifted his eyes.

She looked at the table and decided it wasn't worth pursuing. She was on the clock, and time was a fickle construct that waited for no one.

"You said this gentleman made a noise. What kind of noise?" she asked.

"Kind of like ..." He looked at the others before continuing. "He made a noise like this: *Ergh!*" He grabbed the back of his head and closed his eyes.

"Did he grab his head just like you did?"

"Yes, ma'am," he continued. "He grabbed the back of his head and got up out of his chair, walked up to the door and—pop! His head came right off."

"Came right off?"

"Came right off, and there he is." He pointed at the body.

"And no one touched him? No one came near him?"

"No. Everyone stayed away because of his weird sounds."

"Did anyone strike him or throw something at him?"

"No, ma'am."

"And his name?"

"Trevin something or other. Came in here frequently, he did."

"Trevin," she said. "What line of work was he in?"

The man shrugged.

"Thank you, Mr. Smith," she said. "Did anyone see differently?" No one answered. "Then I ask that everyone step away from the crime scene, please and thank you."

The men stepped away and watched her. She glanced at the upstairs windows. The constable supervisor sat and chewed the stub of his cigar.

Coyle put her hands on her hips and chewed her lip, ticking off the facts inside her head: a man sits in a pub, has a drink with someone, grabs his neck, walks to the exit. His head comes off. And she was supposed to solve this. She rubbed the bridge of her nose and squeezed her eyes shut. How did this man's head just—pop off? Now she understood the previous investigations dilemma.

The more obvious fact was that the Academy had piled obstacles in front of her progress. They didn't want her to get the position of detective. They didn't want her to succeed. Which was why they gave her the unsolvable crime. They wanted to prove a woman couldn't do men's work.

I've got to prove them wrong.

Every crime was solvable. One couldn't rely on evidence found in the light. You had to look in the hidden to find the solution. This incident may have been unsolvable to them, but this was her chance to use her giftings. Her motivation wasn't pride or womanhood—no, it was much simpler than that.

She wanted to find her murderous fiancé, the Ripper, within the accordance of the law and bring him to justice.

Just like he dared me to.

"You have fifteen minutes, Constable!" Master Detective Meys called out.

She ignored the warning and went back to the table, knelt, and peered underneath. Nothing unusual. No weapons. No wires. She circled the table and sniffed the glass of Scotch whisky. No poisons. Nothing useful. She examined the other glass. Vodka. It was mostly empty. She crossed her arms and studied the table before taking the dead man's seat. Her eyes searched for answers. There had to be something. Some clue as to how this man had been decapitated with no visible means.

I suppose a last prayer would be appropriate.

For every one that asketh receiveth; and he that seeketh findeth; and to him that knocketh it shall be opened.

She paused and looked straight up.

Do you hear me? Or am I—

"Oh," she whispered, turning her head sideways and squinting. She looked down at the table and spread her hands over the smooth surface. Then she traced a finger along the line of her jaw, staring at the mirror behind the bar. Her finger moved down to her neck and stopped.

She pushed herself away from the table and knelt by the body. She mumbled to herself and spotted something interesting. Pulling back his pant leg, she studied the soles of the man's shoes. Blood on his soles and at the edges of his pants. But not *his* blood. Interesting.

She scooted over and examined the decapitated head, using her fingers to search his bushy hair. She knew what she would find and was thrilled when she found it.

"Oh," she said, examining a tiny hole at the crown of the head. The judges had left the gallery now and were standing a few yards away. They stood silent and studied with her as she used her fingers to run along the inside of the skin of the neck.

Her finger moved slowly along the edge where the skin had been cut. She stopped and rubbed her finger and thumb together before raising them to her nose. She breathed out and paused before smelling the blood on her fingers again. Her eyebrows scrunched together. She wiped her fingers on her handkerchief and stood to inspect the blood-spattered wall.

"Six and a half minutes, Constable," said Meys. Some judges were mumbling in hurried, excited whispers while others scribbled on notepads.

She studied the wall from different angles, training her eyes on each spray of blood, placing her finger on a few spots along the wall. And then she said, "Oh."

She held a spot on the wall and traced a single, straight line that raced away from the doorway. By now, the judges had filed inside the large room and stood directly behind her. All eyes followed her fingertip along the wall until it stopped. She picked at a spot on the wall until her fingertip caught something. She tugged carefully until she could pinch it between her thumb and forefinger and finally pulled out a curious object. It was as long as a threading needle, wide as a shoelace and flat as a razor. In fact, it was a razor. She inspected the object in the light when she heard the announcement.

"Time's up, Constable Coyle," Meys said. He dismissed the actors and waited until they were outside the gates before proceeding, "Constable Coyle, you may present your findings and supporting evidence to the judges and myself. Usually, the gentlemen wait at the stands, but in your case, they have arrived for a more intimate view."

She turned to face the judges and a wash of ice water flooded her veins. Butterflies danced in the pit of her stomach. Someone cleared their throat.

This was it.

"I found..." she said. She waved the razor between her fingers, but the lump in her throat made it difficult to speak.

Perhaps they can hear my heart pounding like a steam-powered train. My cheeks are redder than roses. Everyone's looking at me. Say something!

"Yes? What did you find?" Meys huffed, and she flinched.

"Right," she said. "The victim, Mr. Trevin, had just arrived from, *ahem*, a house of ill repute."

"I'm sorry, Constable," said one of the older judges. "Could you explain how you know his whereabouts?" He tilted his head and frowned.

"Yes, sir," she said. "Two things. There were bits of wool-carpet fiber on the soles of his shoes and near the bottom of his trousers. The carpet fibers were different colors, including purple, the most expensive dye in wool carpets. He—or rather, his body—smelled of spiced citrus with floral accents. Being a constable, I have had my share of run-ins with prostitutes and am quite familiar with this perfume. Ergo, he most likely visited a house of ill repute."

She didn't tell them everything, though. There were spots of darker, older blood on the inside of his left trouser leg, and the same blood was smeared across the soles of his boots. But she had learned to hold her cards close and only reveal essentials. This man, Trevin, had been involved in some other altercation earlier that evening. Over what? She couldn't say for certain. Not yet, anyway.

All of the judges turned and inspected the shoes and trousers of the victim. A rush of excitement burst through her chest and arms.

Finding facts others had passed over filled her with the confidence she needed so desperately. It was a good feeling. Things were looking up. A tight smile crept across her lips, but she looked down and forced it away.

"Thank you, Constable," the older judge said. "You may continue."

"Yes, sir." She swallowed. "He sat at the table for roughly seven minutes before—"

"Seven minutes?" another judge asked.

She walked over to the table and pointed at the glass of whiskey. "He ordered a double single-malt whiskey and took two sips." She paused when she received confused looks before continuing. "The average gentleman will wait between two and a half and three and a half minutes between sips. The measured whiskey in the glass would be the same amount as a double serving, minus two sips. For now, we will ignore the other glass, which obviously belongs to a patron who is out of this storyline."

She did find strange fingerprints on this other glass. Though the imprints were most certainly produced by skin oils, there were no ridges and dips characteristic of human fingertips. She found this most curious. Trevin had apparently been involved in another possible death and then met with someone without fingerprints. But she didn't have all the facts, just circumstantial evidence. And her excitement was overshadowed by the stress of passing the test.

"Yes, sir," she said. "He had sat at the table for about seven minutes when he was shot." She pointed at the ceiling. "From directly above into the apex of his skull."

The men stared up at the two-story ceiling. Mumbles peppered the air, and fingers pointed at the hole they had just discovered.

"Yes, gentlemen, an assassin was at work," Coyle said.

"An assassin!"

"Goodness gracious!

"What on earth?"

"Please." She raised her finger at them, her neck bristling with heat. "Please allow me to continue, thank you." She was in her element now, and she detested when people showered her with their inane questions. The mumbling faded to whispers until she shot the last two murmurers a look. Their mouths closed, and she continued.

"I know this may seem confusing, but I will be thorough in my explanations and will be pleased to answer questions after I finish.

Now." She motioned to the head, and they followed like obedient schoolchildren. She knelt and lifted tufts of hair. "Do you see this hole?"

Some of the men reached for their glasses as she spread the victim's hair to the side.

"This is an entry wound, see?" She pointed at the crown before motioning to the neck. "And here." She slid a finger along a portion of the torn skin and stood. "Who wants to smell?" She shoved the bloodied fingers into their faces.

The judges recoiled and shook their heads. A few had their mouths agape in horror or shock that a woman would willfully stick her fingers inside a decapitated head.

She lifted her finger to her nose. "Blood has its own organic scent, mostly of iron. But during my investigation, I discovered another altogether inorganic scent: hydraulic fluid." She sniffed at her finger and offered it to the nearest judge. He glanced to his side before leaning in to smell. He inhaled and pursed his lips.

"Hydraulic fluid," he agreed, and leaned back. "Jeremy, have a whiff. This is remarkable." The judge next to him leaned in and sniffed. His eyes went wide. Now all of them wanted to smell the fresh clue. Some nodded, but most were awash with confusion.

"The hydraulic fluid," she continued, "was found inside the victim's neck, and it came from a tiny device which shot out these tiny blades." She held up the object she'd pulled out of the wall.

"Remarkable!"

"This is quite something!"

"I can't wait to tell Peter."

"But who would assassinate him?"

"Can a device that tiny be—"

She cleared her throat. "Gentlemen, please, please!" The judges abruptly shut their mouths. Someone mouthed, "Beg your pardon."

"And so, dear gentlemen, judges of the Academy"—she nodded to Meys—"and Master Detective Meys, here is my synopsis: Mr. Trevin met with unknown persons at a, *ahem*, brothel and came here to discuss whatever it was they were discussing." A trickle of sweat ran down her back, and her fingers twitched. She felt confident with her solutions, but would they really let her into their world?

"He was shot by an assassin from above. The precisely engineered round penetrated his skull and sank into his neck. The device rested inside before it followed its design, which was to open and burst outward in a counterclockwise fashion. Two flechette razors were released from a tight coil, spinning with great speed. The resulting action cut his veins, muscle, tendons, and bone until all flesh was severed and his head was decapitated. The blades exited from the right and left sides of his neck and buried themselves deep into the walls here." She pointed out where the blades had been buried. "Seemingly never to be found. The device used was a specific and professionally engineered item of which I have never seen the likes before."

"That's quite extraordinary, Constable Coyle. Extraordinary, indeed," Meys said. "But please provide the judges with proof of your evidence."

"Sir?" she asked.

"Your synopsis is truly interesting," he said. "But where are your recorded findings for submission of evidence?"

"Well, I used my brain to deduce probabilities and collect the—"

"Constable Coyle, are we to understand you do not have your pad of paper to record the evidence?"

She cleared her throat, "Well, sir, I don't actually have a pad of paper. It seems someone pickpocketed me earlier."

"Constable, are we to believe you allowed someone to pickpocket you? And do you suppose you could enter a court of law and offer a brief synopsis of the evidence you gathered… using your brain?"

Someone chuckled. Her skin prickled. She was going to lose her only chance. All because they couldn't stand to let her into their detectives club! But she had to remain professional no matter the circumstance. She cleared her throat and took a breath.

"Sir, I understand the importance of gathering evidence for submission to a court, but we are standing in a facsimile of an unsolvable case, which I have almost certainly solved," she said.

"Watch your tone, Constable! I simply asked if you had a way of gathering evidence during the mock investigation. A simple pad of paper and pencil. Basic, rudimentary tools used by a detective to gather and provide evidence when necessary."

"Sir, I gathered evidence using my eyes, fingers, and mind." She counted her trembling fingers in front of them. "I found the hole in the ceiling used by the assassin. I found—"

Meys raised his hands. "Constable! You are turning down a path you don't want any part of. Now, due to your lack of basic tools to collect evidence, I must disqualify—"

"Disqualify?" Her hands clenched into fists. Heat rushed into her face, and this time she didn't care who noticed. "What? How can I be disqualified when I solved your unsolvable riddle? Could you answer me, sir? Do you know how ridiculous this sounds?"

"Please check your tone, young lady, or there will be stiff consequences."

"Oh! So this is what it's all about! Time to disqualify the 'young lady' because she doesn't belong with the men who didn't have the common sense to solve this case. Is that it?" She tapped her finger into his bony chest, her Irish heritage threatening to make an appearance.

"Constable Coyle, you are now under arrest for assault on a master detective and contempt of an official during the process of testing."

"What on earth are you talking about? Have you gone mad? An official of what, sir? An official of the collection of half-assed, pompous misogynists?"

Meys pointed at her right hand. "You're holding that razor in an aggressive fashion, and your feet have shifted into a fighting stance. Now drop the weapon."

Her fingers spread apart, dropping the flechette and raising her open hand.

"I'll show you an aggressive fashion." Her open fingers tightened into a fist and she punched his face. He stumbled back. Blood spurted from his nose. She took a step forward, but they grabbed her arms and dragged her back. She cursed. Manacles wrapped around her wrists.

It was over.

They led her through the open square as tears streamed down her hot cheeks. The bright sun beat on her face. She heard the judges grumble behind her.

"How on earth did that come about?"

"It's too bad. I thought she would have made a fine detective."

"Too much fighting spirit for her age. Older, but still pretty. She'd make a great wife."

"What time is bridge tonight?"

"She probably never wanted this to happen."

***

Fang slid her fingers over her fake mustache and shook her head. She walked back to the judges' stands with the others, disguised as one of the older men. She squinted up at the sunlight and took a deep breath.

She had to kill Trevin from a distance, that's why she shot him from above. Yet she wanted it to be clever, make sure to take his head off. And ever since then, she had been on the hunt for one very special person to uncover his death. Today, Fang watched with fascination as Sherlyn Coyle found evidence of her work, things she hadn't even considered at the time. The hydraulic fluid from the razor-rotor?

Brilliant.

And Coyle was a fighter. What an impression the constable made. Fang shook her head and took her seat with the judges who had no idea there was an assassin vampire in their midst. It may have seemed cruel, but she was glad Coyle was disqualified. Fang smiled.

She had finally found her detective.

CHAPTER 4

San Francisco City Hall

Prisoner cell no. 18

Fifteen days later

Lord, humble me for not being as holy as I should be, or as holy as I might be through Christ. For thou art all, and to possess thee is to possess all.

Amen.

Another night in a jail cell. Coyle shook her head, certain God was not listening. *Does He even listen to the black sheep? Those who turn away from His shepherd's crook? Those who end up in a jail cell because they were stubborn and selfish and foolish and bad-tempered?*

She ran her fingers through her hair and rubbed her scalp, trying to fight back another round of pity tears.

"Well, Mother," she said. "Here's your daughter. Alone in a jail cell. Finally, I suppose. I was never one to follow direction well, was I? I have to wonder if that was the reason you made me memorize passages when I was young. Maybe you believed I wouldn't stray from the flock if I was filled with Scripture.

"Well, I was wrong too. I believed if I memorized what you gave me, Father would pay more attention. Play with me. Hold my hand. Help with my lessons. I devoured everything you gave me: Bible pages and prayer journals and books devoted to God and His works. For all that, both of us were wrong. I fell in love with a murderer, and Father barely knew I existed.

"And this is the fruit of my planting." She spread her arms out and huffed. "I don't live up to what the church implores: holiness and righteousness. I always find a way to act contrary to Scripture. And because of my stupidity, I'll never find Ronan."

She slid down against a wall, buried her warm face in her cold hands and sobbed. She had been so close, so very close. She should have been working alongside men in the department, men who could help her find the Ripper.

Instead, she stepped onto a frozen lake and plunged into its icy grasp. And now she was trapped. No escape. No second chance. She wiped her wet eyes and looked up before leaning her forehead against the iron bars.

"My temper drove me here," she said. "Not the imbeciles. Father, forgive me. The judges were only doing what men do. I should have expected all this. Mother, I should have listened to you, too. I should have let myself be courted by a rich, arrogant man who wants a quiet wife." She laughed. "Who am I kidding? I'm not worthy of their ilk. What's the point in even living now? It's all gone. Everything's gone."

Something moved in the dark corner. She wiped her eyes and stared. Ambient light spilled through the window but stopped short of the shadowed corners. Nothing stirred. There were no sounds but those from the inmates further down the hall. She stood and walked to the window for some fresh air—freezing mid-stride.

Someone is here.

She took a step back, heart jumping in her throat, fists clenched. Her eyes shifted back and forth. Oh, how she hated the dark. Her mind tried desperately to balance logic with the flood of adrenaline. She closed her eyes, remembering what the doctors had taught her to calm her nerves.

Nothing is there. You have an overactive imagination is all. Nothing is there.

"I'm alone in a cell," she said. "All by myself, surrounded by iron and stone and correctional officers. No imaginary beings, no monsters and certainly not *him*."

Her breathing steadied, and she took one long, deep breath before she opened her eyes into slits. Her gaze shifted to the same black corner.

Are those eyes staring back at me?

Panic cascaded through her mind, her breathing turned to gasps, her mouth opened to scream. A shadow rushed from the darkness, and a thin, cold hand clamped her mouth shut. A beautiful, pale woman with eyes like living embers stared into her own terrified gaze.

My judgment awaits.

But then a curious thing happened. The stranger held a slim finger to her lips, squinted, nodded.

"No need to call out. I'm not here to harm you," she whispered. "Understand?"

Coyle shifted her gaze, studying the creature who was asking for understanding. She shook like a frightened rabbit in the stranger's powerful, iron grip. But, if the woman wanted her dead, she would have done it already. Right?

Coyle nodded, and the woman slowly lifted her hand away. They stepped away from each other, Coyle to the wall at her back, the stranger to the far side, allowing Coyle to study her.

A simple black dress covered her lithe frame. She was taller than Coyle and stood with the posture and build of a prima ballerina. Straight locks of short, dark hair framed a heart-shaped face. Her smile was at once both charming and disturbing. Her glowing amber eyes were full of savagery, cunning intelligence and focused will. A chill crept down Coyle's back, and she crossed her arms.

Is this my overactive imagination coming to fruition in the guise of a mysterious woman?

"Before we make standard introductions, I must confess I'm still in wonder at your attention to detail," Fang said. "How old am I, and where am I from?"

Coyle said nothing, still trying to decide what was happening. Maybe if she played along, the aberration would dissolve and she would shake herself awake. She gave the woman a glance before answering.

"Twenty-three, and your accent is southeast England. If I had to guess, you were raised near Buckinghamshire."

"I'm a bit older than that."

"Now to more important questions. If you're real, how did you get in here?"

"I can shift into a Shade. Vapor and shadow. It makes getting to my targets much easier."

"What are you?"

"That's a question I ask myself from time to time," she said. "I'm not entirely sure you would believe the answer."

The burning eyes. The ability to morph into a phantom shroud. Unnatural strength. All of it made horrible sense, but she didn't want to believe any of it.

"You're a vampire," Coyle said.

"You are quick, I'll give you that. But I do have a name. Why don't we start with the introductions?" she asked, and smiled. "Hello, my name is Fang."

"Fang." Coyle raised trembling fingers to her lips and immediately shifted her hands to her throat.

"You're not my type," Fang said.

"What are you doing here?" Coyle asked. She wiped her damp palms together, trying to stay afloat between madness and curiosity. *What in the world is a vampire doing in my cell? A vampire who doesn't want to harm me?*

Fang sat on the bench and clasped her hands together between her knees. She looked out the window and sighed, her eyes glimmering like hot coals as she stared at the stars.

"I need your help finding something."

That's not what I expected.

Coyle took a deep breath, letting out her nerves. "Your honesty is refreshing," she said. "But, I really have to ask, why me? I'm not a detective. I'm not good for anything." She motioned to the stained walls.

"Your value is based on your environment?" Fang squinted.

Coyle looked at the floor.

Fang continued.

"I need to find a dangerous book called *The Curse of Shadows.* It was written by the fae thousands of years ago. It's a book that, if used correctly, can change people into creatures or something worse. The scientists couldn't find it, but that didn't stop them from making me into this. They shaped me into their version of a nightmare: a vampire with military enhancements, complete with the ability to kill me when necessary."

"Sounds as if you've been through a lot. It also sounds like you need a librarian or antiquities dealer to find this book."

"It was stolen by two dangerous men, Trevin and Moreci. I killed Trevin six months ago, but Moreci is still out there somewhere, and he's going to use the book to kill hundreds of thousands of people."

"How... how can a book kill that many people?"

"There's a lot more going on in the world besides what you see on constable patrol."

"I don't like the way this sounds. We should go to the authorities. Maybe the government has resources."

"I killed my way out of a special weapons facility that used to belong to a group calling themselves the Templars of the Unseen Path. They're the ones who shaped me for their clandestine operations. Besides, you know none of those options will work. Look at me. Look at what I am, Coyle."

"Wait. *You* killed Trevin?" Coyle's fingers combed through her hair. "I solved that case fifteen days ago." She raised her hands in disbelief. "And here I am. Stuck in the same cell with the very murderer whose work I was tasked to decipher. Unbelievable."

Coyle paced. She was left with two options: help a vampire find a dangerous book, or tell her to leave. And everything in her liked the second option. She had always considered herself intelligent, despite her imagination and fear of the dark. She wasn't prone to incredulity or tall tales, and this tale was as tall as Eiffel's new Tower.

"Do you understand how... how mad all this sounds?" Coyle asked. She twisted a lock of hair around her finger. "And I'm supposed to believe a secret organization—Templars—have been creating your ilk for clandestine operations. The entire affair is quite unbelievable. How many men did you kill the night of your escape?" Coyle asked.

"I don't like the tone of your voice."

"Too accusatory?"

"Too self-righteous."

"I am a God-fearing woman listening to the ravings of a lunatic or a vampire, which I almost can't believe. I follow the law and adhere to our state's mandates of protecting lives and property."

Fang motioned to the cell. "And look where it's brought you."

"That's beside the point."

"You have trouble keeping the point, don't you? The point is, Constable Coyle—or rather *former* Constable," Fang said, tilting her head—"that you wanted to solve riddles by becoming a detective. You uncovered the clues to my work—"

"Your murder."

"—and now you sit in a charming cell, awaiting judgment. Here I am, offering you a dandy of a case. And it's one of a kind, I promise you that."

"And why would I trust a vampire?"

"Ah, so you're a believer, then?"

Coyle stomped her foot, hands on her hips. "You're quite vexing."

"Most vampires are."

A long silence passed as they stared at each other. Each of their wills was as strong as the bars that surrounded them, and yet Coyle couldn't deny she was indeed interested. A missing book of ancient curses wasn't something to pass up. And she did appreciate the modicum of trust and respect she'd established with this creature.

Only a modicum.

"Hold on. Why would a vampire want to save innocents?"

The vampire's face softened before answering. "Not all of me is a murderer."

"You're the epitome of disarray."

"You don't know the half of it." Fang snapped to attention and stood, gliding to the window.

"What is it?"

What would make a vampire distressed? Coyle wondered. Electric lights glowed through windows in the distance. A lone dirigible passed through the starlit sky. But no unusual noises. What was wrong?

"Men are coming," Fang said. "Two of them." She closed her eyes and held her breath before continuing. "They're going to take you."

"Who? What men? Take me where?"

"They have good intentions. They want you to find the book, too. Curious." She turned to Coyle. "I wonder if they're Templars."

"I thought the Templars are—evil?"

"It's complicated. Listen, I can't go with you for obvious reasons. But I'll keep in touch."

Darkness enshrouded Fang as a rusty door opened and heavy footsteps echoed through the hall. The mysterious visitor vanished, and Coyle was left with more questions that she couldn't possibly answer by herself.

They're going to take you.

All of this was madness. Yet, Coyle stepped away from the window, wrapped her thin, light-brown hair up in a bun and swept her bangs out of her face. She patted her dingy dress as best she could. She had to put on a new face. The face of someone grateful and excited to be taken away from here.

Do I actually believe this vampire? Is she telling the truth? Does that mean she's telling me the truth about everything?

She shook her head and looked up. A guard led two gentlemen to her cell. She examined them as the guard worked the lock. They were dressed the same: thick, black overcoats with dark-gray suits and expensive shoes. Simple gold rings bearing a Templars cross around their index fingers.

She stood away from the iron door and waited with her hands behind her back. The handsome one with the strong jaw and thin mustache spoke first.

"Constable Coyle," he said. "I am Detective Louis Vonteg, and this is Detective Kade Duone. We're here to grant you an early pardon from your sentence."

"My good sirs," she said. "I truly appreciate being released sooner than expected! What a gracious and wonderful surprise." She clasped her hands together and smiled. She knew what they wanted to see and gave it in earnest.

"We'll have a more frank discussion on the way to our destination." He turned to the guard. "Does she have any belongings?"

"No, sir," the guard answered. "Just what she's wearing." The men glanced at each other.

"Constable Coyle, you were admitted to this cell with no clean clothes to wear for…"

"Fifteen days, nine hours and a few minutes, but who's counting?" She beamed.

CHAPTER 5

The Treece mansion

Sausalito

The soft chime of midnight welcomed Coyle as she was escorted to her suite. The mansion was the complete opposite of her hard-walled cell in every way. Beautiful green-and-gold paper covered the walls. Custom engraved wood graced the ceiling. Brass and crystal sconces held electric-lighted lamps. Hand-carved furniture rested on rare carpets. And her room was just as marvelous.

Cream-colored silk sheets and down pillows promised a good night's rest. A full private bathroom with a steaming tub waited close by. Burning candles filled the room with lavender and rose oil. Steamed towels sat in a covered bin. A tray of chocolates rested on a table, waiting to be eaten. Every square foot contained a detail Coyle had never experienced. And there, by the bedside, were two wonderful tokens: a violin case and a pipe next to a small container of tobacco.

She opened the case and gasped. A Stradivarius. She inspected the tiny writing inside and beamed. 1719! She set it down gingerly. She was in no condition to touch such a remarkable object.

She slipped out of her dingy clothes and boots and sank into the tub. Her overwrought senses welcomed the heat, scented oils and fizzy bubbles. She took a deep breath and eased underwater, letting her body slide down where it was completely quiet. Safe.

Despite the comfort, she couldn't help but think about the past couple of weeks. She was nagged by her failure. All her work, snatched out of her hands. Or did she release it with a clenched fist?

She breathed out and forced herself to think of her surroundings, wondering if she would experience this again. What did they want with her? Was Fang giving her false information? Was she being led into a devious plot? Could she trust anyone here? Could she trust Fang? Could she trust a *vampire*?

Someone watches me.

Her eyes opened underwater and fixated on a dark silhouette. She shot out of the water, eyes flashing around the room before settling in the corner. Shadows from the cabinet danced in the candlelight.

She was alone.

She rubbed her face, silently cursed and closed her eyes. Seeing things in the dark was not uncommon, the consequence of having dark scars in her life, her mind always pulled away from what was real, stretching into the fringes of madness. But for once, her imagination came to fruition: a living shadow named Fang had emerged from the dark and pleaded for help.

A pleading vampire wasn't something she had heard of before. And they hadn't necessarily agreed to terms. But Fang had promised to keep in touch.

She opened her eyes into slits, scanning the room again. No, she was alone. She stretched and reached to the tray of chocolates, slipping one into her mouth. Strawberries and cream. A soft moan escaped her lips. She didn't want to leave this place. Wherever she was, whatever job they asked of her, she would make sure to remain close friends with them.

The men who picked her up had told her this was a government operation. A government-owned building. But she knew better. Fang had briefly mentioned a group calling themselves Templars, and their rings proved it. Besides, she knew wealth when she saw it, and this was not a government operation. She was inside a private mansion belonging to someone with great wealth and influence.

She picked another truffle from the plate. Honey nougat with a touch of lavender. A glance at the clock showed over an hour had passed. She pulled herself out of the tub and wiped the mirror. Her gaze hovered on the long, jagged, pink scar down the center of her body, but she turned her eyes away. She grabbed a brush for her hair and pulled out the tangles before wrapping herself in a thick, heated towel.

She blew out the candles and walked into the bedroom. This one room alone had cost more to furnish than she would make in five years. But what kind of money could provide all this? Shipping. Oil. Gold. Textiles. Real Estate. Old money. All valid explanations. Yet these Templars were a secret organization. Did they pool their money together? And what would they want with a washed-out constable with a temper, who couldn't sleep peacefully before the nightmares took her?

She let the towel fall away and picked up the violin. They must have given this to her. As a gift? As a bribe?

Her fingers fell into place and she played an easy melody, background noise while she thought. Her eyes searched the room. There was plenty of food, well-tailored clothes, and hot baths. All of this was a temporary comfort. Besides, this is not what she wanted for the rest of her life.

She preferred solving riddles, untying knots, and shedding new light on crime scenes. Each case studied and solved, and then on to the next one. And the next, and the next. Knowing humanity, there would never be a shortage of ugly crimes to solve.

She stopped playing and ran her fingers through her hair as she thought of the future. After she found Ronan, she would sit at her desk, with a steady supply of chocolates at hand, and pore through files of evidence, solving crimes until she was an older woman. That sounded like happiness. She'd lost the opportunity; but now, she may have another. She shook her head and studied the wooden sculptured ceiling tiles, trying to guess where they were from. Franciscan church, late seventeenth century. The furniture was more recent, early Edwardian. Rug, Persian, ninth century? Tenth century. She caught herself in the mirror, her eyes sliding down the scar he gave her.

She stopped playing and set the violin back into its case before lying in bed. Her fingers touched the space where her collarbones met. The skin was bumpy from his suture marks. She traced the scar down past her belly button, where it stopped. She frowned. Fang had said she was created by this organization. Created for a specific purpose.

Was she, Coyle, made as well? Did she have a specific purpose?

Four years since his cruelty.

A lump grew in her chest, and her shoulders tensed. She pressed her fingers into her eyes. She'd spent her time as a constable learning the law, dealing with criminals, all to become a detective. She had no idea how that would happen now. Not a clue. She sighed and closed her eyes to think. Just a few more ideas, hopes, and prayers before she would fall asleep.

***

She breathed him in...

Ronan wore the cologne she had given him for his birthday. His strong arm wrapped around her shoulder. Light showers soaked into the sidewalk, reflecting the orange glow from the electric streetlamps. His warm breath on her neck gave her butterflies.

"Let's go to your apartment," he whispered. "I have a hankering to pierce you."

She slapped his arm. "Look at you! Don't be a brute, Ronan. Just because you put a ring on my finger doesn't mean you get to 'pierce' me before our wedding." But her smile was as mischievous as his.

"Oh, it's not like we haven't before, sweetie." He pressed his lips into her neck the way he always did, ingratiating her lust. His kiss lingered, sending her to another place entirely, far away from the cold San Francisco fog and into the warm weightlessness of passion. This was her favorite place. Heart to heart. Skin to skin.

She pulled away, whispering, "Let's go, then. I'm ready to be pierced. Gently."

Someone knocked on a door. She looked around, but no one was there. The knocking persisted.

Coyle shot up and grabbed her chest, panting, her eyes wide with terror. The pillows and comforter were scattered on the bed and floor, and sun poured in from the windows. Her hair was a tangled mess.

Where am I?

Another knock on the door.

"Yes?" she asked.

"Miss Coyle?" a girl asked from the other side of the door.

"You're needed immediately. Please get dressed as soon as you can."

"Yes, of course. What time is it, please?" She rubbed her face.

"It's two in the afternoon, miss," the girl answered.

Two in the afternoon. She'd been asleep for over twelve hours. And now they wanted her immediately.

What have I gotten into?

CHAPTER 6

WIRE projection facility

Potrero Point

San Francisco

Thou hast begun a new work in me and canst alone continue and complete it.

Amen.

Coyle was handed a small bag marked with her name and ushered outside to a large carriage. It was painted glossy black with gold accents. Six large, knobby tires were affixed to the sides, and a curious steam engine quietly chugged at the rear.

"Everyone is waiting inside, miss," the butler said, motioning to the carriage's double doors. There were no horses to draw the transit, but she skipped the questions and stepped inside.

She joined six gentlemen on a plush leather bench. The interior was spacious and luxurious, with room for at least five more. An older gentleman tapped a metal-tipped cane on the cabin wall. A shrill whistle and hiss of steam announced their departure. She noticed the Templar ring on his finger.

"I do apologize for the abrupt start, Miss Coyle," he said, adjusting small-framed glasses over inquisitive brown eyes. Thick, steel-gray hair surrounded his pink face. "We were caught between letting you sleep most of the day or waking you up earlier to get started. I voted the former, and since this is my operation, my vote counts." His smile was cheerful. "But we do have an investigation to consider, and we must get moving. The bag is a picnic lunch to eat at your leisure."

"Thank you so much," Coyle said, stuffing the bag next to her. She wasn't going to eat in front of strangers. "And I apologize for sleeping so soundly."

"Not to worry, Miss Coyle," he responded. "I believe you are the strongest of our group and thus the most important. I wanted to make sure you were well rested."

Heat bloomed into her cheeks, and she gave a polite smile. She darted a glance at the other passengers, instinctively focusing on their body language, tone of voice, and eye contact for hints about their personas.

And whether I can trust them.

"Ah, where are my manners?" he said. "Let me introduce who we are. My name is Adrian Treece, and I am your humble host."

"Treece? You own Dawn Industries," she said. "The technology company."

"I also lead the North American division of a worldwide secret organization," he added. "Templars of the Unseen Path. We keep the denizens of Hell at bay so innocent people can sleep at night. Now, I'm confident in telling you all this because of your marvelous work a few weeks ago. Very impressive, I must add. We are in a bit of a bind. Our other detective has disappeared, leaving an opening for a formidable replacement. We only take in the best, and your remarkable work during the test scenarios was brought to our attention."

"What if I don't want to join these … Templars?"

"Well, if you do, I'm sure we can help you achieve your personal goals."

She glanced out the windows before answering. "This is another test, isn't it? To see if I'm good enough for your group."

"Sharp as a razor, she is!" he said with a twinkle in his eye. "Let me introduce you to your teammates." He extended his hand. "This is Professor Peter Quolo, emancipated slave and expert in ancient languages. Earned two master's degrees at Yale. He's head of Research and Development."

She smiled and studied him. Quolo had an honest smile and kind eyes that held stories that would put all of theirs to shame. His handsome, boyish face hid great wisdom and intelligence.

"I believe you've met detectives Louis Vonteg and Kade Duone," he said.

She nodded at them. Their boots, their accent and the scruff on their rugged, tanned faces spoke of experience chasing outlaws through deserts.

"My name is Rafael Boltuego," a thick-necked, barrel-chested man said out of turn. "Call me Bolt. My specialties are engineering and head cracking." There was a dangerous gleam in his eye, something dark and malicious. He flexed his hands and flashed his smile.

She ignored his wink and nodded at Treece.

A slender, handsome man spoke. "Chance Poes, investigating attorney. Pleasure." He refused to look away until she did. His face was unreadable. Plain, yet polite and professional. But nothing further. The mark of a good attorney.

"My name is Sherlyn Coyle," she said with a polite smile. "I am—I was—a constable with the San Francisco Police."

"And we're on a tight schedule to visit one of our gnome facilities," Treece said. "You remember the WIRE projector during your scenario?"

Coyle nodded. "The World Image Reconstruction Evaluator." She felt heat in her cheeks and turned away for a moment, trying to forget the embarrassment altogether.

"Well, we're going to visit another crime scene at the Baldwin mansion," Treece said. "The WIRE projection has a shelf life of less than eight months, and we're a few hours away from losing any shred of evidence."

Coyle frowned. "Baldwin mansion?"

"Seems there was a dinner party, followed by a massacre. An ancient book called the *Curse of Shadows* was taken from the residence," Duone said with a gentle Texas drawl.

"I had arranged the meeting between fae and humans," Treece said. "It was a political endeavor between the two peoples. I was in France when it was scheduled. When I heard of the tragedy, I rushed back as quickly as I could. Some of them were my close friends. Given the circumstances, I believed this was a case for the Templars. The book that was taken is quite dangerous, and we must do everything we can to get it back."

Coyle nodded. All of that sounded horrible and tragic and absolutely interesting all at once. And, of course, it was exactly what Fang had mentioned.

She wasn't lying, then.

The men discussed small details, and she caught and studied every word. Important visiting fae dignitaries had brought fae relics as a sign of openness and trust. But a mysterious group of people had slaughtered everyone and stolen the book of curses.

The idea of impressing Treece turned into a bright opportunity. Another chance at solving a difficult riddle? Another chance of becoming a detective, albeit with a secret organization? Her fingers twitched. Yes. All of this was possible.

Possibly.

She glanced outside. The rolling hills of Sausalito were thinning out, and she squinted.

"Are we approaching the shoreline?" she asked, gripping her seat.

"Miss Coyle, this carriage is equipped to transit land." Treece smiled as pebbles crunched beneath the wheels. A shrill whistle sounded, followed by mechanical clunks and locks and switches. "And water."

Her mouth dropped open as bay water lapped against the carriage. The floor vibrated.

"The wheels turn into propellers, Miss Coyle," Treece said. "The cabin is double-walled, providing adequate floatation, and a small rudder unfolds to provide steerage."

Strange hums and clanks came from behind and below. She pressed herself back into the seat and tried not to look nervous. A flock of terns scooted away as their carriage navigated the water, hugging the coast. A cargo ship lumbered close, and Coyle noticed most of the crew squinting, pointing and shooting curious stares. The air was chill off the dark water, and Coyle pulled her collar around her neck.

Finally, the carriage pulled up onto a launch ramp near a shipyard. Men, ogrek and a few gnomes carrying tools and lumber turned and looked, their jaws slack. But most didn't give the strange carriage a second glance as they continued their tasks. A sign on a weathered building read *Pacific Rolling Mill*.

Coyle mumbled to herself, "We're at Potrero Point."

"Yes, I own a few of the warehouses in this district," Treece said. "We should arrive in a few minutes."

The carriage stopped, and the carriage pilot opened the double doors.

"Here we are," Treece said. "Ladies first."

Coyle smiled and stepped out onto the street. The carriage pilot connected a water hose to the building and began rinsing off the underside of the carriage. A few passersby gave curious glances as the group collected themselves and walked into the warehouse.

A pug-nosed ogrek greeted them at the door. Most were intimidating due to their sheer size, and this one was no different. His massive muscles bulged under a simple gray shirt. Tribal tattoos stretched across his green skin and past his shirt collar. He nodded, gave the politest, yet awkward smile his oversized jaw could offer, and took their coats and hats before escorting them through a network of hallways filled with small offices.

He led them out of a large door and into a very busy warehouse where the air was filled with pungent ozone, hissing steam and incessant hammering. Thick-muscled ogreks held huge pieces of iron and waited as goggled, short gnomes welded them together, spraying gold sparks across the floor. Most of the ogreks were hairless, as opposed to the gnomes, who wore stylized, colorfully dyed beards and pointed mustaches.

"Gnomes are always a busy bunch," Treece said. "I have most of them working for my company. Pleasant to work with and quite loyal. I do pay them handsomely, too."

"Don't listen to him," said a gnome with a bright red beard. "We don't care as much about money as we do about getting new materials to work with."

"Ah." Treece laughed. "And here's Mr. Sullywether, manager of all of my warehouses in San Francisco. Can you take us to the WIRE projection room, please?"

"Right this way, folks!" Sullywether waved and plodded ahead of them. He was adorable in his blue sweater and overalls, but Coyle kept her mouth shut.

Vonteg leaned in. "I don't think they'd do too well on horses," he whispered. Coyle smirked.

"We do have excellent hearing, though." Sullywether turned and winked. Coyle and Vonteg glanced at each other.

Sullywether turned a few corners before opening another set of wide doors, leading them into a three-story warehouse. Tall WIRE projectors stood high above the floor in each corner, pointing their lenses at the empty center. Catwalks connected the projectors together, and Coyle could see small silhouettes working, making small adjustments on their respective projector devices. Everyone seemed to have a specific job and purpose, and they were doing their job well.

Coyle looked down at her fingernails, heart slamming against her ribs. She squeezed her trembling hands into fists.

***

High above the rafters of the same warehouse, a different kind of opportunity was coming together. Veiul slipped between the metal sheets of the roof and melted into the darkness. She froze and waited, eyes scanning for threats and potential threats. Her body was merely a shadow amongst shadows.

No one saw her.

Her muscles tensed as she scanned the busyness of the warehouse. Automatons clunked back and forth, gnomes crawled over everything, ogreks lifted heavy machinery. All of them were too busy to see her rail-thin, dark-clad form crawl into the massive projection room. Her strong fingers gripped thick cables and her legs wrapped around rafters, shifting and sliding until the gnome projectionists were beneath her. Four of them were double-checking their equipment, making sure everything would go right.

Veiul was there to make sure things went wrong.

She shimmied to a far corner, quick and quiet as a spider. Gnomes did have excellent hearing, but Veiul was a professional, and she wasn't going to let one of them ruin her objective.

She removed a thin, iron-silk cable from a pouch and tied it around the rafter. Lowering herself with one hand and with a dark blade with the other, she sank closer to her prey.

The gnome working this projector stood and yawned for the last time. Her knife slipped into his neck, and her other hand covered his mouth, just in case. He twitched once and was still. She lay his small body on the catwalk, stuffing his wound with combat gauze to keep his blood from spilling below. She tugged away the leather covering her pink, shapeless face, took another look around, and pulled out a small device with a blue glowing switch. She inserted it into the projector and waited.

***

"You ready?" Sullywether asked, and looked at a pocket watch with multiple faces. "We have less than three hours before the image degrades and becomes useless."

"We're ready, sir," Treece said. "I will stand by here, and the five of you need to find as many clues as you can. Apparently in less than three hours." His eyes rested on Coyle.

Coyle smiled. The burden of finding everything herself made her knees shake. She took a long, cleansing breath and flexed her hands. Treece was the most powerful, influential man in her sphere, and he was watching like a hawk.

That didn't work for relaxing, now did it?

"Let 'er rip!" Sullywether shouted. Loud cracks and snaps filled the air before a hazy shimmer of light flashed. Coyle covered her eyes as tendrils of bright, gold light wrapped around each other. Bursts of heat rushed past, her hair flying with each powerful pulse. She brushed her hair back and sniffed, then squinted and looked down at Sullywether.

"I know, I know: toast," Sullywether said. "Believe me, it's better than smelling four and half million units of boomwatts. *Bleh.*"

The air vibrated in steady, rhythmic waves until a large mansion appeared in front of them. Opalescent colors shifted on different parts of the structure until the palette settled into browns and tans.

"Markers?" Sullywether pointed to each projectionist. One by one, they gave Sullywether a thumbs-up. The one in the far corner gave a slack wave of his hand.

"It's a go, Treece," he said. "Once the time has passed, the image will fade. No harm to your team, just loss of evidence."

"I know you will do your very best," Treece said to them, but he gazed at Coyle. "The reenacted image you are walking into is situated roughly thirty minutes after the crime occurred."

Coyle's heart raced as they stepped through the projection. He was depending on her skills. She rolled her eyes. On one hand, this was an excellent chance to dig herself out of the proverbial grave. On the other hand, she was pressed into a performance of substantial consequence.

An abrupt change in the air grabbed her attention. The rapid drop in temperature slapped her skin, and she dug her hands into her pockets. White curls of breath rose from their mouths as they approached the front door.

"Why can't these incidents occur in the warm sun?" Poes said next to her.

"I'd take creosote bush, baked dirt and bright sun any day of the week," Vonteg agreed.

***

They stepped through the front door and into the parlor. As soon as the door closed behind them, Veiul pressed the switch on the molecular transference device, making it hum.

"They're on the timer," she said, pressing the transceiver switch in her ear. "Twenty minutes until they're killed."

"Excellent," said a deep, mechanical voice.

CHAPTER 7

A deep breath brought the familiar scent of fresh bread, smoked meat and steamed vegetables. Candles rested in wall sconces and on tables throughout the rooms. But the silence was eerie.

Unnatural.

They walked closer to the dining hall, and Coyle caught a single note of lilac perfume amidst the pungent cigar fumes. Duone and Vonteg saw the mess before anyone else.

"Good God Almighty," Duone said as the rest stepped carefully into the large room. The scene was shocking to behold. Blood spattered the sunshine-yellow wallpaper. Dark-red spots peppered the crystal chandelier. The wounds were fresh, yet the volume of spilled blood littered the air with a heavy, sweet, bile odor. The second time in as many days and Coyle would never get used to it. Removing her handkerchief, Coyle covered her nose and studied the eight bodies that lay in various poses. Two gentlemen, six women. Throats slashed. Eyes frozen in terror. Coyle turned away.

"It's a lot to take in," Poes said.

"I suppose I'm more used to bodies lying in a similar state due to the consequences of criminal activity," she said. "But these people were just having supper."

Poes nodded.

"I've seen massacres out in the flatlands of Nebraska," Duone said. "Between Paloma and Army, mostly. Both sides usually warriors. But Coyle's right. This is beyond savage."

"Fae dignitaries," Vonteg said. "They were meeting with our side, trying to work something out. A mutual benefit of sorts."

Coyle focused on a nearby display of simple-looking objects: a small statue, a mirror, jars of clear, luminescent liquid. Poes followed her gaze.

"Those are the fae relics," he said. "They brought them over as a token of trust between the two species."

"What's missing is the book." Quolo had joined them. "*Cuanteff Eme Burlsekwa,* loosely translated as *Curse of Shadows.*"

Coyle's mind shot back to Fang's plea. "Do we know anything else about this book?" Coyle asked.

"Not without fae," Quolo answered. "And the fae have sealed their gates until we get this incident sorted out."

"Miss Coyle," Bolt said. "Isn't your specialty digging around dead bodies? Maybe you should be over here."

He was right, of course, but she didn't like the tone of his voice.

Stop jibber-jabbing and get to work.

She cleared her throat and stepped closer to the slaughter, her eyes covering the details of the room. Everything was bathed in red. She couldn't even see the color of the rug. A lump grew in her throat.

Poes glanced at her. "There can't be too many female constables in the city, let alone the state of California. You must have an interesting story."

"It's not that interesting," she said as she knelt near a man. Her cheeks warmed. Poes was trying to get friendly. *Just what I need in an already uncomfortable situation.*

"I've learned to ask the right questions when searching for answers," Poes smiled. "And I can always find something interesting if I poke enough." He was an attorney. Making people uncomfortable was his pride. And she was uncomfortable.

"Right now, I need to find something interesting in these bodies, thank you." She turned the dead man's head and peered at his neck.

"Gentlemen, let's give Coyle a few moments alone so she can work," Vonteg said. "This here's a big house, and there are plenty of other places to look for something useful."

Their footsteps grew distant after a few moments, and she glanced over her shoulder. She was alone. In a sense. She let out a long breath of air and her shoulders slouched. She rolled her neck when a small noise caught her attention.

It was soft, just barely a whisper. But, what—or who—was it? She leaned over and studied the faces. Who could be alive after this? No one. She was hearing things.

Right?

And then she locked eyes with a woman. Her lips moved. Coyle pulled up the hem of her dress, keeping it away from the blood-soaked rug, and stepped over the bodies until she was next to the woman with lavender eyes. A thin line of blood seeped from the corner of her mouth. Her skin was pale, without life, yet she was alive. Her pupils were constricted, focused and locked onto Coyle's gaze.

The woman's lips formed shapes, struggling with words. Coyle leaned in close and dabbed her handkerchief at the woman's mouth.

"Keep this safe," the woman said, pushing each word out. "Keep this safe."

"I don't understand," Coyle said. "Keep what safe? *Vonteg!*" she called out, regardless of the fact she was standing in the aftermath of a crime that had occurred over six months ago. She didn't understand what or how this was happening, but she had to treat the situation as if it were happening right now.

The woman patted her waist. A bulge was under the material, and Coyle carefully lifted the woman's cool, soft fingers away. She tugged a pouch away and pulled out a large metallic ring with smaller concentric rings inside it. Runes were engraved along the outside. Coyle pushed a gemmed knob on one side. The rings came apart and hovered next to each other, tethered by a single blue, glowing strand. She switched hands, and the rings floated into a different formation but still held fast to the blue strand.

"What is this?" Coyle asked.

"Reciter. For the book. To read it." The woman's hand slipped away, and her eyes rolled back. "They don't know. Keep it safe." She let out a long sigh, and her body went limp, her eyes vacant.

Coyle held up her palm, and the rings returned to their original formation and collapsed into her hand. She pressed her finger into the woman's neck. No pulse. Coyle's eyes shifted to the Reciter.

What have I found?

***

Veiul's pulse quickened, and she pushed the switch on her transreceiver.

"They found the Reciter. Repeat, they found the Reciter," she said.

"Then it wasn't in Trevin's lair?" the deep, mechanical voice asked.

"The woman named Coyle just found it. Do you want me to single her out of the projection equation?"

"Yes. Send her to me. I'll take it when she arrives."

"Singling her out means there won't be enough power to kill the others, you understand," Veiul said.

"We do whatever is necessary to reach the objective. Let Death have her way when she wishes."

Veiul removed the device, adjusted its knobs, and returned it into the projector.

***

Coyle stood up and looked down at the other bodies, wondering if anyone else was still alive. She carefully inspected each of their faces and called out to Vonteg again. They would have to know what she found and what happened. She patted her pocket and felt the heavy rings inside. She smiled. She couldn't wait to see Treece's face when she shared the news. She was definitely on her way to becoming a detective.

The floor shifted underneath her. She steadied herself and looked down, but nothing appeared to have moved. She stepped out of the bloody mess and was about to call out again when Vonteg and Duone arrived from the staircase. She frowned when the staircase shifted colors.

"Coyle," Vonteg said. "What's wrong? Did you find some—"

She gasped as Vonteg and Duone shifted colors. Their mouths moved as if they were speaking, yet there was no sound. Portions of the walls and furniture shifted colors and disappeared for a moment before reverting back to normal. The air vibrated and made a scratching noise.

"Should we leave?" Coyle looked around the room. The walls and floors and ceilings were disappearing and reappearing all at once.

What's happening?

***

"We still have over two hours to retrieve any evidence, Coyle," Poes said as he rounded a corner. "What's wrong?"

Coyle's mouth moved as if she were speaking. The men frowned at each other. She looked at her hands and arms as her body shifted colors, from black and white to shades of blue and green, before changing back to normal. Dismay and shock washed over her face.

"Coyle?" Poes asked. He walked toward her. She shifted colors again, faster and faster until she burst into a flash of light. The men shielded their eyes. There was a loud pop and the sharp odor of hot metal.

Poes opened his eyes into slits and stood before a motionless, three-dimensional image of Coyle, the color of blue sky. The details were blurred, but Coyle's hand reached out to him, mouth was frozen in a scream eyes wide in terror. By instinct he reached for her, but the image melted into nothingness. He looked at the floor, then at the ceiling, but she was gone.

"What's happened?" Vonteg shouted. "Treece?"

The others came running until they were all standing near the crime scene. Treece and Sullywether exploded through the door.

"What's going on?" Bolt asked.

"Something happened to Coyle," Vonteg said. "She was flashing colors and then, poof, she's gone."

"But where?" Quolo asked.

"Sullywether?" Treece asked. All eyes settled on the gnome.

"Sounds like the work of a molecular transference device, and not one of ours. That means there is only one place she could have gone," Sullywether said. He shoved the cigar back in his mouth.

"She's at the original Baldwin mansion."

CHAPTER 8

The Baldwin mansion

Presidio Heights

"What happened?" Coyle asked. Her heart slammed against her ribs as she searched for Poes. But he'd vanished right before her eyes. All the others had vanished, too.

And that wasn't the half of it.

She stepped back, looking into the empty dining room. Everything was--different. No bodies. No gore. No blood-splattered walls. The furniture was missing. The walls were vacant of oil paintings, and the house smelled like dust and old wood. Warm sunlight poured into the empty spaces through bare windows.

"Am I...? Am I in the real Baldwin mansion?" She swallowed. Her eyes darted around the empty space. "How on earth did this happen? And where is everyone else?"

She stepped toward the front of the house, but the door opened, making her stop. A tall cloaked man stepped inside, flanked by two masked men with pneumatic rifles at their sides. They raised their weapons at her.

Her strength evaporated, and her knees trembled. She raised a hand to her mouth. The man closed the door behind them.

No one to help me.

The cloaked figure stood taller than the others. His bald head was covered in scars, and a brass-and-steel mask covered his mouth and nose. Thin tubes ran from the mask to a heavy contraption on his back. A small speaker-box rested under his chin. Eyes the color of sea grass displayed a bright, intelligent fire.

"So good to see you," he said. His mechanical voice dragged like an iron bar on a gravestone. "My name is Sigfried Moreci, and I've just learned your name is Sherlyn Coyle. Pleasure to make your acquaintance."

She shook her head. "This isn't happening. This can't be real." She stepped away from him all the same. "Vonteg? Duone? Treece? *Someone?*" Her voice bounced off the walls of the empty house.

"It's quite the shock to realize you're alone, isn't it, Miss Coyle?" he said. He lowered his chin and stared at her.

"You're not real. None of this is real."

"Give your rifle to her." He nodded to one of his men.

"Sir?" the man asked.

Moreci said nothing.

The gunman lowered his rifle, walked to her and handed over the weapon. He pulled out a semi-automatic handgun from his hip-holster and stepped back to Moreci's side, glancing up at him.

"Does that feel like a real rifle to you? Test its weight. Smell the gun oil."

She glanced down, shifting the rifle in her hands. It felt real. She blinked.

"Use it. Pull the trigger."

She tried to swallow. The strangers stared back at her. She lowered the weapon until it dropped to her side.

"Shame." He held out his hand, and the gunman handed him the pistol.

She tensed, her heart caught in her throat.

Moreci raised the weapon and shot the gunman in the head, spraying the wall with gunpowder and brains. The man dropped in a heap. Coyle backed into the wall and the rifle clattered to the floor.

"Now that we've uncovered the reality before us, let's change the subject. I heard you were interested in acquiring a detective position, but you failed. You've also failed to believe you're capable of killing when given the chance." He shook his head and chuckled. "You're not cut out for this. And it's not for lack of testosterone. It's more about the need, you see?"

"The need? To kill?"

"To survive."

"What do you want?"

"A chance to prove myself in the world." He held his hands behind his back. "Isn't that what you want? Yes, of course it is. And is it any wonder that we both get what we're looking for? We have a lot in common, you and me. Both of us have needs, desires."

"I don't think so." If she could buy just a few seconds, maybe she would be rescued.

"On the contrary, Miss Coyle. We both need something very important. I need a special key called the Reciter. It's used to read certain ancient tomes written in the fae language. We thought it was in Trevin's home until your excellent detective work popped up. You didn't think Treece and his ilk were the only people interested in what you could find, did you?"

The only people?

"I don't know what you're talking about." Her gaze flashed around the room, and she inadvertently pressed her fingers against the ring in her pocket.

"Treece is the worst kind of backstabber you can imagine. He uses all his money to get what he wants, and when he's finished, he'll destroy you." His eyes hovered over her pocket.

"That's not true." She hoped.

"I have proof." He motioned his hands to present himself. "Here I am, barely alive."

"Yet able to slaughter innocents."

"Tell me. Is there anything you need so desperately that you would do anything in your power to get it?"

She paused too long. "No."

"Don't take me for a fool." He stepped forward. "I certainly wouldn't take you for one."

"If you're not a fool, then who are you?"

"The long answer is that I was once a good, hard worker. Treece noticed something in me that others didn't and hired me to do his work. Does that sound familiar? But I digress. He wanted me to create an army, one that could fight against the powers of darkness that plagued mankind—under his control, of course. And I created marvelous soldiers for him, absolutely marvelous. Stunning showcases of what could be wrought from my laboratory. Alas, my brilliance was overshadowed by my naiveté, and by the time I realized I was expendable, it was too late. Treece was finished with me, and I was discarded like a used tin can.

"I survive now with the help of oxygen scrubbers and medicated baths. I certainly will never forget the enormity of what happened to me, of how he changed me. There's real power in change, isn't there? Why, you have the same look in your eye, as if someone changed you. Yes, curious. For the better, I hope. Yes, I think so, I think so. For now we have this power within us. It's our impetus for change, swooping in to capture and strangle what was so close to destroying us. Yes, you and I are the same, aren't we?"

"We're nothing alike."

"We're more alike than you care to perceive. It is curious, though. I wonder who changed you. It had to be someone you were close to you, someone you trusted. Someone of great value. Betrayal does that to a person: it drives them beyond their own limits and fears to become something new."

She needed to keep him talking. "You said that was your long answer. What's the short answer?"

He tilted his head. "The shorter answer is that I am mankind's reckoning. I was changed into this for the better. If Treece represents a bulwark for humanity, then I happily represent its impetus for change. I am going to change people, turn them into *my* soldiers, for *my* purpose, under *my* control. And I can't continue without the Reciter. Now, are you going to give it to me, or do I have to change you too?"

Ice slid down her spine. Her hand reached back to the stairwell and she ran. Up one flight, then two flights, then down the hall. Every room was empty. No furniture to hide behind. No dressers to push against the door.

No place to hide.

"There is no escape, Coyle." His amplified voice echoed off the hardwood walls and floors and ceilings. "Just as surely as mankind has no escape from me."

She searched room after room. She paused for a beat and heard the other gunman plodding up the stairs.

"Give me the device, and I give you my word to let you live. I need the Reciter, and you need to learn to survive."

Every room she tried was a dead end. Finally, she shoved herself into a closet and shut the door as heavy boots clomped down the hallway. She heard a mechanical clicking noise and turned, frowning as two blinking eyes stared back at her.

"Are you an automaton?" she whispered.

"This is my hiding place," it answered, shoving her out the door and closing it just as the thug grabbed her.

She was dragged back downstairs where more gunmen waited. Fighting was useless. Two of them rifled through her pockets until they found the prize. She met Moreci's hard gaze.

"I am the victor here," he said.

"I don't have to like it," she retorted. "And that doesn't belong to you."

"And it belongs to you?"

"It needs to be returned to the fae. Give it back!" She reached for it, but strong hands yanked her back, and cold steel muzzles pressed against her body. She froze.

Moreci opened his hand and let the rings spread out in a configuration. He waved his hand, and the rings rearranged in the air before they slipped back into their original position.

"Miss Coyle," he said, "I extend my generosity to you. Though you didn't hand the device freely, I will let you live another day. Let me know when Treece wants you exterminated, and perhaps I can help."

"I prefer not to work with monsters."

He chuckled, the sound of it like gasping, and then he leaned over in a fit of coughing. One of his men adjusted knobs on his apparatus, and Moreci took a deep breath and stood.

"Monsters. You don't really know Treece, do you?" he said. He waved his hand. The rifles pointed at her head lowered. "I'm very curious, Miss Coyle. If you don't mind, I'm going to learn everything I can about you. Until then."

They left, their boots thudding against the wooden floors.

She collapsed against the wall, breathing out a long sigh. A tight knot grew in her chest, and she clenched her fists. She wasn't going to cry over this. Not now. She'd lost something very important. She'd given it away, practically.

It's gone.

The opportunity to prove her worth had been snatched out of hand—again. And now she was her old self, an incompetent buffoon.

Her head thumped against the wall before she remembered the automaton.

He's going to answer for this.

She went back upstairs and yanked open the closet.

"You," she growled.

"But there wasn't room for the two of us!"

CHAPTER 9

The Treece mansion

Sausalito

"It's a wonder you are still alive at all, Coyle," Treece said. "This Moreci character sounds incredibly dangerous, and he's working with a former soldier of mine, Fang."

"Fang killed one of my projectionists and used a molecular transference device to suck you out of the warehouse and into the real Baldwin mansion," Sullywether said. "Those devices can be tricky, seeing as how they weren't invented by gnomes."

Coyle nodded and puffed from her pipe. The group was in a large workshop, standing around the automaton Coyle had found. Most automatons were plain brass and steel, but this one was polished to a high shine with intricate silver and gold filigree. Bright green gems mimicked eyes, and a small rectangular speaker-box formed its mouth. Various switches and buttons and pipes with pressure gauges covered its chest and back.

"It's a Model GEM-9," Sullywether said. "I thought you recalled all those?" he said to Treece.

"We did," Treece answered. "Though we were told a handful had been lost."

"Looks like someone was fibbing," Quolo added.

Sullywether pulled himself into stilted metal legs and tightened the leather straps so he stood at a similar height to the rest of the group. He slipped into metal exoskeleton arms and flexed the metal fingers.

"What does GEM stand for?" Vonteg asked.

"Gnomish Engineered Mech," Sullywether said.

"Why were the GEM-9s recalled?" Poes asked.

"They were a ninth-generation prototype of artificial creation and intelligence," Sullywether explained. "Marketed to the rich. They did fine for the first few months, but then they got mouthy, brewing up their own ideas of their place in the world. Some started naming themselves. We found a couple out in Colorado that called themselves bounty hunters."

"Mr. Baldwin kept my name as GEM," the automaton said. "And we had an arrangement: I would keep most ideas to myself, and he wouldn't turn me in. I kept watch over his family as a faithful servant for 1,095 days, and I would never hurt a fly."

"You pushed Coyle out of the closet," Poes shot back. "What was that all about?"

"I told her: there was only room enough for one of us. I saw what happened downstairs. Someone with daggers switched all of the dinner party guests off, one by one and in quick succession. I certainly didn't want that to happen to me," GEM said with raised hands.

"And you've been hiding upstairs in the closet ever since?" Coyle asked, relighting the tobacco.

"Wouldn't you?"

"Wait a minute," Poes said. "You were there when the Baldwin mansion was attacked. What do you know about it?"

"I suppose everything," he answered. "I am required to record all emergency incidents. More for proof that I wasn't the cause of them."

"But you said you were hiding upstairs," Coyle said.

"I prefer to call it surviving, thank you," GEM said, and blinked at her. "But I am synchronized with the other automatons who were downstairs and recorded what they saw."

"We can hook him up to the roto-display," Sullywether said. The gnome grabbed a long, thick, flexible tube and connected it to the base of GEM's polished dome. After a few clicks, Sullywether moved

to the table and flipped a few switches. A long, dark metal rod with

joints popped out of the center of the table before splitting into

branches and spinning. Sullywether pushed a knob, adjusted the speed

to something he liked and flipped another switch. Small arcs of

electricity jumped between the rods until a blue globe appeared.

"Ready," Sullywether said, glancing at Treece.

"I suppose we should watch from about fifteen minutes prior to

the incident," Treece said.

Sullywether turned a couple of knobs, and the globe hissed and

crackled until images appeared.

"Moving pictures? Like Edison's kinescope?" Vonteg asked.

"Pfft. this is nothing like Edison's work," Sullywether said.

"Tesla designed this. He's got all sorts of gadgets no one's seen. I'm

ready to believe he's just a tall gnome, because no human on earth—"

"Let's just play the image, shall we?" Treece said with a tight

smile. He shot a polite glance Coyle's way, but he was obviously

disappointed in her. She looked down and shook her head.

The moving pictures were different shades of blue, but amidst

the crackle and hum of the moving parts, there was recorded sound.

Everyone, including GEM, stared at the globe and watched the entire event.

Coyle's ears perked up when the dinner guests began talking about fae history. An older woman named Dame Graethe did most of the talking. Coyle recognized her as the woman who was still alive.

"Keep it safe."

"We live in peace and harmony with almost all of the other races and species," Dame Graethe said through the speakers. "Ogreks, mudlucks, sprites, vamperion and gnomes are our friends. Most of the time. But there have been factions of fae or vamperion who split off to follow a deranged leader who's so inclined. One such fae deviant was Arch-general August, who wanted more power than he held. He joined with the vilest race, the frost wyches, to walk our nether-realm. They built an army and set out to destroy us."

"To destroy fae-kind?" someone asked.

"To destroy everyone," Dame Graethe said. "Fae magic is particular, non-threatening. We won't use magic to kill. But vamperion are different. If the fae are wardens of the day, vamperion are of the night. Their magic is visceral, unyielding and deadly."

"So, vamperion are—benign?" someone asked. "Or are they violent?"

"They're no more violent than any other species when pressed to survive," she answered. "They were quiet and kept to themselves and complemented the fae in every way. But the August War threatened everyone, and they took the lead in stopping his army. Vamperion mages created a book of spells powerful enough to defeat our enemies."

"*The Curse of Shadows*," Coyle said to herself.

Dame Graethe continued, "The vamperion unleashed destruction, and August's armies were wiped out—but not without consequences. Our sky and moon became one, erasing the familiar lavender sky of day and dull crimson of night. Our world no longer rotates. It's as if our eight seasons became one, and our crops have steadily declined over the past 1900 years, as have our races. We do what we can, but life has become difficult."

The dinner table was silent for a time before someone asked, "And what of the vamperion? Heralded as champions?"

Dame Graethe shook her head. "The vamperion went mad, whether from the change in our world or from the book itself. They turned into the creatures you call vampires, cursed to drink blood to survive, cowering from sunlight. They saved all of the nether-realm but lost their rightful place. Once a proud people, they now survive as frightful, pale shadows of their former selves."

The slaughter erupted soon after she spoke those words. Furniture was smashed against a wall. Screams erupted. Coyle looked away from the carnage, but the audio continued to play out the last horrid screams until all was silent. She turned back and looked at the bloody scene she had walked through. Then she watched as a familiar woman pick up a book from the table. Her posture, build and shape were certainly familiar. Coyle pictured the glowing ember eyes, she could hear the clipped-British accent. The woman in the images searched the room for a bit before leaving with Trevin out the back door. Coyle's skin chilled. This was the woman who'd visited her in the cell, who wanted help finding a dangerous book. The same vampire who said she would keep an eye on her. She glanced to the sides, studying the dark corners.

"Stop the roto-display." Treece sighed. "It's obvious the dinner party was ambushed by two people." He rubbed his face and stared at the floor.

"One witness described a young female—fair skin, short dark hair, dressed in dark leathers—using daggers. This is the assassin known as Fang," Duone said. "Not too much is known about her except that she's ruthless, cunning and a dangerous vampire." He showed everyone a photograph of a lovely woman with short hair, her dark eyes vacant.

"She's definitely pretty," Bolt said.

"And deadly," Duone added.

"No doubt." Quolo said.

"Do vampires use daggers to kill?" Poes asked. "Don't they have--teeth?"

Treece answered. "She was part of a secret project called Archangel. We thought, what better way to kill monsters than with our own, created and put carefully together in labs? Fang was the most successful of this new breed of soldier. But the manner in which she was created didn't sit well with the rest of the Templar leaders—and they were right. We shut the project down and set the whole thing for eradication. These man-made soldiers were supposed to be transported to a research center in the New Mexico Territory, but most of them disappeared. We got wind that the US government had placed these missing creatures into a secret location. After a few years of fruitless leads, we stopped looking.

"Just over six months ago, a warehouse burned into the bay," Treece continued. "Witnesses described hearing strange howls and moans coming from the structure. We had our suspicions, until Miss Coyle unraveled the mystery of Trevin's death and confirmed our deepest fears: Fang was responsible for all of it. The burning warehouse, Trevin's death and now this. She was made to be a one-of-a-kind unstoppable weapon and we're witnessing the devastation she's capable of."

"Well, she's on the move with this book of curses," Quolo said. "A dangerous book in the hands of a dangerous killer. I think we need more people."

"Possibly," said Vonteg.

The discussion turned to Trevin and why he would be involved, but Coyle stared at the last frames of the image and lit her pipe. She sucked a long draw until the tobacco tinged orange and she exhaled smoke. She squinted, staring at the images. Something wasn't right.

"I apologize," Coyle said, interrupting them. "But can you go back a few seconds? I thought I noticed something."

Sullywether shrugged and turned a knob. The images reversed. Coyle leaned in and pointed with the pipe stem.

"There, see?" she said.

"What do you see?" Vonteg asked. Everyone squinted at the moving images.

"Play it again, just these last few seconds," Coyle said. "The light changes shape on Fang's face. See? She looks back, and the light and shadow are different on her face. The nose and jawline melt into a different position, almost as if she were wearing a featureless mask."

The images reversed and played back again. It was plain as day to her, but no one else agreed.

"I think it's a trick of the light," Duone said. "Hard to make out with these visuals."

Coyle's observations were dismissed, and discussion turned to newer technologies and the differences between Tesla's inventions and gnomish engineering. Coyle stared at the images as they flipped back and forth. She was positive she was right. The images proved Fang was telling her the truth. But she wasn't ready to tell them the assassin vampire had visited her in a jail cell and asked for help. Then they wouldn't believe or trust her, and she would be turned out onto the street, left to figure out another way to make detective. Best to keep that card close to her chest. Yet she had to try to open their minds.

"Are there fae or vampires who can change the shape of their face?" she asked. "Maybe this isn't Fang. Maybe this is someone else."

The men turned to her with frowns.

"Preposterous!" Bolt said. "Any of us could easily see the vampire's face throughout the incident. She is a trained assassin, apparently full of madness, and we just watched her slaughter."

"But what if there's another assassin at work here? What if Fang is innocent?" Coyle asked. The question hung in the air like a rotted apple no one wanted to pick. Odd looks shot her way. Someone cleared their throat.

"Let's get back to the real meat. The book gets stolen, and Moreci wants to kill a few people?" Poes asked.

Coyle was glad for the diverted attention. First, she'd lost an important piece of evidence, and then her hypothesis had been brushed aside. *Such a fine start.* All she wanted to do was crawl under the table and hide in the dark. There would be no more talking for a while. A long while. She leaned against a table, her cheeks warm, vacantly staring at her nails.

Just how important did you think you were?

"The book was used to kill an army," Duone said. "Why kill tens when you can kill hundreds of thousands?"

"He means to wipe out a large population," Treece said, and bowed his head. "Possibly an entire city."

"So a murderous vampire slaughtered innocent guests and stole a book," Bolt said. "And apparently Coyle gave them a device to use it. How thoughtful of you." His dark eyes bored into Coyle. "And now you seem especially forward in claiming Fang is innocent. Are we to believe you and Fang are in collusion together?"

"That's ridiculous," Coyle said, her voice cracking.

"Is it?" Bolt asked.

Maybe.

"How dare you insinuate a vampire and I are working together?" Coyle said. She squeezed her hands into fists. Her body shook with anger and fear all wrapped together. He was right, of course. They were working together, just not in the sense he was talking about.

"You may have fooled the others, Coyle," Bolt said. "But you're not fooling me."

"It does sound a bit odd," Duone said. "Why are you trying to defend this vampire?"

"I believe she's just trying to investigate all possible avenues," Quolo offered. "It's what she was trained for."

"Yet she failed," Bolt added.

"Gentlemen," Treece said. "We know nothing else at the moment, and what we need is unity, not division. Miss Coyle did the best she could, I'm sure. Why don't we adjourn for a moment and let me have a discussion with our esteemed guest?"

The others left the room amidst a babble of murmurs. Poes was the only who looked back and gave her a slight nod before he left her in the room with GEM and Treece.

"I'm so sorry, Treece," she said, setting the pipe down and running trembling fingers through her hair.

"Miss Coyle, I'm more happy you're safe than… anything worse."

"It's just that, well, I feel like a failure. I was supposed to help you in this mission, and I keep failing."

"On the contrary, Miss Coyle. You found a peculiar device no one else found before you were confronted by Moreci." He rested a hand on her shoulder. "I'm happy to have your services, and I believe you're the perfect fit for the Templars."

She smiled politely. Her skin prickled.

You really don't know Treece, do you?

How many times would she fail before Treece decided she wasn't worth keeping around?

Let me know when Treece wants you exterminated.

She pulled away from him and wiped her face. "I appreciate everything you've offered me. If you feel I should resign from—"

"Absolutely not."

"I don't feel I'm pulling my weight here."

"If you feel deficient in pulling or pushing weight, you can count on me to help," GEM said. He blinked his emerald eyes. "After all, you helped me in my time of need. They would have found me if it weren't for you."

Coyle frowned.

"There, see?" Treece patted her shoulder. "Even the automaton would like you to stay. You're needed here, Miss Coyle. I believe you can do a great amount of good."

"I don't know what else I can do," she said.

"Why don't we send you and the others to Trevin's place to have a look around? I know you could find something useful. And GEM will help take care of you."

"Absolutely!" GEM said. "Where is Trevin's housing located?"

"Fort Alcatraz," Treece answered.

GEM blinked and swiveled back and forth between Coyle and Treece.

"Fort Alcatraz is surrounded by a cold, deep ocean with surprisingly strong currents." GEM gently patted Coyle's shoulder and leaned close. "All that to say—I can't swim. I believe it's in all of our interest if I sit this one out. Best of luck!" he said, and headed to the doorway. "Gentlemen, who wants sandwiches?"

CHAPTER 10

Let me never slumber, never lose my assurance, never fail to wear armor when passing through enemy land.

Amen.

It was close to noon when they embarked on the magnificent waterborne horseless carriage. Three volunteered: Poes, Vonteg and Coyle. The others opted out, giving her a wary eye. She wasn't sure which was more hurtful, the fact that she wasn't trusted enough by the other men or the fact that Poes and Vonteg were basically forced into working with her.

This was nothing new. In her former line of work, not too many men wanted to work with the "weaker" sex, and those who did were mostly interested in the possibility of intimate relations. She found it infuriating all the same. She just wanted to be the best candidate for promotion, and since she wasn't going to heed their desperate urge for relations, she had opted for the test scenarios with her peers.

She hunched over, shoulders slouched, resting her chin on her knuckles, eyes gazing out at the bustle of the streets.

"How are you feeling so far, Miss Coyle?" Poes asked.

"Fine, I suppose," she answered. "I've never been involved with an investigation on this scale."

"Do you feel like you fit in? Or not?" Poes asked.

She paused. He was an attorney; she had to remember he was trained to get to the point.

"Truthfully, I do not. But I also suppose it's natural since I'm the only person unfamiliar with the Templars and Treece. I can't say anything bad, of course. I mean, he's invited me into his amazing home and provided every furnishing I need, even new clothes."

"He's generous with what he has," Vonteg said.

"I've never seen so much of it in my life," Coyle said. "My father is rich, too, but he never shared any of it with us. We lived in a simple home outside of Sacramento. He was always away and too busy building his shipping empire."

"Treece is a good man," Vonteg said. "Gives to charities, supplies hospitals with equipment, helps build farms for the poor. Not a mean bone in his body."

"He's kind to his... employees?" she asked.

Vonteg nodded. "And members of the Templars. He gave me a small bonus when my firstborn came into the world. And then he sent a nursemaid to help with the first year. I'm lucky to be working with him."

"And you?" Coyle asked Poes. "How long have you been working for him?"

"I got picked up by Dawn Industries less than a month ago," he answered. "I haven't seen as much, so I'm in the same sort of boat you are."

"Every Templar in North America works for Dawn Industries, but not every employee for Dawn is a Templar. Treece runs a world-renowned conglomeration. He uses Dawn Industries to create what's necessary for agents in the field, who in turn protect assets owned by Dawn."

"What are the Templars all about?" Poes asked.

"Lots and nothing at all," said Vonteg. "I know this all sounds strange, but there are a lot of dark things out there. I've fought against a small army of mummies in Peru, a swarm of tentacles in Lake Okeechobee. The most frightening thing was probably a para-demon in New Mexico. Took eight Templars out before we could banish it."

"That was the 'lots,'" Poes said. "What did you mean about the 'nothing'?"

"No one outside of the Templars knows what we do. Not our neighbors, not our families, not our children. All of our work is kept silent, and that's the way it's been for thousands of years. We're of the Unseen Path, the path no one knows about, the path that's used most by the enemies of mankind. But that's the rub. So much of our work is quiet, we lose people sometimes. People disappear, and sometimes people die, and people turn against us."

"What does he need an investigative attorney for?" Coyle asked. "No offense intended."

"None taken," Poes said. "The Templars operate as their own agency, their own business. And as such, they have need of everything a business needs: phone operators, radio operators, pilots for airships, and the list goes on. I'm needed on this case because apparently an employee had not been truthful with his work schedule and hid potentially valuable information."

"Trevin?" Coyle asked.

Poes nodded.

She studied his face. His eyes. The pulse of his jugular veins. Something was off about the man, but she couldn't put a finger on it. Or maybe it was something else.

Overactive imagination.

"What do you know about Trevin? Was he a Templar?" Coyle asked.

"Trevin?" Vonteg said. "No, strictly an employee of Dawn's Industries. As I understand it, he supervised a lot of research and development, but not like Quolo's work. Trevin worked with a small team that studied problems and resolutions from older cultures. They collected art, books, writings, relics, that sort of thing. They hoped that learning from the past would help create a better Dawn Industries."

"Apparently he found something along that kind with this book," Poes said.

"So we're on our way to his offices?" Coyle asked.

"He moved around, but he did spend a lot of time at Fort Alcatraz," Vonteg said. "The Union used it for training during the Northern Aggression. Right now, it's less an army outpost and increasingly more of a jailhouse. But there may be something there to tell us why he was targeted and killed."

"I wonder what he was researching out there," Coyle said. The men glanced at her with blank faces. No one answered because no one had the answer. But finding it was the main purpose of their visit. She rubbed her fingers together at the prospect of discovering fresh clues, new opportunities to make things right.

"Everyone hold tight," the driver said.

"Bumpy roads?" Coyle asked, looking out the window and expecting to be jostled.

Poes nudged her side with his elbow. "I've got you," he said. Coyle threaded her arm through his and held tight, her heart rate thumping along with the bumpy road and the warmth of him. She was receiving mixed signals. He was challenging but thoughtful. Masked yet disarming.

Men.

She would never understand them.

"No, just getting into the bay," Vonteg said. He smiled playfully at both of them as the carriage rolled down a steep slope.

Water splashed against the hull as the carriage drove into the bay, the craft becoming weightless. She glanced outside and saw the wheels fold upon themselves and retract under the chassis. Long tubes protruded from the sides and opened horizontally. Canvas material emerged from the tubes and filled with air until they expanded. Clicks and whirrs came from below their feet until a steady hum vibrated through the cabin. The craft bobbed from side to side but glided through the water without trouble.

Poes glanced at Coyle, and they both noticed they were grasping each other's arms. They pulled away and straightened themselves out.

Vonteg laughed. "You two are the first I've seen cling to each other like little kittens when their momma runs off."

Coyle turned as far away from the two as possible so they couldn't see her smile.

The dock became visible, and the carriage slowed to a stop before the driver tied the line to the cleats. He opened the door, and Coyle got out first, followed by Poes and Vonteg.

The air smelled of sea-lion waste and dried seaweed, and she never got used to it. She huffed out a breath and glanced around. A tall, whitewashed lighthouse rested on top of rolling hills and stood tall over the other structures in the distance. Long-fingered succulents with bright purple flowers covered most of the ground. Just as Coyle was wondering if they were even allowed to be on the island, a small group of Army men arrived on horseback, their weathered blue uniforms dulled by the sun and ocean air.

"Names?" asked a man with a yellow hat, tanned face and grayed mustache.

"Detective Vonteg, Miss Coyle, and investigative attorney Poes," Vonteg replied. "We're here to search a former employee's quarters and office space."

"I'm Sergeant Tanner, US Army. You talking about Trevin? Heavy guy, always wearing white suits?" the man asked.

"That's the one," Vonteg said.

Tanner spat a line of tobacco juice. "We gathered as much stuff as we could find and set it aside. These gentlemen will escort you to his building. I'll have to ask for your firearms while you're on the property."

"Oh, sir, we don't have any…" Coyle's voice trailed off as Poes and Vonteg pulled handguns from under their coats and handed them over. She pretended to be busy straightening her skirt and wondered when the weapons were handed out. Then again, the weapons were undoubtedly their own. Their line of work would require appropriate means of self-defense when called upon. She wasn't allowed to carry a firearm as a constable. Most of that was police policy, and some of it was chauvinism. Between the two, she wouldn't be issued a gun anytime in the near future. Which was fine all the same. She wasn't even sure she could be a decent shot.

They followed the soldiers over small hills until they arrived at the mesa that was Fort Alcatraz. Barracks, storehouses, and walls were built in the Spanish mission style. Whitewash over curved natural stone. Coyle noted the lighthouse and some smaller residences were made of wood. Tanner pointed to a house.

"That's his place right there," he said. "We set his belongings out for you to look through."

"Thank you kindly," Vonteg said.

"How long do you think you'll need?" Tanner asked.

"Not long," Vonteg answered.

"Listen, we're not your babysitters. Just don't go through the other houses or any other buildings and you'll be fine. Got it?" They nodded, and he and the soldiers left.

They walked toward a heap sitting in front of the house. Furniture, clothes, cabinets, utensils and everything else between had been tossed into the pile.

"I'm not sure what to look for," Coyle said.

"Paperwork, journals... anything that had to do with his studies and work," Poes said. He moved into the pile and began sorting through the mess. Coyle and Vonteg followed.

The air was chilly despite it being the middle of June. Coyle kept herself warm by digging through clothes. Her fingers searched through every pocket, looking for notes or anything worthy to be called evidence. She still wasn't sure what they would find. She was also aware that the others didn't know about the bloodstains hidden on Trevin's pants and shoes. That was Fang's blood, if she was telling the whole truth. And Coyle had a feeling she was telling the truth, but still--

"Find anything?" Vonteg asked.

She frowned at a stack of folders in his hands.

"A few dollars is all," she answered. "Looks like you found a few items." She tried to sound encouraging.

"A few work orders and receipts for things he needed. Hopefully, we can find more," he said.

Coyle looked around. "Where's Poes?"

"He went into the house a few minutes ago," he said. "I think we're done out here, so let's join him."

Tall, thick bushes surrounded the small, one-bedroom, craftsman-style construction. Windows with thin drapes were set on either side of the open door. The walls and wooden floors were bare. Coyle walked to the small kitchen out of curiosity and glanced outside the small window above the sink.

The bold blue of the bay was a stark contrast to the tan bluffs of the island. Foamy wakes from passing ships glimmered in the sun. She looked down at the gas range. It was too clean. He probably never cooked. She opened the oven door and peeked inside, expecting to find a manila folder filled with all the secrets she could hope for. It was empty, of course.

"Anything in the kitchen?" Vonteg asked her.

"A nice view is all," she answered.

"There's nothing in the house except a few built-in bookshelves," Vonteg said. "Poes, what are you looking at?"

Coyle walked into the bedroom. Poes stared at something in the closet, silent. They followed his gaze at a blank wall. She looked back at him. He wasn't looking at the wall, but something else entirely.

"Poes?" she asked. He blinked and looked at the floor.

"Sorry, just ruminating," Poes replied. "There's nothing here."

Coyle wiped her finger along the wall and looked at the dust on her fingertip. She glanced at each of the four walls and said, "Doesn't look like he hung any pictures or paintings. He hardly used the stove. It's like he didn't really live here."

"Well, he's got a yard full of belongings out front," Vonteg said. "Someone must've lived here. May as well be him."

"You're right, of course," she said. "I guess I'm thinking about how a person makes a place their home. Pictures, plants, things they enjoy. Wouldn't all these things be in a place you live? And not a single one of those are in the yard outside."

"What's that tapping sound?" Vonteg said. They stepped back into the living room and found Poes tapping the floorboards. "What are you looking for? Buried treasure?"

Poes didn't answer as his foot tapped different parts of the room. Coyle guessed what he was looking for and tapped the floor in the hallway.

"Both of you think he's got a trap door here? They're usually hidden under a rug, but there's no hiding anything on this floor," Vonteg said. He shook his head at the idea, but Coyle noticed he walked into the kitchen to explore cabinets.

Vonteg was right about this particular floor. There weren't any perpendicular lines across the wood boards. She walked to the built-in bookshelf and checked for openings, cracks, anything that would give away a possible trap door. Finding nothing useful, she stepped back and stared down at the lighted floor. Tiny bits of dust swirled around her dress and glowed in the sunlight. When she was a child, she used to imagine the dust particles were angels. Thousands and millions of angels dancing in the air. And now they danced around her dress.

Are they not all ministering spirits sent forth to minister for them who shall be heirs of salvation?

As she grew older, wiser, she knew the truth. It was just dust. Not angels. But even dust has its purpose. She frowned at the dust, dancing at the edges of her dress—she had an idea. She scraped her hand along the wall, gathering dust and dropping it in front of the bookshelf. The dust settled gently to the floor and she waited. Nothing happened.

She walked into the living room where the other two bookshelves were and found Poes also scooping dust into his hand and dropping it. He had thought of the same thing. Vonteg stepped into the room.

And then it happened.

All three watched as a steady puff of air blew dust away from behind the bookshelf.

"There, see it?" Poes said. He pointed at something along the floor. "There's an arc here, just barely etched into the surface. This is the door."

"To where? And why?" Vonteg asked. No one had the answers yet. Poes checked each of the shelves for a mechanism of some kind, but nothing happened. Then he tried lifting the book case and a dull crack echoed through the room as the bookshelf glided open. All three of them stared into a dark, narrow staircase.

Coyle's heart froze.

It was a simple staircase that led down. Yet it was a dark void drawing her nearer to death. How could such a simple point of access be so threatening? And here she was, barely able to move, let alone take a step into her worst fears. She backed away.

"I guess smoking cigars has its benefits," Vonteg said as he lit a small lighter. "You always have a light." The flame seemed weak and insignificant compared to the vastness of dark waiting to swallow her.

"Maybe… maybe we could wait for some more help." Coyle gulped. "Or a brighter light."

"Well, this is our investigation, Coyle," Vonteg said. "And I'm fairly certain the Army doesn't know about this."

"We'll be fine," Poes said. "Between the three of us, we'll take care of whatever we run into."

"But we have no weapons," Coyle said. She squeezed her dress with trembling fingers. "How are we going to take care of anything with no weapons?"

The men looked at each other and shrugged. Vonteg said, "We should get down there before it gets dark. No telling how far or how big this is going to get." He stepped down into the abyss with his tiny light. Poes followed.

Coyle's breath shrank away to nothing, her shoes slipping backward, away from the mortal dangers and creeping tendrils of the eerie. She glanced outside. She made out shapes of horseback riders in the distance. Three armed men in all the daylight. She glanced at the front door.

"Coyle?" Poes asked, and she turned to him.

Terror crossed her face.

"The dark isn't one of your favorite colors, is it?" Poes smiled and offered his hand. She looked outside but reached for his hand, grasping it tightly. He was the anchor amidst the rising storm in her soul.

***

Over fifty yards away, Sergeant Tanner was joking with his perimeter patrol when someone caught his attention.

"Say, who's that?" he asked.

"Where, Sarge?" one of them asked.

"Looks like a female over there," he answered. "Kinda looks like that pretty lady who arrived earlier… What was her name?"

"Miss Coyle, Sarge."

"And how did Miss Coyle end up over here? I thought I told her to stay around the residences."

"I don't know, Sarge."

"I have no idea why Captain Sievers allows citizens on this property, but if they looked this nice, well I'd let them come all day."

"Sir, she's getting within hearing range."

She walked up to them and squinted in the sun.

"Miss Coyle?" asked Sergeant Tanner. "How in the world did you get away from your group?" He looked behind him and then at her.

"Yes, silly me. I got bored and went looking at the sights." Veiul's eyes narrowed at the soldiers. "Can you point me in the direction of my friends? I seem to have gotten a little lost."

CHAPTER 11

Coyle counted the steps to keep her mind busy. Logic, prayers and anything useful were washed away in the midst of gnawing panic, but she had to grasp onto what was real and the grated metal beneath her boots fit the bill. She focused on Vonteg's tiny light, trying hard to remember Scripture about the light of God and trying harder not to imagine what was waiting in the horrible dark.

She counted two landings and two more flights of steps. Sixteen for each flight, thirty-two total. She barely felt Poes's hand in hers, but she was thankful she wasn't alone. The doctors said it was nyctophobia, a severe fear of the dark. But she knew it was all in her mind. The same mind where thousands of possibilities spun into compelling deductions and applicable calculations. The same mind that hid sinister fears in the spaces between logic and reason. When triggered, these fears grew chaotic, and she spun out of control like she was sliding on an icy lake toward an open hole to nowhere.

She breathed in through her nose, out through her mouth. In and out. Counting the steps one by one until they stopped at a wide, flat landing.

"This is the floor level," Vonteg said, and stepped to the side. "There's got to be a switch here somewhere."

Coyle winced at a loud snap, and electric lights flickered. Most of them stayed on. She released herself from Poes's grasp, nodded to him, and stopped chewing her bottom lip. She shook the nervousness from her hands and took notice of her new surroundings.

They were in a wide hall with rooms and hallways veering off in every direction. It smelled of damp earth and seawater. Large, rough-hewn timber logs braced the ceiling and corners.

"This was made during the Civil War," Vonteg said, tapping a log. "Union soldiers cut their timber like this for their fortifications."

"What would the purpose of this place be?" Coyle's voice cracked.

"Reckon we'll find out," Vonteg said. "The lights should hold. Good thing Edison picked San Francisco to introduce his electric lights. Looks like the Union took advantage of it, like they did everything else."

"There are a lot of rooms," Poes said. "As long as there are lights, it may be a good idea for us to separate. We can cover more area. Sound good?" He looked at Coyle, and she nodded without thinking it through. She shivered and picked a room.

Coyle found herself in a workshop. *Perfect.* She would use discovery as a distraction from the fact that she was holed up in an underground tunnel system built twenty years ago.

A large table rested in the center, papers scattered across its surface. Large scrolls lay strewn and stacked throughout the small room. She took a deep breath and busied herself by unrolling them one by one. They were all blueprints of airships. None she recognized. But she logged each of the ships' names into her mind for future use. She searched through other papers: memos, notes, journals. The lights flicked off.

God, no!

Adrenaline rushed through her, and panic flickered through her mind. She gripped the papers, and the lights flickered back to life. Breath escaped her lips, and her damp, trembling hands smoothed out the papers. She looked around the room again. Two cabinets stood next to each other. She pulled out the drawers. There were loads of files, all filled with notes of machines and devices. She tried to keep an eye out for names and locations, but nothing was useful. She looked down at the blueprints again before she left the room and walked down the hall to the next room.

Poes sat on the floor, silent, examining a picture. Coyle glanced over his shoulder. It was a portrait of a young girl and a smiling man with kind eyes. The girl was about ten years old with thin, pale, dark hair and a pretty face. Her eyes looked drawn, heavy, as if she had just finished crying. Coyle stepped in the room, making Poes shift.

"That's not Trevin, is it?" Coyle asked.

Poes dragged his finger across the picture. He shook his head and stared for a few moments before answering. "I haven't seen... I don't know who they are."

"Do they remind you of anyone?" Coyle asked. She noticed Poes's eyes no longer held the hard edge but were instead soft, deep in thought.

"I have a relative I haven't seen in so long. A niece."

"Is there anything on the back? Date or place? Names?" Coyle asked.

"No," he said. He tossed the picture onto the overturned desk. The room was a small study, but papers were scattered everywhere. "Someone's already been through here."

Coyle remembered Moreci's words: *"We thought it was in Trevin's home."*

"Moreci was here," she said.

"Ah, yes. With Fang, looking for the device."

She nodded, despite knowing Fang's involvement was different. They both looked around at the mess. Drawers had been emptied and tossed. File folders were thrown everywhere. Furniture was broken apart.

"I wonder if there's anything else to find." Coyle asked. She picked up another picture. Two men shook hands and faced the camera. Creases and age obscured most of the image, making identification impossible. She tossed the picture on the table and scanned the papers. After a few moments, she found something familiar.

"A lot of these papers have the same heading: *Project Archangel.*"

"I noticed," Poes said. "Along with the Templar's crest."

"So Trevin was working for Dawn Industries," Coyle said. "But apparently he had something to do with this Archangel project, too."

"He wasn't supposed to, but I agree with your observation." Poes said. "And now we need to find out why."

They sat on the floor, rifling through papers. Each with their stack of notes, memos, reports. Both were mumbling as they sifted through folders, setting papers aside and stacking others.

Together.

Coyle's heart had settled into a normal rhythm. Her hands no longer shook. She was back in her investigative mode where she was comfortable, safe. Happy.

Her eyes scanned as much as she could, but most of the information was blotted out with black ink. She set her stack aside and gathered a new stack from the floor.

"Here's something. A name," Poes said. "A telegraph. Let's see. Inspector Mortis Burngrove wrote a telegraph to… someone blocked it out. Let's see…"

Coyle half listened, sorting out what she had in her hands, until something caught her eye. She read it quietly to herself.

Memo to: [redacted] Date: May 9, 1874

From: Prof. Moreci

Re: Project: Archangel

I have received three more potential subjects, though all were human. We understand testing is necessary for all species, but after discussions, we had agreed humans are too quickly diminished through the extended regimen. I have repeatedly requested more fae and vamperion, especially after our marked progress with Subject 0120, aptly code-named Fang. Thus far, she has responded to the program with exceeding merit and would be a remarkable presentation next spring. Our next meeting concerning new protocols and safety measures will be [redacted].

Please speak with [redacted] regarding more appropriate acquisitions. We must also consider a viable method for the disposition of the failed experiments. After one of the bodies was discovered on the shore, we can no longer assume "burial at sea" will be adequate.

"Well, here's something very interesting. Moreci was quite involved in the Archangel project," Coyle said. "Along with someone else."

"I couldn't find anything useful with this one," Poes said. "There's so many redactions."

"They're all copies. Everything here is copies of originals. Come to think of it, why would someone redact their own work?"

"True," Poes said. "So who else are we supposed to investigate?"

Coyle squinted. "How about that Inspector Burngrove you mentioned?"

"He was killed at the dinner party."

"No good, then," Coyle said and looked at the ceiling. Finding clues that led to other clues could be disheartening. But it also invited a broader method of approach to a narrow search. Coyle loved it and smiled inside herself. All these puzzle pieces were strewn across the room, and she was in the middle. Her favorite place to be.

She looked at Poes. "Do you like puzzles?"

"Do I like puzzles? In a sense. When I was younger, there was a game I used to play with my friends. An adult would show us a rabbit, and we would note the shade of fur, the length of ears and feet. While we were inside the cabin, the rabbit was released in the woods, and we had to find that exact rabbit, right down to the bushiness of its tail. It had to be the same. The other children were excited and ran off in every direction, searching under rocks and bushes, yelling and cracking sticks against the trees. I was patient, though. I looked for places the rabbit had run through, noticing a trail of fur here and a footprint there. I always found the rabbit. Always the exact one."

"So you're a hunter?" Coyle asked.

He smiled. "I hunt for the truth. I ask the right questions, find out where someone has been and what paths they took to get there. And then, when they're discovered, I bury them under enough evidence that they can never get back out."

There was a fire deep in his eyes, but it wasn't aimed at her this time. It was a passion for his work. The same kind of passion she had for hers. Maybe he wasn't as bad a chap as she originally perceived. "And you? Do you like puzzles?"

"Some girls played with dolls," Coyle said. "I tried to study fingerprints as best I could. I would try to guess the weight of dinner guests and when I became too accurate, I was told to leave." They shared a laugh. "But, yes, I do love puzzles. They give me something to work towards, pieces fall into place when you least expect them to." She shared a long glance at Poes. She wanted to enjoy the moment, yet—she couldn't. She barely knew the man and yet she wanted to know him, that much was sure. And yet again, she wasn't sure if there was any room in her life for--

"What did you find in the other room?" Poes asked.

"Blueprints of ships," Coyle said. "Airships."

"As in dirigibles?" Poes asked.

"Here," Coyle said as Poes helped her up. "Let me get a few, and we can sort them out."

Coyle walked down the hall and had the distinct feeling of being watched. She turned, expecting Vonteg or maybe—

Fang?

The vampire would surely be down here, wouldn't she? She'd promised to stay in touch. What better meeting place than a hidden network of tunnels? Her eyes were playing with her and she swore there was a shape—a shadow—there. In the corner. Watching her. Coyle's heart thrummed in her ears. Her fingers grasped her dress. She should say something, but then Fang would be discovered. What was she to do? She took a step closer when something creaked and she turned away and snapped her head back around to the corner. She took the few steps and reached out into the darkened corner.

Nothing was there.

The lights flickered again, and she hurried to the workshop. With nerves on edge, she walked into the room and grabbed a handful of papers, but before leaving, her eyes spotted a small wooden box with a curious brass piece on top. She set the papers aside and placed the wooden device on the table. There, a word stamped across the top: "Kinetoscope." A small red button sat next to a raised, brass peephole. Edison had been recently showing off this invention: moving pictures in a box. She pushed the button and heard a series of clicks and whirs that made the wood vibrate as she looked into the lighted eyepiece. There was no audio, only a soft mechanical whirring and the sound of her steady breathing.

The pictures were choppy and distorted before they cleared. Rooms full of young men and women, no older than fifteen, all wearing the same dark gray clothes. Men walked around them in lab coats. She stopped.

"Humans are too quickly diminished through the extended regimen."

She wanted to leave. And she wanted to stay, but not out of morbid curiosity. Out of duty. She clenched her jaw and pressed the button.

The children, seemingly selected from all walks of life, appeared normal. And then abnormalities were shown. Thick patches of coarse hair, and long nails that resembled eagle's claws. Others stood in pools, displaying webbed hands and feet, their faces sallow and thin, their genitalia missing. Still others had long, distorted arms and legs. Men in lab coats assisted them to stand and walk across the room in front of the camera.

A girl was brought into view or what Coyle assumed from the shape of her body. But the girl's face was smooth, without features. She had only slits for eyes, nostrils and a lipless mouth. Her skin shifted, and her appearance changed to that of an older lady, complete with shaggy, white hair and thin, wrinkled skin. She changed again to a beautiful young woman with lush lips, full cheeks and thin, arching eyebrows. She sat in the lap of a man in a lab coat and smiled. The man looked at the camera—there was something familiar about his eyes. But, her focus returned to the girl.

Coyle remembered the roto-display in Treece's workshop. The assassin's features had changed in the light, shifting into someone else. This had to be the same person, the one who had disguised herself as Fang. She looked into the box.

An operating table appeared with the body of a woman on it. Coyle winced and looked away as someone pulled a scalpel down the center of her body, dissecting her. Coyle grabbed her own chest, took a breath and looked again. The photographer focused on the woman's mouth. A rod was placed under her upper teeth, displaying long, sharp fangs. Her skin was covered in horrible welts and burns.

The following pictures showed rows of operating tables, all filled with bodies, all of them with their chest cavities opened, organs set aside, men digging through their flesh. Coyle's gut squirmed.

The pictures changed to a girl no older than thirteen, with short dark hair and eyes, pacing in a small, padded room, screaming, crying. Madness and confusion etched her face as she pleaded with the camera operator.

Fang.

Coyle gasped. Fang was tied to a bed, and a robed priest sprinkled holy water over her nude body before displaying a large silver cross and pressing it into her skin. But nothing happened. Her haunted eyes stared into the camera, and Coyle's heart ached.

The pictures changed, and the camera peered into a padded room. Fang was a disheveled form, dressed in torn rags. She paced the room, glanced at the camera and looked away, her fingers picking at her skin. And then she rocked back and forth on her knees, talking and laughing to herself. In another set of pictures, she leaned down, hands on her knees, whispering to the air in front of her before hugging herself. Men in lab coats shook their heads and made notes, arguing with each other.

The pictures changed; they were outside. Men escorted Fang into bright sunlight with the tall, white lighthouse of Fort Alcatraz just behind them. A scientist displayed one of her arms and smiled. Her pale skin appeared untouched by the rays of the sun.

Then she was inside a concrete jail cell, pacing. Wild, wet eyes shifted back and forth at the men outside, and she shook her head and mumbled. Men held rifles. Someone in a lab coat gave them directions before he stepped away. The riflemen raised their weapons at her.

Fang froze and backed against the wall, raising her thin, trembling hands. Her lips quivered and moved soundlessly. But Coyle could read lips.

"Not again."

They opened fire. Coyle gasped. The girl screamed, covering her face and body, but the monsters kept firing. Blood sprayed out, staining her gown dark, her skin tearing apart. She curled into a ball, seemingly about to die. But no! Fang glared at them with fire in her eyes. With broken fists clenched, she burst into a dark-purple vapor and slipped between the bars. Shock washed over the riflemen's faces. The cameraman backed away.

Violence ensued.

Rifles were snapped, limbs were torn off, blood gushed from necks, and within seconds, four of the men were corpses. Others rushed into view and struck her with rods with glowing orange tips. She fell down and writhed and screamed. Bile crept into Coyle's throat.

The pictures changed, scratched and distorted, but she could make out two men in suits congratulating each other. Coyle couldn't quite see who they were no matter how hard she tried. But she had to guess one of them was Moreci. He may have been in charge of creating these horrid experiments—and, ultimately, Fang.

She looked up at the ceiling, rubbing her eyes, hoping to erase the evil she witnessed. For the first time, she wanted to help Fang, the poor creature. No one deserved to be put through that. She sighed before gathering the papers and moving-picture box. She never heard the shapeshifting Veiul approaching from behind.

***

Poes leaned over and sifted through Coyle's pile. Every paper contained notes regarding the physical and physiological training of young men and women.

"What were they getting at?" Poes asked himself. "What were they looking to do?"

The silence from the other room had been drawn out too long, and Poes listened intently for a long few moments.

Nothing.

"Coyle?" Poes got up and dusted off his trousers. "Coyle? Are you–"

"Hello," Veiul said, brushing her hair back. "Sorry, I got a little lost there." She stood in the doorway with her hands behind her back. Her disguise was perfectly complete, able to fool the Templars.

"Coyle, good heavens, you were gone for a bit longer than I thought. Where are the blueprints?"

"Ah," she said. "I don't think we'll need them. A lot of them didn't make sense to me. Engineers could make sense of all that, but not us."

Poes frowned. "I thought that's why we had Bolt. He's the aeronautical engineer."

"Ah," Veiul smiled. "That's right. That's right. So what did you find here?"

Poes glanced behind him. "Well, that's what we were about to talk about. Wait. What's that smell?"

There was a shout, and Poes saw flames licking the ceiling at the opposite end of the hallway. Vonteg ran up to them, coughing.

"There's a fire! We need to get out of here!" he shouted.

"Back up to the house, quickly!" Poes shouted as hot, smoky air rushed toward them. Spouts of flame leapt from another room as they ran down the hall and up the staircase. They pushed open the bookshelf and discovered tongues of flame licking the ceiling and walls.

The three of them rushed outside into the yard. Vonteg and Poes were coughing through their hands, the heated smoke nearly killing them in their escape. Veiul waved at the arriving soldiers.

In moments, soldiers and federal prisoners were dousing the remaining timbers with fire hoses and pails of water. Vonteg, Poes, and Veiul sat on a low wall, catching their breath.

"You three are lucky to be alive," Sergeant Tanner said.

"We appreciate all the help, sir." Veiul smiled. "But we really need to get back to our people and sort everything out."

"One thing at a time, miss," the soldier replied. "One thing at a time."

And as soon as I get all of them together, I will slice their throats. One neck at a time. Veiul smiled.

***

She breathed him in…

He smelled of manic sweat. The air was filled with impatient purpose and madness.

"My wrists hurt, Ronan," Coyle said, tugging at the restraints. "I thought you were going to make love to me, not tie me up for the asylum."

"Hush," he said, extinguishing the candles one by one until only the faintest glow from the streetlamps reached through the dark. Ronan's face was tinged with cold light, his visage becoming a nightmarish phantom. His eyes studied her as if she were an experiment. He held something in his hand. Small and bright. Sharp and deadly.

"What's that in your hand? Ronan, let me go. What's happening?"

The eerie dark collided with rising panic in her mind, creating terrors she had never experienced and yet, she knew, would never leave her. With every tug and pull, she became overwhelmed by the obvious: there was no escape, and she was going to die. He shoved a rag in her mouth.

"Stop fussing. I just want to give you my reason, understand? I respect you, and now you will respect me."

He thumbed the scalpel while her muscles strained against the leather wraps. Her hands and feet were cool and numb, but her chest, neck and face were blazing hot. He sat next to her in the shadows, his voice nothing more than an echo in the dark.

"I've always been curious as to how my mother carried so much power. Everyone, including my father, respected her. Gave her the attention she deserved. She was like that ever since she spit me out. So much power, respect, fear. And, like I said, I was curious where her power came from and guessed it was from something inside. Deep inside. I had to find the answer to this mystery, right? If it was inside, I just needed to find it, and then I could have it too.

"So, I had to kill Father first, because he certainly wasn't going to let me find power. He was easy to kill. And then Mother. I opened my mother up and looked. Humph, couldn't find anything. I was so sure it was there. Baffling and frustrating all at the same time." His eyes searched the ceiling, the scalpel tapping against his lips.

"Time went on, and I grew older, wiser. I noticed some women held the same power over a man, but in a different way. Mostly prostitutes or the occasional wanton wife. I knew they had the same power deep inside, and I opened them all up, right down the middle the way I opened up my mother. I still haven't found their power, so... elusive. Yet I know if I keep searching..."

He leaned in with his blade, and his fingers slid across her skin. The warmth of his touch brought hope.

Just for a moment, she knew all of this had to be a joke, and he would stop and untie her and laugh at all the silliness and fright he had given her, and they would hold each other until the sun appeared on the horizon, and everything would be safe and wonderful.

And then the tip of his blade pierced her skin.

Coyle jolted awake and grabbed at her chest. She rubbed her face and looked around, but *he* wasn't there. Just the nightmare again.

Where was she? She sat up, caught her breath, and her head flared in pain. She rubbed her head and looked at her palm.

Blood. My blood.

She'd fallen. What had happened? She touched a thick lump behind her ear and winced as she stood on shaky legs.

Was there a fireplace nearby?

Tendrils of black smoke curled through the ceiling. She leaned against the table. The maps and Edison's moving-picture box jolted her memory. She remembered she was looking through the rooms for evidence. That meant Poes and Vonteg were somewhere.

"Poes! Poes, what's happened?" She stood at the doorway and listened. There was the crackling and popping of a roaring fire nearby, but she didn't remember a fireplace. She glanced around the corner and cried out. Flames crept along the old timber ceiling and fortifications. The growing heat and smoke forced her to her knees, and she crawled to the room Poes was in. She screamed his name again, but there was no answer. She covered her head as the ceiling collapsed in a shower of flaming debris. Bits of charred papers and folders flew into the hall. Something fell from above and struck her knee. She glanced at a worn leather notebook and grabbed it. Better to take something out of this than nothing.

The metal grate dug into her bare hands and knees, but it was better than sucking in black, scorching air. She crawled away from the room and looked for the staircase, but couldn't remember. The smoke was getting darker, thicker. Flames were growing by the moment. Her eyes stung. Her head pounded. She tore her skirt, wrapping it around her mouth and nose. The others must have escaped, but why had they left her? Was this some kind of trap? Did they leave her to die? Was Treece finished with her?

She crawled to a closed door, reaching for the doorknob. The handle was warm, but hopefully there was no fire inside. She opened it and shut the door behind her. No flames. Clean air. She coughed and wiped the sting out of her eyes. The lights began to flicker, and she was suddenly aware she may be in the dark again.

The room was spacious, with a long hallway on one side that led to more rooms. She collapsed on the plush, expensive carpets and caught her breath. Oil paintings hung in antique frames, and beautiful furniture pressed against the walls. She stood and limped down the hallway, glancing into the next room—and froze.

In the uncertain light, her eyes recognized the sight before her, though her brain begged for an alternative answer. Shelves covered the walls. On each shelf were rows of large, glass bottles filled with something horrifyingly familiar.

Run!

She didn't need to know. She was better off without knowing.

But the detective in her *had* to know. Had to be sure of the evidence before her. She crept closer the shelf and turned the glass bottle. Revulsion flashed through her mind like the flickering lights above. Her hand pulled back.

Fluid strands of thin, reddish-brown hair.

The scoop and curve of a small ear.

The long, tender curve of a jawline.

Lips curled, misshapen.

A mouth hung open, frozen in a scream no one would hear.

Dull, gray, staring eyes with spots of green.

Bits of pale flesh pulled away into the broth of proteins and embalming fluid.

She turned away and screamed with her hands to her mouth. The faulty lights cast a macabre lightning storm across the shelves of decapitated heads. She turned away, crying out for Poes, but no answer came. She was alone, and there was no one to help her.

And she was going to die alone.

She shook her head at the lie she didn't want to believe. She was dizzy, her legs weak, but her desire to live was more powerful. She was a survivor, and she would find a way.

Like I did that night.

She opened her eyes to the silent audience and bumped into something low to the ground. A table full of paperwork. Ledgers. Notebooks. Scattered papers. Pencils. She scooped them up, shoved them into a leather briefcase leaning against the wall, and pulled the strap over her head.

There was a loud crack. A quick glance at the front door told her there was no going back.

The fire had broken through.

She kept her eyes down, heart pounding in her ears, and turned the corner to a small bedroom. A rifle leaned in the corner, and she slung it over her shoulder. Her eyes searched every inch for escape. She glanced across the hall into a bathroom with a toilet and bath but nothing more. No more doors. No more windows.

She was trapped.

Hot air spread above, and fire crackled louder. She covered her mouth and nose. Time was running out. A loud pop made her peek around the corner. Fire covered one of the shelves. There was another loud crash, and she ducked behind the doorframe as flaming shards of glass sprayed the hallway.

"Oh, my God," Coyle said in terror. Formaldehyde was flammable. And the whole room was full of it. Another crash sent flaming shards of glass everywhere, each piece alighting the floor.

She shut the bedroom door and pulled aside the drawers, the chest. Nothing. She pulled up the rug.

A trap door!

She yanked the handle. Darkness and cold, salted air slapped her face. She looked into the black pit and froze. Her skin crawled, and her stomach rolled.

Anything but this.

The walls shook, and her hands groped down, finding metal rungs. She stepped inside the blackness, sinking into the void, closing her eyes as madness greeted her. And then was she stopped. Something was caught. She pulled, but couldn't go lower. What was happening?

The rifle lay across the opening, preventing her escape. Glass exploded, and the heat became unbearable. She fumbled with the rifle strap, trying to untangle herself.

She yelled and grunted, but the leather strap wouldn't give. She slipped between the straps as the room erupted. The trap door slammed shut, throwing her down the tunnel. Her hands reached out, scraping rough stone she couldn't see. Then her scream was cut short as she plunged into freezing seawater as dark as the fears that haunted her.

***

Thick, black smoke marred the blue sky. The flames reached to other wooden structures, creating a tremendous challenge for the fire suppression team. Soldiers escorted them away from danger and back to the safety of their transit.

"I can't wait to get back and go over what we've learned with everyone," she said. "I want all of us there in the same room."

So I can slit your throats.

"Well, we certainly need a wash-up first," Vonteg said. "Aren't you the least bit harried by this ordeal?"

"Of course I am, sir." Her eyes shifted between the two. "And I'm forever grateful to the both of you for protecting me, especially you." She patted Poes on the shoulder.

He glanced at his shoulder. "For?"

She turned and met his gaze with teasing eyes. "Maybe that's something we can talk about later."

Poes blinked.

The driver helped each of them inside, mentioning a series of safety checks to go through before they could leave. The assassin sat comfortably and pretended to be interested in Treece's water-borne carriage. She had much more pressing engagements, though and her daggers itched to be used.

Veiul looked around. "Charming, isn't it?" She had a bright smile and sparkle in her eye. "When do we leave?"

"In a couple of minutes," Vonteg said. He glanced at her. "Say, you feeling healthy? Head in good shape? There was a lot of smoke back there."

"Perfectly fine, I say," she said. "I guess I'm just eager to get back and share with everyone what we've learned. All together as a team, and all in the same room would be nice."

"You sure make it a point to have us all in the same room," Poes said, squinting at the woman who smiled back.

The carriage hummed, and they heard a series of gears turning before the machine rattled to life.

Poes shifted in his seat and studied Coyle for a few moments.

"What?" she asked.

"Do you like puzzles?"

"Sure, they can be fun."

"Fun?"

She nodded, her smile tight.

Vonteg frowned. "You two want to tell me what's so interesting about puzzles?"

"Go ahead, Coyle. What's so fun about puzzles?"

"I'll let you share. It was your question, after all," the woman answered.

Poes and Veiul studied each other.

"The thing about puzzles is that you won't know the piece fits until it falls into place," Poes said.

"What are you talking about?" Vonteg said.

"He's saying I'm not right for the team," she said, pulling out a pistol.

"What the hell?" said Vonteg.

Poes knocked the gun away and slammed his fist into her face. Veiul kicked once, crashing Poes into the wall, and kicked again, knocking Vonteg out cold.

Veiul shifted in her seat, grabbed Poes's arm, and shoved her boot into his neck. He punched her knee, but she held fast. Poes's face reddened, his veins bulging.

"Not," Poes gasped, "Coyle."

"No," Veiul dropped her guise, shifting into a formless face. "She's dead, and you will be too."

"No." Poes struggled to breathe. "Not. Dead."

Water splashed, and a woman called for help. Veiul glanced outside. The real Coyle was swimming toward them. The driver shouted.

Veiul turned to Poes, sneering, and then she glanced down. He pointed the pistol at her and squeezed the trigger. Her dress tore open, spilling blood. She screamed, released her grip and evaporated in blue smoke and light. Poes clutched his throat, gasping and coughing.

The carriage leaned to one side as the driver helped Coyle into the cabin. She climbed in, splashing water and sputtering, and plopped onto the bench in a sopping heap. She leaned into the corner, breathing hard. Her eyes met Poes's, and they both shook their heads, words escaping them.

Vonteg stirred and opened his eyes. Blinking at Coyle, he hopped up and clenched his fists. Coyle shrank back. Poes stopped him before anything else could happen, and he spent the rest of the journey explaining the situation to both of them.

***

Nearby, a sloop skimmed through the surface of the bay. Its crew busy with lines and sails, though one member kept a steady eye on Treece's curious water carriage.

"Status report," chimed the radioed voice.

The agent set the spyglass aside and held his fist in the air for the skipper: *stop.*

"Yes, sir." He cleared his throat. "Veiul had an altercation with Mr. Poes on——."

"Tell me about Coyle."

"Of course, sir. I'm unsure how this happened, but she ended up swimming from the shore before she was rescued."

"By whom?"

"Mr. Poes and Mr. Vonteg. From the, uh, water carriage, sir."

"Then she found the sea-cave exit from Trevin's underground lair. Interesting. I do hope she's not too badly put out by Veiul's assault. I also hope she found the materials I left for her. Goodness, the mystery of not knowing if she found my clues is almost more unbearable than the mystery itself."

"Well, she was carrying the satchel you left, and she swam about twelve meters, proving she was strong and healthy."

"Good news, then, on both queries. I expressly told Veiul not to kill her, so it looks like she didn't have trouble following orders. Have you ever asked a trained killer not to kill someone? I tell you, it's like herding cats."

"I can't say I have, sir."

"Speaking of trained killers, did you spot Fang?"

The spy cleared his throat. "No sign of her, sir."

"Goodness, she is keeping a low profile. She's doing exactly what she was trained to do, and I don't like it one bit."

"It's worrisome, sir."

"While on her side, I was quite happy to have her as an operative. But now we're on the business end, as it were, and I'm afraid it's unnerving to be hunted by a weaponized vampire with a righteous motive for revenge. Has there been any word from our contacts on the streets? Any criminals drained of blood turning up?"

"No word on the street, and our contact at the morgue says it's been business as usual, sir."

"And we haven't seen her since she visited Coyle in the jail cell, correct?"

"That's correct, sir."

"She's somewhere close, and we have no idea where. Humph. Makes for a frightful situation. Especially considering I'm the one who put her in the iron cage and I'm the one who broke her out."

"I'm sure you're safe, sir."

"Am I? Are you? Such good questions to ask oneself. Thrilling, actually."

The agent glanced to the sides. The crew was busy tying lines and affixing the rigging. No one paid him any attention, which is exactly what they were paid to do.

"Well, that's enough conjecture for now. I'll remain in radio silence until our parties get airborne on the ship. Over and out."

The agent twirled his finger in the air, prompting the captain to resume sailing. He glanced at the crew one more time before rubbing his throat and raising the spyglass to his eye.

CHAPTER 12

The Treece mansion

Sausalito

Treece and the others lounged in the main hall, sipping drinks and discussing the incident. Vonteg pushed a small pack of ice against his swollen lip. Poes's complexion was this side of ashen, his trembling hands rubbing his bruised neck. The rest of the group argued civilly about what had transpired and what had happened to Coyle.

"Why was she targeted?" Bolt asked.

"Why not?" Poes answered. "She was by herself when it happened. It was just a matter of opportunity."

"Opportunity for what?" Duone asked.

"Disguise," Poes said. "I'm not sure what that creature is."

"I suspect she's fae," Treece said. "And I suspect she's a mimic of some kind. I'll have to do some investigating with my contacts. But, you say she disappeared when you shot her?"

"There was a flash of blue light—and poof! She was gone."

"It could have been a molecular-transference device, the same kind used on Miss Coyle," GEM added.

The room sat in silence. Each man ruminating about the past events. There were more questions being raised than answers given, and it would take some time to discover what they found. But, each knew they didn't have much time.

"We could have been walking around with this thing since the beginning." Bolt gently tugged on his waxed mustache. "I knew there was something about her."

"There is something about her," GEM chimed in. "She wants to help a group of men who haven't found a way to trust her yet. Not yet, anyway."

Bolt side-glanced the automaton.

"I'm not wrong, am I?" GEM asked.

"It could have been any of us," Duone said. "Right?"

"No, I believe this fae can only mimic other females," Treece answered. "But I do wonder how long this has been happening."

"Not too long," Poes said. "Coyle had left me to find some papers, and when this impostor returned, things took a wrong turn."

"But how did you know it was… this thing and not the real Coyle?" Bolt asked.

"It was little details," Poes said.

"So the devil's in the details, is it?" Bolt cracked his knuckles. "And it fooled Vonteg, but not you?"

"What made you change your mind about this one, Poes?" Duone asked.

He took a few moments before shrugging. "It was a hunch."

"Well, we can't continue with this kind of work based on hunches, Poes," Bolt said.

"And yet I did." Poes set his drink down. "And it looks like my hunch paid off."

Bolt walked around the room and huffed. "This changes things, though, doesn't it? This really changes things."

"Such as?" Duone asked.

Bolt turned to them. "What if there are more of these impostors? How do we know Coyle and this fae weren't conspiring together? And how do we know one of us isn't going to be next because of Poes's hunches? What if he offs me next?"

"You're not making any sense," Poes answered.

"But you said it yourself." Bolt snorted. "All of you were separated for a time. That means any of you could have been taken by this creature."

"I'm not interested in your baseless accusations, Bolt," Poes said. "I'm interested in finding the truth, not distorting it."

"She had to have started the fire," Duone said. "Set the whole place ablaze. Burned away any evidence we needed."

"Not everything," Coyle said.

They all turned to the doorway. Coyle leaned against the doorframe with a bandage wrapped around her head.

"Not everything was destroyed," she said, holding a stack of papers.

"Miss Coyle!" Treece said. "The doctor's orders were to rest. You need to get back into your bed."

"I finished going through what we found, and we need to do a proper debrief," Coyle said, walking inside.

The men looked at each other. Bolt studied Coyle, his finger tugging the end of his mustache. Poes studied Bolt in turn, and the two glanced at each other, their eyes challenging the other to turn away first. Bolt grunted, looked at his drink and finished it.

***

GEM helped Coyle move a chair and small table to the center of the room. She asked for a Scotch and soda, and the automaton went to the bar. This would be her second since waking up. The first had kept her company in the study where the papers had been taken to dry, as she gleaned everything she could and arranged what was available into something coherent and usable.

GEM handed her a tumbler, and she took a big gulp, hoping to numb the grotesque evils seeping through her mind. She needed to be sharp if they were to listen to what she'd discovered. No more naive washout walking around the boys; she knew she had to prove her worth tonight, and she was fully confident of her findings.

She pulled the glass away from her lips as the men made themselves comfortable. GEM freshened their drinks and made sure the fire was adequate. Though she looked like she could use a long day off, all ears waited for her to speak.

This is my chance. Again.

"Has anyone ever heard of Project Archangel?" She glanced around the room for answers. Hearing nothing, she continued. "It appears it was initially funded by the Templars. They were trying to forge an unstoppable warrior. Treece? Sound familiar?" All eyes settled on the older man, who suddenly appeared aged and frail. His shoulders slumped and he sighed before speaking.

"Moreci and I were colleagues. Both of us young and foolish and eager to become notable scientists in our work. I, in engineering and he in biology. We were recruited by the Templars, who were interested in finding a supplemental group of individuals from the nether realm," Treece said. "I became transfixed with the beauty of their kind and the marvels of their own wonderful engineering. I was too busy with my pride to acknowledge this new program was heading in the wrong direction. By that time, tremendous damage was done to the few individuals we were given to test. We soon learned the government was also involved and wanted fae and vamperion to be used a new, more powerful army. Those from the nether-realm were wary of such an endeavor, citing misuse of trust. I raised my concerns to the Templars and promptly left. Moreci assured us they would put a stop to the project. But, we suspected Moreci continued their work under the guise of merely studying aberrations from those of the nether realm. I should have known he was continuing creating … monsters. I'm ashamed I didn't stop this project long before it got out hand. Please Miss Coyle, tell us what you found out," he answered.

"During the dinner party at the Baldwin mansion," Coyle continued, "Dame Graethe mentioned that the fae had begun reaching out to the United States government for assistance. This led to meetings with the military, and Professor Moreci was given full control over the project. It seems the original intention was to create warriors for the fae realm. Instead of complying with previously agreed upon terms, Moreci went rogue, testing fae and vamperion for unique abilities. Through his vile experiments, they were empowered with pharmaceuticals, scientific enhancements and psychological fortitude.

"This led to multiple failures and setbacks among the test subjects. The numbers of those tested dropped dramatically, and on the surface, the government disavowed any involvement, but kept pushing the project along. Moreci continued working until he created his version of a perfect nightmare."

"Fang," Vonteg said.

Coyle nodded. "She was conditioned to become a powerful weapon and clandestine operative. Once they discovered the correct formula, more test subjects were successfully completed. Moreci's project became a smashing success, and the government sent a small group of them all over the world with Fang as the leader," Coyle answered. She finished her drink and raised the empty glass for another.

"This is unheard of," Quolo said. "Are you trying to say that Moreci created a... a group of vampires responsible for assassinations all over the world?"

"Not all of them were vampires." Poes thumbed his nose. "They were a mixture of fae and other unknown entities as well."

"I found a small note mentioning Alexander II of Russia," Coyle said, glancing at Poes.

"He was assassinated in 1881," Quolo said. "They caught the culprits. Three men were said to have used explosives."

"So we were led to believe," Coyle said. "There were also notes involving the Tonkin War, the Aceh War, and the Mahdist War."

"This group Moreci created would have been older children. Didn't anyone think this was unusual?" Quolo asked.

"Think of it," Coyle said. "They were a highly trained group of weapons masters and experts at artful subterfuge. They could have scooped ice cream and overthrown a small country in the same afternoon, and no one would have been the wiser."

"And Trevin?" Treece asked. "How was he involved in all this?"

"He used his expertise to help Moreci with his creations. In fact, he seems to have been key to the transformation of Fang, and they made certain she's not the garden variety vampire. Garlic, sunlight, holy water, crucifixes, running water: none of those hinder Fang. And I know, because they tried everything through their experiments." She closed her eyes and thought of all the test subjects who didn't succeed, ending up instead in a jar on Trevin's shelves. How many died so they could create the perfect weapon?

Coyle's hands were moving slower. Her mind had trouble keeping up with the words she wanted to use. She wasn't sure whether to feel ashamed or glad. Why not both? This was her opportunity to show just how smart, how brilliant she was. They would all see how much she deserved to be a detective.

So there.

"Sounds like a nightmare," Quolo said. "I can't think of anything worse."

"It gets worse," Coyle said. She shuffled through the paperwork. "The government supplied Moreci with people from asylums and prisons all over the country, and he created more and more preternatural creatures. Until, eventually there were problems within the original group itself and possibly with Fang. The government officially declared the project finished. In fact, here's a memo, dated more than two years ago regarding the status of the project, 'Project Archangel is set for full termination, and all working for the project will be under quaerite et conteret status.'".

"Seek and destroy," Poes translated the Latin phrase. "They were going to destroy and kill everything and everyone involved."

"Since the program created aberrations, the Templars took it upon themselves to roll up their sleeves and finish what Moreci started. I should have remained with Moreci, to keep him in line. This was my mistake and I won't forgive myself for what happened," Treece said.

"Professor Moreci was supposedly killed years ago. Shot in his lab. Four plugs in his chest." Vonteg said.

"Obviously he lived," Coyle said. "He was right in front of me a couple of days ago."

"And apparently Fang broke free and killed all the other creatures before taking the *Curse of Shadows*," Bolt said. "Now she's bent on revenge, with the perfect motive: kill them before they kill her. Makes perfect sense."

"She's unstoppable," Duone said.

"Except for aurorium," Coyle said.

"Aurorium? The mineral that creates its own energy?" Quolo asked.

"Yes. Apparently a defect was purposely embedded into Fang's genetic build. Some felt she was made too powerful and wanted a fail-safe so she could be killed when necessary." Coyle swallowed her drink and caught the automaton's attention for another.

"Easy now, Coyle," Vonteg said. "That's a lot of alcohol."

"Please. I've had quite the day," she retorted, ignoring the strands of hair covering her eyes. The liquid courage kept her tongue loose, and the chance to think out loud for a change felt freeing. And brave. Mostly brave. And smart.

Very smart.

Yes. She would show them how her mind worked, show them just how capable she was, just how important she was to the team.

Coyle stared at the far wall that tilted sideways, trying to keep her thoughts straight and orderly.

"We're going to have to make a list of people working against us," she said.

"Fang, of course," Bolt said. "Coyle, aren't you paying attention?" He motioned to the others. "I thought she was a smart detective."

"No. Fang's not against us, see? She's the one who killed Trevin, the head collector," she said. "Ugh! Trevin was a horrible, horrible man. Kept heads in glass jars. Why? Why did I go into that room?" She slurped from the glass. The walls kept trying to turn sideways.

Duone shook his head. "Those drinks are gettin' to ya, friend."

"See, Fang killed Trevin because… Hmm. They… Well, see, let's try this instead. He stole the book with the impostor, and they—" She stopped and covered her mouth in shock.

"Coyle, I believe you've had enough drinks. It has been a long day for you," Treece said. "The doctor said—"

"No, no! The Baldwin mansion. Hear me out. The Baldwin mansion." She snapped her fingers. "Treece, you said the woman who attacked me was probably fae and could probably impersonate other women, right? Tell me I'm right. Yes? Good. Of course I'm right, I'm a detective. Of sorts.

"Listen, listen. The impostor fae woman-thing impersonates Fang. Fang! She slaughters the dinner party. They want her to... They frame her. Right? Yes! Why? Because she's the best operative Moreci created, his shining example of what he could accomplish, and how did they thank him? The Templars tried to kill him. But he's alive—somehow. So many mysteries here." She chewed her bottom lip, her mind slipping through different possibilities of how Moreci had survived and who could have helped him.

"Doesn't it make sense? Do I have to explain everything? I mean, come on, isn't obvious? But, no, they don't want a lady detective working with them, really."

"Miss Coyle," Treece said.

She ignored him. "Moreci wants to get back at the Templars, at the people, at everyone who betrayed him! That's why he took the book and framed Fang. For *revenge*."

"And then?" Bolt asked.

She snapped her fingers and pointed at Poes. "And then the real Fang found out about their plan, I don't know how, perhaps because she's an amazing… person at what she does, right? She's amazing. And she hunted down Trevin at the pub. Boom!" Coyle used her hands to tell the story. "She shot him with the amazing gadget that only Treece could have designed for her. Did you see it? No. Did you find it? No. I did. But never mind, they don't want a lady detective. Heaven forbid they solve more crimes."

A few shot glances toward Treece, before he said, "Yes, Dawn's Industries designed the special weapons meant for Templars. It appears Moreci supplied her for his own purposes, but let me assure you: Fang has never been, nor will she ever be a Templar. She is a vile monster, and besides, one can never trust a vampire."

"Unn-unn," Coyle said. "Never say never, silly." She wagged her finger at Treece and steadied herself.

"She's completely smashed," Duone said.

"Amusing, though," Poes said. "And it is a great hypothesis."

"They took the book! Moreci and—what was her name, the one who attacked us? Veiul or Veil or something—they took it. They're working together, you know?" she stammered.

"Veiul? How did you know her name was Veiul?" Bolt asked.

"Fang told me, but that's not important now," she said. "They didn't like the way they were treated, Moreci and Veiul and the others. After all their hard work, see? What was that thing, that saying, Poes?"

"*Quaerite et conteret.*" He smiled.

"Quote and concert. That one," she said, and smiled at him. "Seek and destroy. You know Latin. I like that. *Latin*'s a nice word, isn't it? But, as I was saying, they wanted revenge for being betrayed. Just like me." Her fingers reached up to the buttons on her blouse. It would make more sense if they all knew about the scar and Ronan the Ripper.

Right?

"Miss Coyle," Treece said, rising from his seat. "Let's retire for the night, shall we?"

"Not before the airships," she said, dropping her hands to her sides.

"What?" Treece asked.

"I found the papers, big papers for this many airships. Down underground. Trevin's big papers," Coyle said, holding up three fingers.

"She found blueprints for airships," Poes said.

Coyle tried to stare at Bolt as she named each one, but his chair kept moving around. Or maybe it was her head. Or maybe it was her eyes.

"The *Starlighter*, the *Aurora* and the *Dawn's Edge*. Which one—which one of these is in the air tonight?" She pointed at Bolt but looked around the spinning, tilting, maddening room for Poes. She grinned when she found him. Why was she looking for him? Oh, that's right. There was something she wanted everyone to know. It was about him, about her. About them.

Bolt frowned before answering. "The *Dawn's Edge* is the flagship of Dawn Industries. It left port this morning. It's en route to Chicago."

"For?" Coyle hunched her shoulders.

"To participate in the dedication ceremonies for the World's Columbian Exposition, set a year before it opens," Treece said.

"So, so *Dawn's Edge* is headed for a big city." Coyle shifted her feet. "Big city with a lot of people with a bad book."

"For a major event," Quolo whispered.

"Sounds like a perfectly grand opportunity to murder a plethora of innocents," GEM said. All eyes stared at him. "What? Am I wrong?"

"I have what's called a Tesla-Vine gate. We use the gates to transport ourselves throughout the world, and I included one on the *Dawn's Edge*," Treece said.

"We need to stop that ship," she said, turning to Treece, but her eyes hovered on Poes, or tried to anyway. "We need to stop that ship. Bad book on big airship thing."

"Then let's get aboard," Vonteg said.

Treece led them through a labyrinth of hallways. Poes wrapped Coyle's arm around his shoulders and helped her walk.

There was something she wanted to say to him. To whisper in his ear. Something about the size of his shoulders, something about the smell of his cologne and his strong, steady gait as they walked. But the words weren't there. She remained content with keeping her eyes on him, but the moving floors and her tumbling stomach weren't helping. They turned a corner and stopped.

"There's a strange smell coming from the Gate room," Treece said and walked down the halls ahead of them.

"Burning metal and wires. Keep an eye on that one." Bolt pointed at Coyle.

"She won't leave my side, I promise you that," Poes said.

"She'll won't leave by my side, promise me," Coyle slurred, a wide grin across her face, her gaze searching for Poes.

The smell of hot metal overwhelmed her, and she stopped at the doorway, leaned against the wall, and got sick. Poes handed her a handkerchief and held her hair away from her face as she coughed out the rest of her guts.

"Oh no, Miss Coyle is ill," GEM said. "I'll retrieve a pail and mop for someone else to clean up."

"What's happened?" Bolt asked.

Coyle wiped her mouth with Poes's handkerchief, trying to look into the Gate room. A smoldering arch sat in the middle of a wide room. Bits of flame covered the wood-and-metal construction, and burning wires jutted in all directions. Coyle turned away, leaning against the doorframe.

"It's destroyed," Vonteg said.

"Who did this?" Treece said. "Someone… someone sabotaged the gate, destroying our only chance of stopping them."

"Well, who was alone? I'll give you three guesses," Bolt said.

"We can't assume it was her," Quolo said. "She's obviously trying to make sense of the—"

"She's obviously drunk! Anyone with half a brain can see what she's trying to do: sabotage our efforts at finding the culprits," Bolt said. The men added their opinions, each trying to shout the other down.

Coyle mumbled something nonsensical. She was weightless in Poes's firm grip. He was so strong. She leaned closer to tell him a secret, something only he would enjoy, something only she knew about him. She looked into his eyes, and he met her gaze.

Those eyes!

She smiled, opened her mouth to tell him, but fell to giggling instead. The secret was so ridiculously, incredibly preposterous. Poes shook his head and turned away.

"Do we have another means of stopping the airship?" Poes asked.

"Besides our transceiver system?" Treece said. "Yes. As a matter of fact, a train leaves in the morning that uses a similar route as the *Dawn's Edge*. We can find another way from there."

Coyle closed her eyes as severed heads in glass jars strobed to life in her mind. She was a mess. Tonight hadn't gone the way she'd hoped. But it was fine. As long as Poes knew the *secret*, then everything…

She dropped to her knees, leaned into Poes's legs, and passed out.

***

"Is she well?"

"She's fine, Embeth," Fang answered.

"Is she sick?"

"Tomorrow, for certain. But right now, she's just sleepy. Very sleepy."

"She had a hard day?" Embeth looked in the mirror and fixed the hair that kept falling in her eyes.

"She had a hard day," Fang agreed.

"Will she help you get the book?"

"Yes. Yes, she will. In fact, she's helped so much already."

"Then, maybe she's your friend?" Embeth hopped up and down on one leg.

"I'm not sure she wants friends."

"But you do."

"I don't know. I don't think so." Fang shook her head. What would she do with a friend? People were meant to be manipulated, trust was meant to be exploited and friends were meant to be betrayed. This had been her training, and her training had kept her alive. Survival was paramount. Friendship created weaknesses and distractions. In her business, survival and the objectives were the only things that mattered. There was no room for friends.

Embeth grinned and tucked her chin into her chest. "You care about her, right?"

"What do you mean?"

"You're watching her sleep, silly."

"I just… want to make sure she's safe. She had a very hard day."

"So you're worried about her?"

"I was with her most of the day, remember?"

"But she didn't know you were there."

Fang shook her head. She had stayed well-hidden throughout Coyle's investigation of Trevin's old place. But certain things had been brought to light during Fang's own investigation that she wasn't prepared for. She was piecing together parts of her memory, and she wasn't sure how to process them. Especially the memories that haunted her.

"You're remembering things, aren't you?"

A deep pressure grew in Fang's chest, and she shot a glance at Embeth through blurry eyes. She nodded. She didn't want to talk about the memories she'd discovered. Especially with Embeth.

Not ever.

"What do you remember?"

"That's enough." Fang pressed a finger against her lips, her voice cracking. "Let her sleep. We need to get ready for tomorrow."

"What's tomorrow?" Embeth's eyes twinkled.

"We're traveling by train."

Embeth hopped on the bed and slapped her hands on her mouth.

"Shush! Get down!" Fang whispered through her teeth, glancing at Coyle. She expected the detective to stir, but of course not. Embeth couldn't disturb anything or anyone because she wasn't there. She looked into Embeth's eyes, her bright, happy eyes, trying to understand how Embeth could be so full of joy given the situation. She wasn't here, but yet—*she was*.

Her little sister hopped in her arms and they left the room. Embeth's excited whispers made Fang smile, despite knowing she had killed the little girl.

CHAPTER 13

Grand stateroom of the *Dawn's Edge*

Twelve thousand feet over the Sierra Nevada

Moreci stood near the row of slanted windows. His breathing apparatus made quiet chugging sounds as he looked at the passing landscape below. A tour guide explained the ship's capabilities and provisions to an exclusive group of investors. Moreci wasn't interested in what the *Dawn's Edge* could provide to its guests. He was more interested in the smaller escape ship, the *Dawn's Point*.

"I say," Moreci said, "how safe is the ship, and do we have a lifeboat of sorts?"

"Actually, we do, sir," the tour guide answered. "It's a lovely, twin-engine flying craft that can comfortably fit all of our passengers and crew."

"What's a twin engine?" a gentleman asked. "Flying craft?"

"Mr. Treece has the finest engineers from across the globe and the nether-realm working with him exclusively," the tour guide explained. "Under his direction, they produce inventions for the modern world, pushing past the limitations of known scientific achievements to provide new wonders for humanity.

"The *Dawn's Point* acts as a lifeboat of sorts." He nodded at Moreci. "And she will carry us to safety when called upon."

A light round of applause from the guests made the tour guide blush. The people were bereft of the coming changes to their scheduled flight. And of their own state of being.

"Can you go over the particulars of the *Dawn's Point*?" Moreci asked.

"Of course." The guide offered his extensive knowledge of the craft. All of it made Moreci smile. "And the most exciting feature are the propellers. Each blade is edged with a titanium-aurorium alloy. They are completely unbreakable—unless, of course, you were to hurl a gigantic mass of aurorium into them. But such a thing doesn't exist." He laughed, and the crowd laughed with him.

The imbeciles.

They had no idea what was coming. He nodded to one of his men, who was disguised as a guest. The soldier removed a sidearm and pointed it at the guide's head.

"What's this all about?" the guide asked, a tremor rising in his voice.

"I'm taking over the ship," Moreci said, and he pushed a small device in his hand. Shouting and gunfire ensued. "Thank you for sharing the information on the escape ship. She will suffice for my own people when the time comes."

The soldier pulled the trigger. The guide dropped in a blood-soaked heap. Screams erupted, and more soldiers poured in, weapons drawn. Veiul arrived behind them.

"Take them to the grand ballroom, and hold them until we're ready," he said to his officer. The soldiers escorted out the assembled passengers, leaving Moreci with Veiul and two of his personal guards. He went back to the window and scanned the valleys below.

"What happened?" Moreci asked.

"I was ambushed by one of them," Veiul explained. "Poes was his name."

"And?"

"All of them are alive," she said. "But our operative destroyed Treece's Tesla-Vine Gate. They can't follow us."

He watched her reflection. She glanced at one of his two guards, who glanced back.

"All of us are soldiers, all of us are expendable. If I wanted you dead for not meeting your objective, so be it."

Veiul said nothing, but her shoulders tensed. He knew she wouldn't be put down easily.

"We've been together ever since I created you," he said, turning to her. "We shared many pleasant memories, didn't we?"

Veiul's face flushed deep pink. He stepped closer, reaching his hand to her face.

"I always thought you were better than her," Moreci lied.

Veiul's hands tightened into fists.

"Even though Fang appears to be more powerful, she isn't. She has her inner demons. Fang isn't fully vamperion. Her spirit isn't as sullied or torn as the rest of her ilk. But her mind was affected, just enough, for me to push her. That's why I created a psychological toy."

"The small music box?"

He nodded. "It helped control her. Put her in a more... agreeable mood. "

"Nice of you. I remember the tune, though I'm not familiar with the composer." Her pose relaxed—just a bit.

"*Christ Lag Todesbande* by Heinrich Bach. It's German for 'Christ lay in the bonds of death.' I thought it was fitting, you know? Her people, the vamperion, were the saviors of the nether-realm, but now they are helpless vampires wearing the bonds of death. Interestingly, she had seen Heinrich in concert and remembered her sister liked it."

He could see Veiul's mind spinning, trying to work the math. It was never one of her stronger points. Not like Fang.

"When was this?" Veiul asked.

"The concert was in 1658. One year before she killed her younger sister, Embeth." He turned to Veiul. "Did I ever tell you their tragic story?"

"No, but why would I need to know?"

"I hope I'm wrong, but I have a feeling you may see her again soon, and if you do, you need to know their story. Just in case you need to hurt her in here." He tapped his chest.

"Tell me what happened."

CHAPTER 14

Southern Pacific Depot

San Francisco

If I am not right, set me right, keep me right; that I may at last come to thy house in peace.

Amen.

The *Pegasus*, a cross-continental locomotive train, was the epitome of luxurious travel. Treece hired the best engineers and craftsmen, resulting in extraordinary innovation and the finest technology available. Passengers rode from coast to coast in comfort and grand style. No other machine in the world had its equal.

Treece's team was given double-decker suites with magnificent views of the rolling countryside. They were spacious enough to hold four people comfortably. Servants were assigned to each of the rooms, providing any amenities available. Expensive liquors, rare chocolates, and imported water were theirs with a ring of the bell.

Coyle sat on her bed upstairs with a cold rag on her head, watching the green hills of northern California roll by. The cold, blue, mountains of the Sierra Nevada jutted into the morning sky far in the distance, with the blue Pacific Ocean behind them.

She closed her eyes, wincing at the events of the previous night. Her bright idea to impress them with her skills may not have worked out. They'd asked for a detective, and she'd wanted to give them a show. And just like the training scenario, everything fell apart. She pinched the bridge of her nose, hoping the sharp pain digging into her skull would go away.

"You're not cut out for this."

Maybe Moreci was right. Maybe she wasn't made to be a detective. Maybe she would never find the justice she sought. Detectives solve cases, one after another after another. Certainly, she could find difficult evidence and put things together in her head. But what else did it take to be a great detective? Because she didn't have it.

And maybe I never will.

She rubbed her eyes and walked to the dresser, pulling a hairbrush through her thick brown-gold hair. She caught her reflection in the large window. Her hazel eyes stared back. She wasn't sure when age lines usually appeared at the corners of women's eyes, but she had them at twenty-two.

And what would she look like at thirty-two? Fifty-two? Would she find Ronan by then? And how many women would die while she tried to figure out her life?

She gazed at the slouch of her posture. It was, no doubt, the result of a lack of proper rest, but she had to wonder if the cost of bringing Ronan to justice was growing heavier on her, especially in light of her recent actions of immaturity.

And what was the secret she wanted to tell Poes? She paused, frowning at herself. Was it something she knew? Something he knew? She shook her head and continued. Nothing made sense. Not yet.

She finished brushing her hair and opened her luggage to find a handsome brown pantsuit and matching waistcoat fashioned from woolen tweed. Soft but firm black leather boots and gloves were set beside the clothes. She pulled them out and found another matching set underneath.

Treece had packed her a week's worth of dress-work clothes. She opened another trunk and found two dresses in the latest fashion resting next to beautiful matching shoes. She checked for a manufacturer's imprint but realized the shoes and clothes were all made in-house by Treece's company. At this rate, she'd soon be owned and run by him as well.

A soft rap at the door diverted her attention. She went downstairs and opened the door.

"Yes?" she asked the attendant, giving the girl a quick once-over. She was young, late teens. Her face was pretty with baby-fat cheeks. Her mousy, brown eyes were both shy and curious. Shorter and a bit heavier than Coyle. Smudge on the left sleeve. Odor of cigars. Soft hands.

The girl hummed and handed her a handwritten card. It read, *I have a note for your husband.*

Coyle frowned. "I have no husband. Who is the note for?"

The girl frowned and looked at her notecard. She pulled out a pad of paper and wrote with a small pencil before handing over the pad. Coyle studied the paper. *This is for Suite number 202.*

"Are you deaf?" Coyle asked, tapping her own ear.

The girl's cheeks flushed red, and she nodded. Her soft eyes shot to the floor before looking back up.

Coyle signed, <Do you know how to sign?>

The girl's eyes and mouth opened slightly, but then she frowned. She signed something vaguely resembling, <Yes, I do>.

Coyle had learned American Sign Language from her deaf aunt and cousin, who were taught at a private school. But when she practiced signing with others during her travels, she sometimes had difficulty understanding them. When she questioned her aunt, her aunt explained deaf people could carry an "accent" of sorts depending on their friend group and the region they lived in. But she'd assured Coyle that for the most part, people eventually found enough similarities to hold a conversation.

Coyle wasn't too interested in making new friends and decided to keep the conversation short and simple.

<Who is note for?> Coyle asked.

The girl handed the note to Coyle and gave a polite smile.

<Thank you,> Coyle signed before turning away.

<I'm sorry!> the girl said. She signed something else, but Coyle wasn't too sure what was said.

Coyle nodded her head and shut the door. The note read, *Meeting in Treece's suite, seven o'clock.* She glanced at the trunk with the dresses and sighed.

More opportunities to embarrass myself.

Her pipe hanging at the side of her mouth, she spent the rest of the day reading and rereading the journal she had found deep underground. The edges were torn, and some of the ink had melted into the pages from the seawater. But she read what she could and guessed what she couldn't.

Most of it was written with constant misspellings and a shaky hand, making reading slow and even impossible at times. She could only guess the author was Trevin, but the journal also contained torn pages from someone else's journal. This author's writing indicated education and excellent penmanship.

She set the torn pages and reread them. The author wrote with a gentle though tortured heart. He and another unnamed cohort had been in charge of modifications within Project Archangel.

There were many entries pertaining to a girl, half-human, half-vamperion. She was brought in wearing a straitjacket. She had murdered her adoptive parents with a knife. The unnamed girl was full of rage, almost untamable. Time went on, and the experiments began. Eventually, they forced her into a semblance of control and gave her the codename Fang.

One entry, dated March 1868, read,

We learned she was born in 1649 in a hamlet near Buckinghamshire. By the age of ten, she had suffered a terrible tragedy during a ship's voyage from England to New Amsterdam (now New York). After that, there is no history of her whereabouts other than the account of her murdered adopted parents. Where had she been for over two hundred years? And now she is mentally and spiritually dismantled.

It is with utmost care and delicacy the physician touches the deep wound. And only the Great Physician Himself could heal the wounds inflicted on her poor soul. Did she suffer them from our own hands? Or when she killed her younger sister? Or were they brought upon by the many deathly tasks for which she was created? Only He can tell, and only He can heal.

And what have we done? Who did we think we were to change the course of her destiny? Our own hubris is but a stalk of dried wheat compared to the fiery Seat of Judgement that awaits. I would do anything to keep this girl named Fang whole, to keep her safe, to keep her away from the evils of this world. But I fear I've done too much already, and these hands of clay are not worthy to protect her cherished soul.

Another entry, dated June 1871:

The other operatives, Veiul particularly, tell us something is wrong with Fang.

It is said she makes conversation with the air, with someone unseen. Whether it is an angel for good or a phantom for ill, Fang won't tell us. But I know Fang is suffering either way, and it tears me apart to know this was our doing. Prof. Moreci is certain the invisible companion is nothing more than Fang's guilty conscience. He says she killed her little sister and can't find a way to navigate through her own storm. Despite my earnest objection, Prof. Moreci pushes to take advantage of her malady by creating a psychological tool to control her.

The last entry was dated November 1889:

Fang has become unusable. She has left many of her peers to die in the field, especially after their campaign in Afghanistan. No one trusts her, prompting her to be shut away in confinement until her broken mind can be repaired.

After much discussion with our psychologists, Fang believes the visage of her sister is real and no device, either psychological or physical, could separate them. The spirit of Embeth is wholly in Fang's hands, heart and mind. She will protect her younger sister, whether phantom or memory, with fierce loyalty. I have little doubt Fang would destroy entire armies to protect the treasured girl. I once asked Fang what Embeth was worth. She replied without hesitation, "More than all the stars in the sky."

Coyle looked outside, past the clouds, past the bright screen of daylight. She knew the stars were there but couldn't see their brilliance. Just like she couldn't see her own worth. She tried to imagine what it would be like to be valued so tremendously, so powerfully.

After last night's exhibition of debauchery, she was positive she would never know. She would not feel that esteem from any of her team and especially not from the One she prayed to.

She closed her eyes, her mind searching for answers. Fang had been ten when she and Embeth traveled across the Atlantic. Then tragedy struck: Fang killed Embeth. But how? Why? And how was

Embeth intertwined with Fang's psyche? Or was she really a spirit? Was she benevolent or venomous? Embeth had to be benevolent; otherwise, Fang wouldn't protect her so.

"You're the epitome of disarray."

"You don't know the half of it."

And where was Fang now? Why was there no evidence of her whereabouts? She said she would keep in touch, and yet she hadn't. Did she change her mind? Did she and Embeth leave and find somewhere else to live out their days?

She shook her head and refused to believe Fang had completely disappeared. After she killed Trevin, she would be in pursuit of the other people responsible. In fact, Fang was much like Coyle. They were cut from the same cloth, weren't they? Each pursued the men responsible for destroying their lives.

A chime rang seven o'clock. Coyle chose the black silk dress with matching light-gray coat and gloves. The neck was high, just under her chin, but the cut accentuated what few curves she had. It fit perfectly, just like all the other clothes. The shoes fit comfortably, and the heel gave her small frame a lift. She glanced in the mirror and removed the choker before stepping outside. The attendant popped up from a chair with a tight smile.

<Watch door,> Coyle signed.

<I will.> the girl nodded and stared at the floor. Pink bloomed on her fair cheeks. Coyle walked a few steps and felt the tug of a missed opportunity on her conscience. She turned back.

<What is your name?> she asked.

The girl frowned and pointed to her chest. <Gibby.> she spelled her name out.

<Age?>

<Almost twenty.> Gibby smiled.

<Where are you from?> Coyle asked.

<San Diego.>

Coyle gave her another once-over and met her eyes. <Your hair smells like cheap cigars. Dark scuff on your left sleeve from brass rail. Stay away from saloon! Men in bars don't want to carry you to your future—they want to carry you to their bed. Stay away from them, understand?>

Gibby nodded and Coyle left the girl frowning, sniffing her hair, and noticing the dark smudge on her left arm. She was young and naive, but if Coyle could try to steer her in the right direction, then maybe Gibby could have a chance at bettering herself.

The hallway was spacious enough for guests to pass each other comfortably. Passengers walked back and forth throughout the cars, enjoying eateries, shopping, small galleries, and museums. Coyle didn't mind the exercise and enjoyed people-watching. Children chased each other back and forth while their parents and nannies chatted with new acquaintances. Younger women than Coyle giggled and blushed at young men.

She wondered if she would be doing the same if—no. Definitely not. That's not who she was. Not anymore. Trying to be the first female detective in the state cemented her place in the astonishing tales of women breaking the mold. No man would have her now. Not even Poes.

She suddenly realized something about last night was nagging her, something about the secret. But what? Something about his eyes, the cologne he wore, his strong arms. Nothing was falling into place. Not yet. She shook her head and kept walking.

Superior engineering kept the cars quiet, and the experience was like riding on air. She took a deep breath and smiled. Freshly baked bread and smoked meats were being prepared for dinner. The thought of buttered rolls with blackberry jam and smoked pork dripping with fat danced through her mind. Her mouth began to water.

She arrived at Treece's suite and found the men had arrived earlier and were sipping drinks. Cigars hung from the mouths of those who fancied expensive tobacco. She grimaced as she remembered her pipe on the dresser. The room was impeccable in design with solid mahogany walls and cabinets, frosted-glass electric lamps and stuffed leather chairs.

As soon as she stepped into the room, everyone stopped talking and turned. In turn, she glanced at everyone else. Smoke hung in the air, though it wasn't as thick as the tension. She had a feeling she had been the topic of conversation. And for some reason, she didn't care. She was used to being outside the circle of her peers, and if that was her place, then so be it. She wasn't here to impress anyone. Not anymore.

"Would you like something to drink?" Treece asked. The look in his eyes suggested this wasn't the time to get smashed again.

"Just soda water and lime, please." She removed her gloves, and GEM went to the bar to retrieve her beverage. Her gaze locked onto Poes's and the attorney nodded to an empty seat across from him but next to Bolt. She sighed and sank into the chair. Everything she had wanted to say last night lay tangled in a jumbled mess. Now wasn't the time for that particular discussion. She'd have to wait. In the meantime, she rubbed her temples, feeling the heat from their eyes as if she had to answer for something. *Well, let them ask. Let's see what inane questions they have for me today.*

"Now we have everyone here," Vonteg said. "Time to find out what we know about last night's discovery."

"The only person we should be concentrating on is Miss Coyle," Bolt said.

"I'm sorry," Coyle said. "What are we talking about?"

"My Tesla-Vine Gate was destroyed last night," Treece said.

"And we," Duone added, motioning to everyone, "Are the suspects."

"We," Bolt said, mimicking Duone's gesture, "were all together, except for her."

"The doctor's orders were that you stay in bed," Poes said. "Yet you left your room and apparently wandered about the mansion until you found the evidence you collected. Care to elaborate?"

All eyes turned to her. The familiar sensation of heat rising in her cheeks wouldn't help her innocence. But she was innocent, of course.

"The constant accusations against me are getting a bit overused, don't you think? But I understand your concern, and I'm only too happy to steer you in the right direction—and away from me especially," Coyle said. "I did leave my room. Based on the excitement I had earlier in the day, I knew there wouldn't be any rest on my schedule. My mind was busy with what I had discovered, and I had to untangle the mess."

"You're talking about the notes," Duone said.

"I am. And I felt I could prove more useful by using my strengths than by resting."

"Is getting hammered one of your strengths?" Bolt asked.

"I had a very hard day, one that will stay in my mind for longer than I wish," she said. "I'm sure you, being a wrencher and all, understand having a few drinks after a long day."

"Yes. I am a man, after all, and it's not so uncouth to knock a few back with the boys." Bolt huffed.

"We are not here to discuss the formalities of social drinking," Treece said. "We are a team of well-trained people working together toward a common goal. But one of us, or someone else we aren't aware of, is hindering our progress."

Bolt harrumphed. Ice clinked against glass. Coyle studied the ceiling, her fingers dabbing the lines of perspiration along her hairline.

"Sorry to say," Poes said, "but Coyle was the only one wandering around the house, while most of us were together."

"Well, I didn't even know the thing existed," Coyle said, "let alone know how to destroy it. The whole matter of my involvement is preposterous. I'm here to help uncover evidence, and I'm doing it the best I can, thank you."

"That you are," Treece said. He gave her a confident smile, but she wasn't sure he meant it.

"Poes, you have the most experience with cross-examination. What do you think of Miss Coyle's explanation?" Vonteg asked.

"I believe her," he said without hesitation. "There isn't a bone in her body that sides with injustice or chaos."

"And how would you know what her bones like or dislike?" Bolt asked.

"She isn't a dislikable character," Poes answered. "And I know good character when I see it."

Coyle shot a glance at Poes, swallowed the rest of her drink and stood.

"Would you care for another?" Treece asked.

"I'll get it myself, thank you," she said. "The smoke in the room is bothering me."

"I'm telling you—" Bolt started, but the others interrupted. Their voices rose against each other, but most, if not all, agreed with Poes's remarks.

I'm only disliked by the one, then.

She entered the private bar and ordered her drink, a real one this time, from the automaton behind the counter. Green lights pulsed in its glass-domed head. Unlike the simpler automatons, this one resembled an octopus. Eight arms moved about with quick, precise movements. Gears and tiny pistons worked synchronously within the brass framework until a highball glass was filled with soda water and Scotch. Mechanical claws set the glass carefully on the counter and pushed a wedge of lime onto the rim of the glass. Coyle picked it up.

"Thank you," she said. Hearing footsteps, she turned to find Treece joining her at the bar.

"My automaton bartenders have won over the tavern community throughout the larger cities." Treece smiled. "It's the tavern girls I can't duplicate."

"Do you have any who can solve crimes for you?"

He turned and gave her a long look before answering.

"What, tavern girls?" He chuckled. "Sorry, I couldn't resist. No, artificial people are capable of many things, but nothing beats human intuition and instinct, or his spirit."

She took a sip and glanced sideways at him.

"Her spirit," he added.

"I know you appreciate my efforts, even when I'm not certain how to present them."

"You're under a lot of pressure," Poes said as he stepped up to the bar. "The way Treece has been touting you, we're expecting you to solve the riddle of the Sphinx."

"Man," she said.

"Ah, yes. Oedipus," Poes said, blinking. "Must have forgotten my history lessons."

"Man is probably always the answer when looking for culprits," Treece said. "Which reminds me: we still need to find out who disabled the gate."

"We've been round and round with the lot," Poes said. "All of us are adamant about our innocence."

"And yet all of us are suspect," Treece added.

"Have you asked the automatons?" Coyle asked.

Both men looked at her.

"I'm not... certain one of my automatons could do such a thing," Treece said.

"But you just said it yourself: they're capable of many things," she said. "Why wouldn't they be capable of destruction?"

Treece and Poes discussed the improbabilities of her suggestion while Coyle looked back at the eight-armed automaton. Each of its arms ended with metal-tipped claws capable of holding a delicate wineglass —or squeezing a throat.

The mechanical bartender whizzed its head around, staring into her eyes with pulsing green lights. In a flash of movement, its arms snapped out, claws reaching for her. She gasped and backed away. The arms extended too quickly, she thought, aiming right at her heart.

"It thinks you want a refill," Treece said. "It's reaching for your glass."

She turned to him and back at the machine.

"Did you want a top-off?" Treece asked.

She glanced down at the glass in her hands, the ice swimming amidst the clear liquid. She looked back up at the automaton, sure of its murderous intentions. But no. It was just a machine, doing its job as a bartender.

Her shoulders drooped and she took a deep breath, shaking her head. She smiled, feeling silly for—

A mechanical hand grabbed her shoulder, the strength of it unhinging her. Without resistance, she was spun around to face GEM. His heavy mechanical hands grabbed both of her shoulders, holding her firmly.

So he can *murder you.*

"Miss Coyle," GEM said. "I believe your presumption was correct."

She stared at herself in his polished dome, eyes wide with terror. She was speechless.

"Miss Coyle?" GEM asked. "Are you well? Perhaps you should have more of the 'firewater,' as it were."

"No," she finally answered. "No, I'm fine. Just startled is all. Perhaps next time you could get my attention with a light tap on the shoulder."

"I apologize," GEM said. "But I discovered something interesting that we should look at." GEM tapped a button and waited until a high-pitched whine rose steadily and the room darkened. He flipped a switch on his collar, and a green-tinted projection shot out of his eyes and onto the floor.

The other men stood round the image being cast, staring with curiosity and wonder. The image displayed someone walking down a hall inside Treece's estate. It turned a corner and stepped into a room.

"That's the gate room," Treece said.

The viewer approached a beautiful, carven-wood arch with wires and strange looking contraptions off to the side. Mechanical hands drew close and applied a small box to the side of the arch before pushing a lever. Sparks flew, and flames spread over the arch in a matter of seconds. The image shifted away as the automaton left the room and returned to its duties.

"So," GEM said, "this proves Miss Coyle's innocence and concludes the baseless accusations against her. I, for one, would appreciate changing the tone toward her. After all, she did save my life."

"By pushing her out of a closet?" Poes asked.

"She saved my life," GEM repeated. "And if someone wants to attack her character, I won't have it."

"There, see?" Treece said. "It was someone other than the lot of us."

"Any more questions?" Coyle asked. "Or perhaps we can get on with our task, as if it weren't unnerving enough."

Dinner was served. Their company steered away from rampant accusations and shared stories and backgrounds before returning finally to the subject at hand. All the while, Coyle kept quiet, chewing her roasted duck without the satisfaction of tasting it. Heat radiated from her cheeks, but she kept her composure, pushing the heaviness away and keeping herself busy, listening and watching and noting every detail and nuance of the rest of the group: whether they used their right hand or left, who fidgeted when certain questions were asked, who looked down at the table or tapped the floor when uncertain about something. Shallow breathing. The pulse rates in their jugulars. She couldn't help it.

It was her hobby.

Some women liked needlepoint, baking or gardening. She wanted to know whom she was working with. Whom she could trust. And yet the person with whom she felt safest wasn't there.

Fang.

The one person for whom she felt a modicum of assured trust wasn't in the room. She glanced around, peering into the dark recesses of nearby rooms and once or twice outside the window. But the vampire remained hidden from their eyes and presence. After all, everyone except Coyle suspected Fang was responsible for the ordeal. Why would she want to make an appearance? Coyle herself had barely survived another rash of accusations, and *she* had been handpicked by this group.

Conversation finally came down to one thing: all of them were nervous about the coming event. The task of finding Moreci and stopping him from using an ancient book of curses was outside their bounds of expertise and bordered on unreasonable. Yet, they were Templars. This is what they did. She was in the same predicament as these men, leaps and bounds out of her comfort zone. Sitting behind a desk and piecing clues together was much more her style. She would have been happy pointing out the villain while other officers made the arrest. Instead, she was in a train on its way to an airship, surrounded by men unsure of who she was and a powerfully rich man she had to impress. She wasn't sure of what they were going to face or whether or not they would survive.

Uncertainty had a way of embedding itself into the noblest of intentions. After all, they were only trying to save a city full of people from being destroyed.

"When do we catch up to the *Dawn's Edge*?" Vonteg asked.

"In just over twelve hours," Treece said.

"And then?" Duone asked.

"And then we'll go from there," Treece said. "I have men working on transit between the train and the airship."

"Can't we use one of your gates onboard the train?" asked Quolo.

"Not at these speeds, no," Treece said. "From airship to airship, it's a strong possibility. But not from a high-speed train."

"I wonder what we'll be facing once we're on board," Bolt asked.

"I'm more concerned about how we're getting there," Quolo said.

"We should be more concerned about what's ultimately required of us," Treece said. "Do each of you understand, to the fullest extent, what your duty entails?" His eyes studied hers.

She looked away, thumbing her glass, still quite uncertain. Stopping a thief from stealing a valuable piece of art was one thing; stopping a vengeful madman from killing an entire city... She shook her head, staring at her glass.

"I guess we'll find out in twelve hours," Bolt said.

"We don't have much time to dilly-dally," Duone said. "We need to go over some basic combat guidelines and survival medicine just in case. We'll get an early start, oh seven hundred hours. See you then."

Coyle walked through the cars, full of mingling doubts. Tight knots gripped her upper back and her palms were damp from the inevitability of facing the unknown. And she had to face these unknowns with people who barely trusted her.

Hard drinks knocked on the door of her mind, inviting her to go numb, to relax, to forget the danger she was heading into.

Death waiting to clutch my hand.

She passed her room and nodded to Gibby, who smiled weakly. The girl was good-hearted, happy to have a job. Ah, youth! She remembered being naive like that. Part of her wished she had remained naive, and happy to have a simple job. Her job now was something she preferred not to think about. Why? Because… she wasn't cut out for this. She had discovered plenty of evidence, but the entire ordeal has been much more involved than she could have imagined.

She wasn't the one. Treece could find others who could do the job as well or *better* than she could. She'd learned who she was during this long exercise. She should have listened to her father: be smart, marry rich. Then she would actually get to enjoy being on a luxurious train heading east through the canyons of Utah. None of her current activities would be condoned by her doctor.

Health, yes. That was her ticket out of this mess. She would tell Treece tomorrow. No more chasing after certain death. She was done.

She passed through a lounge car and noticed a woman sitting at a small table studying a chessboard. Short dark hair, fair skin.

Beautiful, dark-red evening dress with long sleeves. A small matching hat with a short, black veil covered her eyes and completed her outfit.

Coyle froze.

She clutched her purse, took a deep, quiet breath, and walked to the table.

"Does asking to play chess with a stranger make you that nervous?" Fang asked without taking her eyes off the board.

Coyle swallowed. "Is anyone sitting here?"

Fang shot her eyes up. *Are you serious?*

Coyle sat and stared at the chess pieces, sitting opposite the most dangerous woman in the world. Yet… yet deep inside, she knew Fang wasn't a threat to her. She exhaled, and a strange, warm sensation washed over her. Her shoulders drooped, and she leaned back.

It felt as if she were meeting an old friend.

An automaton waiter approached.

"Whisky straight, Glenlivet," Fang said.

"Lime. Scotch. And water—soda," Coyle said.

The automaton contemplated for a moment before leaving.

"That's quite the drink," Fang said.

"I'm sorry," Coyle said. "My mind has been a bit harried lately."

They sat in silence, listening to the rhythmic tapping of the tracks and the light chatter around them. Coyle swallowed, still unsure of everything.

"Maybe if you moved a piece," Fang said.

"I haven't played in some time. And I think there are more serious things to talk about."

"Move something, or those men in the corner will think you're just staring at me."

Coyle sighed, picked up the white knight and took Fang's pawn.

"I don't feel like I belong," Coyle said. "I'm in constant fear of being accused of things I didn't do or say. I'm doing my job exactly as they asked of me. Yet..." She shook her fists.

"Yet?"

"Yet it's like I'm being punished for doing it so well."

"Sounds familiar. They ask you to do a job, then they become frightened at just how well you do it."

Coyle brushed a knuckle against her lips, studying Fang as a person, a woman. A peer, not a vampire.

"Yes," Coyle said. "Frightened is the best word to describe their reactions."

"Ignorance is what I would call it."

"I read pages from a journal about you."

"Do tell."

"They locked you up in an iron box of some sort with a date to exterminate you."

"Hmm. Looks like I missed another appointment."

"Doesn't that frighten you? Because it terrifies me to the point of paralysis, and my life isn't even threatened. Treece's team doubts my abilities and who I am as a person. They believe my moral compass is flawed. But you? These men are ready to kill you on sight without hesitation."

Fang tilted her head, a subtle smile playing on her lips. She removed a pawn with a bishop. She stared at the board and spoke.

"Years ago, I was on assignment in Bangladesh—during the summer, I might add. Miserable wet heat, and I was constantly sopping wet. I'm glad it was only once. Anyway, our... *objective* wasn't due to arrive for fourteen hours, so I had to find entertainment. I found a carnival taking place in a large village, and I watched from a rooftop. This man brought out a cage with a tiger inside, and he was warning the crowd to stay back. There's danger inside, but he's tamed it, he assured them. And he's going to show them tricks he taught this tiger."

The automaton arrived, served the drinks and left. Coyle took a small sip, the liquor calming her nerves. Fang continued.

"He opened the cage door, and the tiger limped out, nice and easy. The animal looked anything but dangerous. It hunched, cowered, loped in a small circle, staring at the dirt. The man was getting ready to show them the first trick when the leash snapped apart. The noise attracted the attention of the tiger, who looked at the baffled handler. And then the tiger became a tiger, slashed the man's throat, chased the villagers and ran into the forest."

Fang leaned in and squinted at Coyle. "I've seen your work. The way you study objects, people, their words. Some may call it peculiar, but you are so much more than just an adjective. You are a ravenous tiger. When they let you out of the cage, you want evidence, justice, blood. And everyone you come across is terrified of what you can do, of who you are. Because, Coyle, you're not one of them."

Coyle stared out the window, her mind gathering the wool set before her.

"My perception needs to change," Coyle added.

"In more ways than one. When a tiger wanders down the street, no one needs to warn you, tell you all about its abilities and how dangerous it is. It just *is*, and it does what it was made to do."

Coyle tilted her head and frowned. "A tiger never needs defending, does it?"

She swallowed the rest of her drink, prompting the mechanical waiter to offer another one. She nodded at it.

"You're not afraid of these men, because of who and what you are?" Coyle asked.

"I respect fear—it keeps me alive—but I'm not governed by it. Are they?" Fang shrugged. "They're not my concern right now. My concern is to find and stop Moreci. And it should be yours."

Coyle was reminded of her decision to quit Treece's team. Of her trivial excuses for not continuing.

"I guess I've been too caught up with what the others think of me, on constant alert for rejections and accusations," Coyle said. "It's exhausting."

"Maybe they're not the team for you."

"And you—we—are?"

"Are you a tiger?" Fang smiled.

Coyle's gaze stared past the window before shifting to the fresh drink, the unfinished chess game and the glimmer of Fang's eyes. She chewed the inside of her cheek.

"Am I?"

"Whose blood do you want? You didn't try to become a detective because it was a Tuesday morning with nothing better planned. You applied for that position without caring what others thought or said. And when you were denied, you made a fist and slammed it into the man who held the prize from you. Sounds like a predator to me. So whose blood do you want?"

Coyle slowly nodded. Yes. She was.

A tiger.

CHAPTER 15

A knock on the door disturbed her rest.

"Yes?" Coyle answered, opening her eyes in a tight squint. Soft gray light streamed through the curtains. The train whistle blew clear and shrill.

She kicked aside the pillows on the floor and slipped into a robe as the knocking grew more insistent. She grabbed the door handle and opened it, expecting Gibby.

"We've just had a communiqué," Duone said with wide eyes. "Someone on the *Dawn's Edge* sent an emergency transmission. All hell's broken loose. We must leave immediately."

Later, Coyle stood in one of the half-empty storage cars with the others, learning their new strategy. Each of them wore a special suit made by Treece's team of engineers and tailors: navy-blue leathers with thick armor at the joints, metal knuckles, steel-toed boots, and a special helmet with built-in radio receivers—all with the Templar's emblem.

So, then—its official is it? I'm a Templar.

She was given a bulky handgun, given basic instructions on its use. It was a special weapon, a Multi-Array Dispersal pistol or MAD for short. Three switches allowed for different ballistic options: *bewilder*, a non-lethal choice; *sleep*, for knocking out a target; and a simple skull for a fatal shot. Or something.

Coyle adjusted her multi-use goggles and caught a glimpse of molten anger in Bolt's eyes. Although he smiled at her, his eyes confirmed her suspicions. There was no mistaking Bolt was a threat.

She looked away, trying to stay focused on the task at hand. They had done their best to convince him she meant no harm and would continue to be a great benefit to the team. But his eyes said otherwise. Fang's assurance—that she would be close by once they got on the airship—gave Coyle a bit of something to look forward to.

"We carry the daunting task of investigating this great mystery and putting a stop to whoever, or whatever, stands in our way," Vonteg said. "I am certain each of us knows the risks. We will arrive at our location, board the ship, and overcome any obstacle that befalls us. We have a team of experienced soldiers coming with us. We will also bring a chief crewman who knows the ship backward and forward. Together, as a team, we will succeed. Treece took considerable care in choosing us. He is a brilliant strategist and creator. He will make sure we have breathable air to succeed in our mission."

Coyle looked down at her gloved hands, flexing her fingers. Adrenaline raced through her blood. The swell of rising panic threatened to tilt her off-balance.

Her mind picked out only a few words of Vonteg's speech: *daunting, risks, befalls, breathable air.*

She closed her eyes.

You are a tiger. Act like one.

She straightened her hunched shoulders, trying to hold on to the positives, the little things, to push away the darkness that crept along the edges of her mind. But with each passing second, her mind swirled deeper into the dark storm of helplessness.

She stepped away so they couldn't hear her labored breaths. Her hands were clasped together so tight she worried her fingers might snap.

God, why? I'm being punished, aren't I? Why do I have to fight against the urge to curl into a ball of fear? Why can't I be the tiger I'm supposed to be?

With trembling fingers, she pressed against her trousers and squeezed her eyes. Her lips parted, and air rushed out again. Her ears picked out a new conversation.

"What? How can we be there sooner?" Poes asked.

"We're less than an hour away from catching up to her. This train is equipped with supply pods. Steam-powered, radio-guided aero-rockets that will propel us to the airship," Vonteg explained.

"Pods? Rockets? Have you gone mad?" Quolo asked with a raised voice.

Coyle's fears became more palpable and less containable. She turned back to the rest of the group.

"The pods were built for supplying airships midflight along with emergency travel, and this certainly qualifies. They're easy to manage, and each will have a pilot to carry us to the airship in perfect safety."

"We sit on top of them and just hold on for dear life?" Poes asked.

"Of course not," Vonteg said. "We lay inside. Like a coffin."

Coyle glanced to the heavens.

CHAPTER 16

O Lord of Grace, the world is before me this day, and I am weak and fearful, but I look to thee for strength.

Amen.

The gnome engineer led the group through the cars to the cargo carriers. He was considerably shorter than all of them, and his hair resembled a thick, blue cloud the same color as his eyes. The lines around his bright blue eyes were deeply ingrained into his tanned face. But his short legs carried him faster than everyone else, and he was full of energy. A line of thick, white cigar smoke trailed behind him as he spoke.

"My team is working on the boosters," he said. "The modifications won't take too long."

Coyle's fingertips caressed the polished wooden cabin doors and beautifully crafted brass door handles as they walked along the plush, carpeted walkway. She looked out the windows over the dry valley of northern Utah rushing by. Snow-capped mountains stood majestically at the edges.

They passed a beautiful, evocative oil painting: John Millais's *Ophelia*. The artist depicted the grieving young woman from

Shakespeare's *Hamlet*. She lay face-up, floating along the river, singing songs to herself before finally descending into the depths.

Coyle looked away and inhaled. The scents of women's perfume, baked bread, and fresh flowers hovered in the air as she breathed in and out as carefully as she could.

Chief Sykes unlocked a door, and a flood of noisy, cold air chewed through Coyle's leathers. They passed over a thin gangway with a small brass chain for a handrail. The speed of the train sucked the air out of her lungs. She gripped the brass chain that separated her from the blur of rushing ground. She breathed in traces of wildflower and oak, but mostly grease, burning coal and the pungent sweat from the men.

They passed into the cargo holds, and the temperature inside was no different. Coyle looked up as they walked through. Long slats of wooden screens let air and light into the hold. Wooden crates and boxes of all shapes were stacked in tight formations. The floor was bare wood bound with strips of iron.

Coyle glanced behind and knew the grand comfort of Dawn Industries would be gone for some time to come. She had to wonder what else she was leaving behind.

She wanted to be a detective. She'd failed the exam, and her future was in the gutter. And yet, here she was, helping one of the richest men in the world stop a city from being destroyed. If she was successful, Treece would be grateful—a grateful man with resources and knowledge of people in the right places. She could get a detective position out of this if she played her cards right. But Fang had also told her they would work together. Two of them against whatever was to come.

Two tigers against the world.

They arrived at the booster-pod cargo hold. Gnomes were busy as ants, crawling over large, polished metal pods lined in rows. Their small hands were deft and precise. Hammers, wrenches, and torches filled the air with noise. Coyle wrinkled her nose against the sharp odor of burning metal. Steam and smoke snaked through the hold and disappeared through the open slats above. She noticed others, fully armed and wearing uniforms similar to her group; Templar soldiers. Some pointed at blueprints, others checked weapons and some kept an eye on her.

Vonteg motioned for them to affix their helmets, face covers, and goggles. Coyle unclasped the buckle on her utility belt and slid the helmet on. Her trembling fingers made it difficult, but she finally clasped the face cover together and pulled the goggles over her eyes. Her finger found the small tab along her jawline, and the soft hiss of the communications channel filled her right ear. The noises and smell faded away to almost nothing.

"Can everyone hear me? Yes? Give me a thumbs-up if you're receiving my transmission," Vonteg asked. "Excellent." He looked at Coyle and gave her a nod. She nodded back and gave him a thumbs-up.

She tried to ignore the adrenaline shooting through her body. The narrow opening of the tube held her gaze for too long. There was space enough for a few of them to fit into, shoulder to shoulder. Cramped.

Like a coffin.

"Coyle!"

She turned. Vonteg was nodding at her. "Coyle, can you hear me? Yes? Pay attention, please. With the amount of personnel we have, each of the tubes will fit three of us. There will be one investigative team member with two soldiers, understood?"

She nodded and kept her eyes away from the pods.

Coffins.

"Now look here." Vonteg motioned to the hastily created craft. "These are usually used for in-flight supplies and support. They are sturdy, dependable and most definitely the only option we have right now. Once inside, you will each have one of these bags." He pointed to a small pile of canvas bags on the floor, and she picked one up.

"In the bag, you will find extra boxes of ammunition, medical supplies, survival gear, emergency rations and signaling devices," he said. "The tube will shoot you into the higher altitudes where breathing is difficult. When we enter the tubes, make sure you push the switch here on your helmet to activate the breathing device on your suits.

"Once in the air, the tubes will be guided to the Dawn's Edge through a series of gnomish array-wave signals. Then, the airship will automatically launch a series of magnetic coils to catch and pull the tube into the cargo bay. Once we are inside the bay, we will begin our search for the emergency activation beacon. Duone and I will stick with Coyle, seeing as how we're the three investigators. Poes, Bolt and Quolo will stick together as the other portion of our team. The rest of the armed men are with us to provide lethal options, if needed." He paused for a short time and looked around the room. "Each of you has an important part to play in this mission. Stay safe, and God be with us."

Coyle flinched as the ceiling pulled away with a screech of metal. The wide expanse of the blue sky was above them, and she squinted through the bright sunlight pouring in. Vonteg pointed, and their eyes followed his direction. A long, dark oval floated in the distance. Thin clouds and a hazy atmosphere made the airship look like a ghost ship sailing along a forgotten course.

The *Dawn's Edge*.

"There she is," he said. "It's large enough to hold four hundred twenty-five passengers and seventy-five crew with multiple decks, wide halls, and grand ballrooms. This won't be easy, but we're going to work together, and we know there is strength in unity. Remember our creed: strength through adversity." He looked each of them in the eye, and each gave a nod in response.

One by one, the gnomes finished their work and set equipment to the side. Coyle stepped aside and glanced around the room as the armed men hurried around them. A pair of hands tugged at her, and she turned. Poes looked into her eyes and nodded. She nodded in turn before being led to one of the tubes. She swallowed and looked back at Poes.

He glanced back, locking eyes with her. With that one, knowing glance, Coyle remembered their secret. Everything made sense now. But now, yes now was too late wasn't it? No one would understand, of course. She would have to wait until this played out to see what would happen. Poes finally turned away and crawled into the pod in front of him.

As her eyes refocused, she had the odd sensation of being stared at. Against her better judgment, she glanced to the other side and saw Bolt, his dark eyes piercing hers. He stared for a heartbeat before pushing himself into the opening. She turned her attention to her own tube.

The space inside looked smaller. Darker.

Like a coffin.

The edge of the opening blurred out of focus. With labored breathing, she pressed the switch on her chest plate. There was a tap and a click and then clean, cold oxygen flowed into her mouth and nose. She bit her lip. Her anxiety forbade her to cross the threshold.

"Everything all right, miss?" Chief Sykes looked up and asked. "Need help with anything?"

"Are you sure these are safe, sir?" she asked.

"We use these almost daily for mail and package delivery to our transport ships," he said, holding his cigar. "Please be assured, these are perfectly safe, miss."

"Safe for people to travel in?"

"…Yes." He patted the tube.

She blinked and hesitated for a few moments more before someone gave her a gentle push. She crawled through the opening, and the soldiers handed over the harness straps. She leaned back, pulling the harness close to her body, and clasped the brass fittings together. The door closed with a heavy thud. She shut her eyes.

Thisisnotacoffinthisisnotacoffinthisisnotacoffin.

"Grab the handrails," one of the men said. "The handrails, Miss Coyle?"

Her trembling hands shot up and grabbed the handholds by her shoulders. Someone outside tapped against something a few times before she opened her eyes, glancing out the portal. She heard a small argument between Chief Sykes and another gnome, something about something-something-something or else it won't work.

Panic shot through her body. She reached for the clasp, but it refused to cooperate with her struggling fingers.

"What's wrong? Miss Coyle?"

She didn't answer. She only knew this was all a mistake, and she had to leave right now. She glanced outside and saw a gnome give them a thumbs-up. He slammed his hand against a switch and loud machinery pushed the pod outside at an angle. Air, light and noise rushed in all at once. She struggled against the tight straps but then looked up through the holes in the tube at the cold, blue sky. And somehow, the bright color soothed her mind. She didn't have to panic. This was going to work.

I'm a tiger, remember?

She shut her eyes again, trying to remember the comforts to which she would soon return: the plush carpets, baked bread, hot baths and beautiful vases with fresh-cut flowers. She was going on a trip and returning soon. Everything was going to be fine.

A strange noise grew around her, as if a thousand people were sucking in a long, deep breath. She sucked in her breath as well.

Plush carpet. Beautiful vase. Scent of—

FOOM!

A giant hand pressed against her, crushing her lungs, her head struggling to turn. Her breath came in shallow gasps. A long, loud blast deafened her, and her ears rang incessantly.

Her eyes shifted out of the small window and caught familiar sights: sun, clouds, mountains, sky. Then the clouds and the mountains and the sun sank out of view as the tube was steered through the sky. The pressure against her body relaxed a bit. She eased forward and breathed long, full breaths.

A flash of silver caught her attention. Another tube in the distance flew through the air. Its metal wings unfurled while a puffy white pillar trailed behind. She shifted her focus and found another pod, and there, just to the right, another.

She found consolation in the cluster of flying craft. They were together, even in the air. Her new teammates, all of them experiencing the same things as her. Renewed confidence slowly surfaced and began to push away the dark thoughts.

The craft shifted direction. The movement was subtle. Gentle. And then her eyes found the massive airship hanging in the clouds.

The *Dawn's Edge* grew larger, more real and less like a phantom. She focused on the ship above. As long she kept her eyes on the goal, she would reach the bay safely and in one piece with everyone else.

It's almost over.

A nagging gleam in the sky caught her attention. Her gaze shifted to the cluster of pods. One of the tubes was shuddering.

CHAPTER 17

She squinted. Was it just the normal movement of the craft? Or more tricks of her imagination? She gasped as gray smoke streamed out of the windows before the pod spun and veered sharply to the left and out of view. Her eyes frantically searched the sky, but she couldn't find it. She waved at the pilot.

"There's something wrong with the tube!" she said.

"What?" one of them said.

She pointed just as the sky erupted in fire and black smoke. The destroyed tube spun like a flaming top with plumes of dark spiral rings pouring out. She watched in horror as the craft slammed into another pod, sending both out of control.

Someone shouted, and Coyle looked over. One of their emergency canvas bags was smoking.

What's happening?

One of the men pulled himself out of the harness, grabbed the bag, and shoved it through the small window.

WHAM!

A violent explosion shook her bones and reduced her hearing to a high-pitched whine. The hatch ripped open. Metal debris flew and clattered against the inside of their pod. She squeezed her eyes shut and screamed.

Her body pressed to the side, and nausea flooded her belly as she gripped the handles.

I'm going to die in a coffin in the sky.

Bitter, freezing air rushed inside, clawing through her leathers. Her eyes opened to a dark-red blur. She wiped her goggles, smearing red across the lenses. A quick glance at her fingers proved her worst fear. She wiped again but wished she hadn't. There was blood everywhere.

She looked at the others. The pilot's head was torn to pieces. Long streaks of crimson crept slowly along the metal walls. The other crew member wrestled the controls out of the pilot's hands. She tugged her goggles down around her neck and glanced out the window. They were almost alongside the ship, but fast approaching the top, far away from the landing bay below.

"We have to slow down!" she screamed.

"The speed dampener won't respond! If we cut the propulsion, we'll fall!" he shouted back.

Another violent collision shook them. She gasped as light and shadow flashed through the open hatch. Her eyes were glued to the chaos.

The pod's steam engines whistled and popped as the craft bounced before slowing to a stop on the soft canvas of the airship. She lay sideways along the wall, her body straining against the straps. Squinting through the bright sun pouring in, she realized they were resting near the top of the huge dirigible. Huge steering vanes were at the far end, dark and jagged against the cloudy sky. The surviving soldier disconnected his harness and dropped to the floor.

"Stay there, miss. I'll have a look." He pulled himself out of the tube and the pod tilted just enough to make her heart jump.

"Get out," he said. "Pull yourself out of the harness. Quickly!"

Her hands trembled, and the clasp refused to come apart.

"Quickly, miss." He looked behind him.

The buckle finally came undone, and a gentle rocking made her stop.

"No, keep moving. Get out of the tube!" he shouted.

She grabbed the opening and noticed the crewman walking alongside the craft.

We're sliding!

He reached inside. "Take my hand!"

Their hands grasped each other, and he tugged her out onto the dark-gray skin of the airship, but her foot was yanked back. She looked down at a tangle of rope around her leg and cried out.

"Hold on," he said. "I've got a knife."

She lost her balance and fell onto the soft canvas. He grabbed a handful of coiled rope and cut the edge closest to her. The craft pulled them, and the knife slipped. His fingers grabbed it and resumed cutting.

Her hands reached out, but everything was moving. She rolled onto her stomach, her fingers stretching across the soft canvas until her fingers found the frame. Her fingertips dug into the metal beam until her hands ached, but the pull on her leg was too strong.

"Hurry!" she screamed. Pain shot through her ankle.

"I got it, miss, hold on!" he said.

The strain was too much. She let go, looking over her shoulder at the crewman cutting furiously at the lines. And then her eyes focused on the pod.

It was moving faster now, hurrying away from them. She turned over, pulling at the knotted lines wrapped around her ankle. Her gloved fingers slipped off the rope. Her ankle felt like it would snap like a twig.

The crewman's left hand jerked. The knots he was holding had wrapped around his own wrist.

They were both trapped.

Coyle watched in horror as the craft dipped and slid out of view. They followed. Faster. Faster toward the edge of the open sky. The crewman's knife cut the final line, and she spread her hands and feet apart until she slowed to a stop. She glanced down and muttered gratitude.

But he'd cut the wrong end and was still attached to the coils. The knife bounced away, out of reach. He stretched back to her and she leapt toward him and grabbed at his wrist, but the weight of the craft dragged him away. She crawled as fast as she could and lunged. Her fingers grasped his and they held fast. Her other hand tried desperately to hold on to something, anything.

And then she realized she was being dragged too.

He ripped free from her grasp, and she watched in horror as he tumbled away and disappeared off the edge. She cried out, spread-eagled across the canvas, and slowed to a stop. Not a muscle moved. One of her feet slid just a hair, and she caught her breath. Her eyes fixated on the edge, hoping to see a hand. A silhouette. A shape.

Her bones shook. She squeezed her eyes shut against the madness storming inside before crying out long and loud. Someone had to hear her. Someone had to know what happened. Bone-chilling air whistling past her ears was the only answer.

After a few moments, she pushed and pulled herself away from the edge in slow, careful movements. Finally, she sat up, crawling backward where it was safe, and lay on her back and stared at the sky. She tried to regain her breath. Her hands and feet tingled, and her muscles spasmed.

She sat up and glanced to the side. The massive steering vanes were arcing into the sky on one side, and she saw nothing on the other. Everything else was soft, gray canvas stretching in every direction.

She was all alone, but she'd survived, and someone must have seen what happened and compelled a rescue attempt. She pushed the communications lever on her helmet, wincing when static burst

through her earpiece.

"This is Coyle. Does anyone read me?"

Static.

She adjusted the knob marked *send* and tried again. "This is

Coyle. Does anyone hear me?"

"Bzzt-es-zzzf-whe-fzzzt-into-rzzzz."

"This is Coyle. We landed on top of the airship. Can anyone

hear me?"

More static.

No use.

Maybe they didn't know what happened. And maybe she

would be left up on top of the ship until it landed. An uneasy weight

settled in her gut, and she gazed at the heavens stretching before her. It

was safer up here, wasn't it? She couldn't go on without the rest of the

team, could she? No, she couldn't wait. She still had a job to do. But

shouldn't she let the professionals do it? After all, who was she? Right

now she was useless, a trembling heap of bones lying on top of an

airship. Everything in her wanted to give up. But wasn't she always chiding herself to do the right thing? And why was the right thing to do always more difficult?

She sighed. She had to finish the job.

No matter the cost?

She scooted to the large tear across the surface, shoving her hands into the canvas. When she was close, she lay on her belly and crawled to the edge before dropping inside.

***

"Status report," the radioed voice said, startling the agent stationed in the high-altitude balloon. He leaned away from the powerful spyglass and answered.

"As planned, two of the pods were successfully destroyed, essentially removing—"

"I need to know about Coyle," the voice said.

"Of course, sir. Detect—er, Miss Coyle—"

"She's a detective, now. Please do not disrespect her."

"Of course, sir. Detective Coyle landed on top of the airship unharmed and made her way inside."

"Can you explain how she landed *on top*?"

"Sir, it appears one of the explosive charges was placed into her pod, and luckily was thrown out the window before it exploded. Unfortunately, one of the sabotaged craft collided with hers, sending them out of control. As far I could see, she was the only survivor."

"That wasn't part of the plan."

"It wasn't, sir. If you wish, I could order the immediate death of Mr.—"

"Not necessary. He'll be dying soon enough."

"Of course, sir."

"I'll have to trust our detective will survive long enough to find the clues I've left for her."

The balloon agent cleared his throat, choosing not to respond.

"You can head back to base."

"As you wish, sir. Would you like me to radio Moreci?"

"No, I'll tell him myself. I'll take over from here."

"Of course, sir. Over and out."

CHAPTER 18

Upper maintenance deck no. 12

Dawn's Edge

To the eye of reason everything is as dark as midnight, but thou canst accomplish great things; thy cause is thine, and it is to thy glory that men should be saved. Amen

The drop was farther than she thought, and pain flared through her ankle. She winced, rubbing away the ache with her hands, and took in the surroundings.

The catwalk ran perpendicular to the airship. Behind and forward of her position were more catwalks. She stood, removed the face mask, and tested her ankles before she climbed down an access ladder.

Unfamiliar sounds kept her mind active as darkness swallowed her. Groaning. Creaking. Small, busy taps of metal against metal. She glanced up. Strong, steady air blew the torn fabric back and forth like fingers running along a heavy curtain.

She reached the landing and inventoried her belt: the MAD pistol with ammunition, resting in their pouches on her right hip; two different sized knives, one on her left side, the other strapped to her ankle, a small lantern on the left. She flipped on the lantern, and tested its brightness, before snapping it onto an attachment on her helmet. Soft yellow-orange light pushed the dark away.

She followed the walkway and found a second set of ladders leading down. She tilted her head, spotting another set and the hint of still another set below. She tried to remember how deep the body of the ship was.

How far down until I find someone?

A strange sound startled her. She froze, eyes searching the dark, but what was it? Metal? No. Something organic. Guttural.

"Hello?" she asked, waiting. Her pounding heart made it difficult to hear, but she waited a few more seconds before moving again.

The ambient light from above grew dim as she lowered herself deeper into the bowels of the ship. Her goal was the cargo bay, where her team was. There's safety in numbers. But to get there, she would have to travel alone in the dark, and she wanted the experience to be quick.

Strange noises kept her alert, and at each landing, she waited and looked for signs of life. Sometimes she called out and hoped for a response. But only silence answered her calls.

A burst of static made her wince in pain, the sharp noise piercing her ear until she switched off the device. She shook her head, stepping down the ladders, rung by rung.

Then she paused.

The metal in her hands pulsed with vibration as if something heavy was tapping it. The sound she'd heard earlier repeated itself, and she couldn't help but look up.

"Hello? Anyone there?" she called out. She couldn't be sure if the metal under her hands was vibrating from her own nerves or something else.

She waited.

The unfamiliar sounds set her teeth on edge: the constant echo of groaning metal, the torn fabric above, her own heavy breathing, her heart slamming against her ribs.

She focused on the opening above, nothing more than a pale dot where she'd dropped in. It would get darker, more dangerous down below. But she knew this was the right decision.

The team was below, not above. If she went up, the sun wouldn't be there for long. The light would disappear, and then she would be in the sky, alone, freezing in the dark.

Her foot found the next rung and she lowered herself, bound by duty, obligation and just a smidge of curiosity. She took another step and realized something: she wasn't afraid of the dark. She rested on the ladder, blinking. Her light wasn't that bright, but for some reason, she wasn't terrified despite being alone in the bowels of a massive airship. She glanced at her steady hands, assuring her heart that everything was fine. This was the way normal people dealt with the dark, which was, after all, only the absence of light.

Everything's fine.

She stepped down, and a scraping sound froze her in place. She looked up, her heart hammering, fingers tightening. Her light remained on the raised landing, the soft yellow globe of light thumping along with her heart. But—nothing. Overactive imagination.

A distorted face peeked over the edge.

She cried out, her feet slipping down a rung. The creature opened its horribly wide mouth, and black drool dangled from its mangled lips. Strips of ragged flesh hung from one side of its head, and a pale, misshapen eyeball jutted out of its socket. A watery gurgle came out of the ghoul's throat as a long, twisted arm reached down.

She shouted, letting go of the ladder and slamming into the metal floor. Her wrists and backside flared with pain, but she sprang up, looking for an escape. Metal clanged and she stared above, waiting for the worst. Spittle fell like shiny metal strings, and the creature's gurgling urged retreat. A modicum of courage ignited deep inside, and she paused.

Was she going to run away all her life? How was this any different than running into trouble on the city streets? She didn't run away from that trouble, did she?

She set her feet, ripping the gun from its holster and pulling the hammer back. She pointed it above, but the ghoul shied away from her light. Her feet inched closer, her eyes frantically searching—

The creature crashed in front of her. She pulled the trigger reflexively, sending tiny bright particles in the air. She took a step back, adjusting the switch from *bewilder* to *skull*, and pulled the trigger again.

Shots rang out, filling the air with smoke. She coughed and waved at the air, her eyes trying to focus.

A twisted nightmare loomed from the smoke, standing to its full height. Its appearance was mostly human, but its arms and legs and hands were grotesquely long, bony and twisted. A third arm rose from its hunched back, long fingers twitching, reaching for her.

She pulled the trigger again. Sparks jumped as bullets crashed into metal and flesh. Deep, unnatural groans bubbled from its throat. Purple entrails slipped out from the wounds, hanging loose and wet against its misshapen legs. The ghoul jerked back, pausing before it took another step toward her. She aimed at a cloudy, yellowed eye and pulled the trigger. A thick stream of blood erupted from the socket, and it collapsed into a twitching heap.

She kept the weapon pointed at the ghoul and backed away. Her free hand searched for ammunition, and she dumped the empty shells out of the revolver. With trembling fingers, she quickly shoved fresh ammo into the slots and took another step back—but her foot slipped into empty space, her hands clawing at the air, and a small cry rose from her throat as she fell backward into the horrible darkness.

CHAPTER 19

Main hangar bay

Dawn's Edge

"Where is our light?" asked Quolo. "Surely there must be a simple switch?" He searched for a pulley or handle along the walls.

The massive bay was easily five stories in height, and wider than it was high, taking up most of the lower center of the airship. A series of doors running along both sides of the bay were open, allowing a constant stream of cold air from either direction. Crates lay in stacks and piles, pushed to the sides to create a wide space in the middle.

"Strange. There should be power," said Chief Sykes. He puffed on his cigar and squinted through the smoke.

"Smells like stale rust and rat turds," Poes said. "Where are the others? Coyle? The detectives?"

Bolt looked confused. "Not here? They left before us. I assumed they'd arrived and were looking for resources."

"They're not here. Look around. How many pods do you see?" Poes shot back.

"Poes," Bolt said. "I would appreciate you watching your tone with me."

"The tone is appropriate, sir," Poes said. "Your level of situational awareness is not."

Sykes finished strapping what looked like metal overalls onto his small frame and stood as high as the others. He pulled up a wire antenna from a gadget near his shoulder and switched on his radio, frowning and turning knobs.

"This is Chief Sykes," he said. "Anyone read me?"

Static and squelches filled the air. The gnome repeated his query and frowned.

"What's wrong?" Bolt asked.

"There's no blasted radio reception is what's wrong," he said. "These infernal devices were probably made by an automaton or, worse, a human. Gnomish engineering never fails, but I digress. With no radio reception, I have no way to get in touch with support."

"But we can hear each other," Bolt said. "Through our radios."

"Ours work through what's called line of sight communications," Sykes explained. "We can radio each other as long as we can see each other."

"Curious," Poes said.

"Sir," a soldier said to Sykes. "Some of our men report three of the tubes were involved in a collision during flight. There appear to be streams of smoke below that corroborate their account."

Most of them stepped carefully to the open doors and peered down.

"Yup," Sykes agreed. "Those aren't coal fires. Hopefully someone's out to investigate. However, with regard to the altitude, the probability of survival is not good."

Poes and Quolo glanced at each other.

"What happened?" asked Bolt.

The soldier shook his head. "Not sure. They saw flames and black smoke from two of the tubes. One spun out of control and struck the others. By deduction, it appears the lost tubes contained Duone, Vonteg and Coyle, along with their crewmates. Nine souls in all," he said.

"All of our law enforcement is gone. Seems like too much of a coincidence," Quolo added.

After a few moments, Poes stirred and frowned. "What would be flammable onboard the tubes?" he asked.

"Determining the nature of the accident isn't a priority right now," Bolt growled. "What is important is determining the nature of this ship's stability and the whereabouts of her crew," he said. He turned to Sykes. "Which way to the bridge?"

"This way," Sykes answered, and the others followed him up flights of stairs until they reached the passenger decks.

As they moved away from the windows, the rooms and hallways darkened. Each of them switched on their lanterns and cast glowing light back and forth across empty spaces. The men kept their weapons trained on the darker spaces where their lights couldn't penetrate. The surroundings changed from slate gray and practical to the rich colors of luxury, resembling the train cars in every way. Their heavy boots echoed across polished mahogany floors and walls. Plush, leather recliners and couches rested in corners, and rare tapestries and paintings hung on the walls. They passed rooms large enough to hold ceremonies, dinners and banquets with ease. But among all the beautiful furniture and accompaniments, there was one thing missing.

"Where are the people?" Quolo asked.

"Let's hold on a second," Poes said, and everyone stopped and listened. Their eyes searched the surroundings, and their ears waited for the sound of life.

"This is unsettling," Quolo said.

"Let's get moving," Sykes said. "They're holding the passengers somewhere."

"How many ballrooms does this ship have?" Poes asked.

"Eight," Sykes answered around his cigar.

"Shouldn't we try to rescue them?" Quolo asked.

"Our priority is control of the ship," Sykes answered. "Then we look for the passengers."

They searched through rooms as they passed and gazed up elegant staircases and around darkened corners. But there was nothing. No voices. No music. No scent of food. No lights but their own.

"When was the last contact," Poes asked, "besides the emergency beacon?"

Chief Sykes thought for a moment. "Two days ago."

"And there was no hint of something amiss? Concerns?" Poes asked.

Sykes shook his head. "The chief mate sent word with their position and a requisition list of supplies about six hours after she launched. That was the last time we heard from the *Dawn's Edge*."

Finally, they reached the bridge level. They were making their way up the wide stairs when short bursts of static filled their communications line. Everyone froze. Garbled transmissions flooded the air for a few seconds.

"Who's that?" Bolt asked.

Everyone waited for a few moments, but there was nothing else.

"The ship's crew?" Quolo asked.

"Possibly." Poes nodded. "Has to be. But where are they?"

"Let's get to the bridge so we can access the power. Once power is restored, we can use that area as a base of operations," Sykes said. They agreed and continued.

"Stop," Poes said. "Do you hear something?" Everyone stood still.

"What are we listening for?" Quolo asked.

"I'm not sure," Poes said. "But it sounded like... groaning. As if someone were trying to speak."

They all stood and waited, but the only sounds were distant taps and creaks echoing through the airship.

"I hear nothing," Bolt said, and continued through the hallway.

Everyone followed when a sharp burst of static pierced their ears. Everyone stopped and grabbed their ears. Poes winced and pulled his earpiece away from his head. The electronic screeching tore through their ears for a few seconds and then stopped.

"Bolt, any ideas on what could have caused that noise?" Quolo asked.

He shook his head. "Could be anything, though all of us receiving the same level of noise is curious."

Another blast flooded their ears, and most of them pulled their earpieces away from their head. The loud squelching abruptly stopped when another sound caught their attention. Everyone stood still and listened.

Scrapes. Moans. Shuffling feet. Sharp objects scraping against the wood.

"Someone's alive and trying to get help," Quolo said. "Up there, in the bridge."

All at once, they hurried up the stairs, their small lamps flashing across the wall and double doors of the bridge. Their eyes fixed on the frosted-glass doors as a shadow passed on the other side.

"There! See?" Quolo said. He stepped toward the door, but Sykes stopped him.

"Something's covering the glass," Sykes said. "It looks like…"

"Blood," said Poes.

Everyone stared at the reddish-brown streaks covering the glass. Traces of handprints and fingertips streaked through the gore.

"There may be poisonous gasses inside," Bolt said. "Everyone, get your masks and goggles on for safety."

Everyone put on the contraptions, their oxygen scrubbers humming to life. After everyone had checked their seals and given a thumbs-up, they were ready.

"Everyone on alert," Sykes said through the radio. "Ready your weapons just in case. Remember: we're here for a rescue operation, so mind your triggers."

As he finished giving them instructions, one of the soldiers pointed at the glass behind him. An unnaturally long, bony hand scraped the glass door before disappearing.

The men glanced at each other. Some stepped away. Heavy breathing, gasping, choking sounds filled the hallway outside the bridge. The floor creaked under their feet, and strange tappings came from somewhere above them.

"All right, men," Sykes said. "Get a hold of yourselves. You two, get on either side of the door. Now, I'm going to open the doors, and the both of you—"

A faint voice jumped through the transceivers, but static drowned out anything recognizable.

"That sounded like Coyle," Poes said.

"Can you be sure? How could she still be alive?" Bolt asked.

"Come in," Sykes said through his transceiver. "Come in, Coyle, can you read me?"

They listened intently for a few seconds and heard no more.

"I'll try to find her. She may be somewhere above," Poes said. "As soon as I find something useful, I'll try to relay the information."

He turned and sprinted back down the stairs into the darkness. The men watched his light float away down the hall until he disappeared around a corner.

"Shouldn't some of us go with him?" Quolo asked.

"We can't afford to lose any more men." Sykes shook his head. "It's too dangerous."

All of them jumped when something slammed against the door. Louder groans filled the air, and someone crashed against the other side of the door, causing the men to step back.

Sykes held his position, pointing his weapon at the door.

"Be ready, men," he said.

But the noise stopped as if nothing had happened. Not a single noise was heard from inside the bridge. Sykes turned and nodded his head, reaching for the handle.

The glass doors exploded, sending shards into the soldiers. Long, pale, twisted hands reached out and dragged a screaming soldier into the bridge. Dozens more of the creatures shot out from the opening and clawed at the other soldiers. Misshapen claws tore away leathers, masks, goggles and limbs, leaving jagged wounds. The creatures emerged from the bridge, revealing their horrible, twisted maws and limbs searching for the men.

Sykes shouted and the soldiers opened fire, darkening the room with gun smoke, muzzle flashes and splintered wood. But the pale ghouls crawled through the eruptions of gunfire, overpowering the screaming men and dragging them to the floor.

A dense fog of spent munitions arose, making it difficult to see anything or anyone. Sykes shouted a retreat, and the men huddled together away from the bridge.

"Reload!" someone shouted. Most of the men leaned against the walls, cycling through their ammunition, eyes shifting between the weapons and the clouded end of the hall where their buddies were screaming.

Ghouls lunged from the haze. Arms of ragged flesh and bone pulled men to the ground and tore them to shreds. Jagged teeth bit and chewed whatever got close.

Quolo shot a creature. It turned and faced him with a bloodied arm hanging from its jaws. He fired again, the bullet tearing its head open, and the thing dropped. He shot another in the shoulder. Streaks of red sprayed out, but the creature lunged and sank his teeth into the neck of a struggling man. He fired again and again before a bullet sank into the creature's head, stopping its attack. Something crashed into him. He spun. The gun was knocked out of his grip, and he fell to the floor. Sharp teeth clamped down on his face, but his goggles and helmet kept his skin from being torn.

Another tore at his leg. Still another bit into his arm. He slammed his fist and kicked with all his strength. He made an effort to stand, to get away, when someone crashed into him. They rolled down the stairs and landed in a heap. Quolo made a fist, rearing back for a punch.

"No! I'm on your side," said a soldier, and they lifted themselves up.

"We need to get out of here," Bolt said as he reloaded his pistol. "We're losing men."

Sykes looked around at the pandemonium. Body parts lay strewn across the floor, soldiers fired blindly at the creatures, and screams from both sides made his blood curdle.

"Fall back to the hanger! Everyone, fall back!" he yelled.

They ran, shuffling and limping through the vacant halls. Some of them kept their weapons trained behind the group, firing at the stray ghouls who managed to follow. They found the hangar bay and fixed the doors behind them. Most of the men were savvy enough to reload their weapons. Some collapsed to the floor, their wounds bleeding profusely.

"Chief Sykes here." He clicked his radio. "Someone read me! It appears there are creatures of unknown origin. No sign of crew or passengers. We have wounded here, some grievously. Expedite medical supplies! Come in! Come in!"

"What are these horrible creatures?" Quolo asked. "And where did they come from?"

CHAPTER 20

Starboard ballroom

Dawn's Edge

Moreci listened to the pleas of Chief Sykes coming over the radio. "Sounds desperate," Moreci said, looking at the waning landscape below.

"These poor souls have no idea what they're facing," Veiul said.

"I disagree," Moreci said. "Every person knows they face a reckoning at some point. I'm only hastening the introduction with their true form: monsters."

"The Hindus would say it is karma," Veiul said.

Moreci nodded. "It appears the bombs took out three of their pods," Moreci said. "The two detectives and our estimable constable. Pity that. She was an interesting one. I would have liked to change her into something more passable than human."

Veiul glanced at Moreci. "I'm more than that woman could have ever hoped to be."

"You are resilient. That's for certain," Moreci said. "And she's dead, so the point is moot."

"I've proven my caliber through the defeat of both Coyle and Fang," she said, clenching her fists. "Neither of them is here, and yet I am. If anyone deserves to be changed into a higher form, it's me."

Moreci studied the fire in her eyes. She was always one for her passion of work.

"You have achieved your highest form, my dear. You are an apex predator, and by my side, we'll capture whatever comes our way."

A knock on the door interrupted them. "Come in," Moreci said.

An appallingly frail man stepped inside, bowing before speaking.

"Sir," he said.

"You have an update, Cavin?" Moreci asked.

"Treece's team landed on the ship. They reached the bridge and were rebuffed by the Turned before they retreated to the hangar. Most have suffered bite wounds, and we should see the effects of the venom very soon."

"They were the last threat. That's the good news," Moreci said. "What's the bad news?"

"Reports of something like gunfire were heard in the upper maintenance decks not too long ago. Would you like to send a small team to investigate?"

Moreci stood silent and looked outside. His oxygen tanks hummed along with the engines of the ship, both of his hands tapping the windowsill.

He finally shook his head. "I'm not going to worry about a lone crewman with limited ammunition. We don't have the resources. Speaking of which, what are the current numbers of passengers and crew?"

"Two hundred were Turned and are roaming the ship. Another one hundred were killed and thrown overboard. That leaves about two hundred crew and passengers remaining in the grand hall, sir."

"Release some passengers into the ship." Moreci smiled. "That should give the Turned something to do in the meantime. And when we get to Chicago, we'll prepare the grand finale."

Cavin left, and Moreci noticed Veiul staring at the floor.

"It's not your fault," he said.

She looked up at him with doleful eyes.

He stepped closer, embracing her before lifting her chin. "I know you were supposed to eliminate Treece's team back in his mansion. But things change, and we must make our adjustments. I would rather have you by my side than dead."

"Fang killed Trevin," Veiul said. "Took his head clean off. That was my fault, too."

"And she's gone. We haven't seen her since," Moreci said. "Besides, we still have our man embedded in Treece's team. He'll make sure everything goes according to plan. Within a few hours, we'll reach our destination and you'll be by my side as we introduce these people to a new god and a new way of life."

CHAPTER 21

Upper maintenance decks

Dawn's Edge

> *She breathed him in...*

Ronan's cologne and sweat became the scent of evil, of betrayal, of *madness*. Her back arched as the scalpel raced down her chest. Thin trickles of blood spread down her sides. She pulled against the restraints until her skin tore. He set the scalpel aside, ignoring her muffled screams.

"Let's see what kind of power you have." He gingerly tugged at her skin—and then stopped.

"I have an idea. What if we change things?" He sat in the dark, tapping a finger scalpel against his chin. She writhed, struggling to exist.

"What if tonight were not a quest for resolution but rather a challenge between rivals? Because like it or not, Sherlyn, you're my nemesis. You certainly have unrivaled power over me. It's true, you do. I never put a ring on a woman's hand before. Wouldn't even consider it. Then you came along, and I felt weightless in your touch, your gaze, your smile. Your eyes captured my heart, and I didn't even know I had a heart. I mean, do you know how many women I've cut open? And I'm not even talking about the ones they found back in Whitechapel. Those weren't women, just working-class beings.

"But I digress. All you did was walk into the room and make eyes with me, and my palms went all sweaty. That is raw, unadulterated power. And what's worse is you never knew you carried it. So naive. So let's run with this idea and see where it goes. What if you could be more powerful than either of us imagined?"

He nodded, staring at the ceiling, light mumbles escaping his lips, before moving to her side. His eyes were dark holes staring into hers.

"Remember the time you discovered the killer of that woman in the alley was her own brother? And you had so little information. It was his shoe imprint in her blood, wasn't it? You followed the little dog, remember? The little dog was licking the blood all the way up to the brother's house. And then to prove it, you bluffed him in front of the police, said you saw how he used his left hand to murder her and he surrendered. The police thought you were clever, but they told you to mind your business. *Tsk, tsk.* Idiots."

"You enjoy untying the knots of enigmas, don't you? Finding joy in discovering clues in the dead. You seem a natural at it, and as you can see, I'm a natural at creating crime scenes. So let's see who's the more powerful between the two of us.

"Come find me, Sherlyn. And I will leave you breadcrumbs of viscera and goblets of sanguine fluid. Yes?"

He removed a small box from his jacket, giving her a cold, reassuring smile as he held a sewing needle and black thread.

"Hold still, dear." His hands worked swiftly and soundlessly, suturing the gaping wound in a matter of minutes. He tied off the end of the thread before cutting it with his teeth and ran a finger along the dark red line with salve. After inspecting his work, he flashed his white teeth, the same smile he'd used many times while they were together. He leaned in close.

"I have one rule." He held up a finger. "Tell anyone—the police or other law enforcement—and I will go into hiding. You will never, ever find me. *Ever*. But I will allow you to join the police force and use their resources. Stretch your boundaries. Work with others, put those brilliant skills to work and show them how moronic they are. You'd enjoy it."

He leaned in and kissed her fevered head before tapping her long wound. "This will heal over time, and then you can pursue me, my sweet. Until then, I'll be leaving bodies in my wake. Hope you find me soon."

He stood, tousling her hair, smiling his smile.

Coyle jolted awake and grabbed her chest, opening her eyes to a dark blue. Soft light filtered down and highlighted the edges of fixtures, pipes and crates, but nothing looked familiar.

Sharp pain spiked through her back and shoulder. She winced and scooted to the wall, looking for her lamp. It wasn't on her helmet; she reached where it should have been but found an empty space instead.

And then she remembered the creature.

Adrenaline rushed through her veins, feeding her senses with heightened awareness. She pulled herself into a crouch and waited. Every muscle tensed, waiting for an attack. Nothing moved except her and the ship in the sky, but her mind refused to believe it. She had shot it—dead? It had slumped to the floor, anyhow. And there were no sounds. It had to be safe.

She stood, unfolding herself, and winced again. But her safety was more important than aches and pains. A quick check of her belt made her grimace. Her gun was missing. The holster was empty. She pulled out a long knife and took a step, when something tapped against her boot. She looked down and smiled—it was the lamp.

She switched it on, and the familiar soft glow burned away the dark. But after a few seconds, the light shut off. She switched it on, and it clicked off again after a few seconds. She sighed. She'd have to make the best of what she had.

She clicked it on. The ladder was to her right. She followed the rungs up into the darkness.

I must have fallen when I was walking backward.

She scolded herself and looked behind. Another ladder led down to where the rest of the crew were, perhaps, still waiting. The light blinked out, and she turned it on again.

She wrestled with curiosity. The creature was above, and she was an investigator, wasn't she? And maybe clues about the creature's identity could help her. A chill rolled down her back. It would be disgusting, of course, but she was on the ship for a reason. Answers above and resources below.

She flexed her fingers and stepped toward the ladder. If she wanted to be a detective, then she had to act like one. That meant going up to the cadaver and inspecting it with a broken light.

She stuck the light between her teeth and flicked the light on with her tongue, illuminating the ladder for a few seconds before it shut off. She muttered a curse and pulled herself up the ladder.

A scrape against metal froze her blood. She stopped, looking up, waiting for something to appear. The rattling of her heart canceled out all other sounds. She flicked the light on to bare metal rungs and darkness. The creaking of the ship prompted her to move.

Light off. Did she see a face?

Light on. No one there.

She climbed, trying to ignore the trembling shadows of her hands. She couldn't help herself, though. This entire ordeal ran counter to the safety and comfort of normal life. Breaths came short and quickened with each rung while her mind whispered dark fears. She flicked on the light. A few more rungs to the landing.

Light off.

Her hand reached the landing, but noises made her withdraw. She hugged the ladder, waiting, listening. What was that? Scraping. Crawling.

Someone whispering my name.

She panicked and stepped down, flicking on the light. She looked up, expecting the worst.

Light off.

She flicked it on again and turned her head. Metal walkways. Pipes. Empty spaces. Dim lights below.

Light off.

She took a deep breath and pulled herself up to the landing and peeked over the edge as she flicked the light on. Light illuminated the sloppy, glistening heap of the body.

Light off.

She ducked down, instinct exhorting her to flee, her ears suddenly picking up every sound. The ship creaked and groaned and rasped.

Something moved beneath her. The light came on, and she looked down. Nothing. She glanced up. It was all in her mind, and she cursed her vivid, overactive imagination.

Light on. She pulled herself up, peering over the edge at the body. It was motionless. She gripped the rail, just in case.

Light off. She wondered if all detectives had to deal with things like this.

Light on. She whispered a short, quick prayer.

Light off.

Light on. She crawled closer and the details came into view: a gaping hole in its head, glistening in shades of crimson; the unnatural shape of its limbs; blood and pink bits splattered the wall.

Light off.

Light on. She drew closer and sat within reach of its skinless, dead hand.

Light off.

Light on. She kicked it. No movement. No sounds.

Light off. The ship groaned.

Light on. She kicked harder. No response. It lay still. For good, she hoped.

Light off.

Light on. She leaned in, poking its head with the knife. No response.

Light off.

Light on. She reached with her other hand. Her trembling fingers were inches away from the head.

"Bzzztt-fzzt—I say, can you hear me? Repeat, Coyle-fzzzzt—"

She jumped back and swung at the empty air.

Light off. Adrenaline blasted through every fiber of her being.

Light on. She stared at the trembling creature, but it was only her light and eyes and imagination.

Light off. She pulled the lamp out of her mouth, flicked it on, and answered. "Yes, this Coyle. Who is this?"

"Heaven's sake, what took you so long to answer? This is GEM. How goes things?"

"GEM," she said. "I've had all the adventures I care to have in my lifetime. There's a million things to share and nothing good. My radio went out after we landed on the ship, and I haven't been able to communicate with anyone." She kept her eyes on the creature. "I'm in the dark and alone. Well, sort of."

"Bzzfsst—I'm sorry to hear that, Miss Coyle. Do you have a few moments?"

She frowned and shrugged her shoulders. "This is as good a time as any, I suppose."

"Fzzss—Perfect. Now listen carefully."

After GEM's lengthy explanation, she tapped a knob on her left hand. Soft white light glowed from tiny bulbs on her shoulders, illuminating the floor in front of her. She leaned back and forth, side to side, testing the lights. She sank to her knees and sighed.

"Do the lights work, Miss Coyle? Everything functioning?"

"Yes, GEM, but I have a million other questions. Why—"

"Fzzsstsss—the suit will take care of you, Miss Coyle. Fzzztt—it's one of a kind. In a sense-fssszzt-have to-szzssst."

She adjusted the radio knobs, but there was no response, and the static transmissions faded to nothing. She was alone again. But she felt much more confident knowing she was wearing a valuable, one-of-a-kind suit. She didn't have resources of people, but she did have what she needed on her person.

She looked down at her left wrist and slid open a compartment. A small button with the words *Tesla Mode* stitched next to it. She stared at the button. GEM said it should be used in the most of dire of emergencies. She wasn't too sure what would happen if she pushed it.

In fact, she wasn't too sure about any of the suit's capabilities. The lights worked, and that's all she needed for now.

GEM's explanations and directions had been rapid and vague. She pushed a knob on her right wrist, and the tip of a dart appeared. She tapped the knob twice, and it slid backward into a slot. There were a few surprises, and she definitely would have appreciated a one-day course on the subject, but this situation had degraded very quickly.

GEM had mentioned some of the choices were voice-activated. It would take some time to know where everything was. But, for now, she had a single job. She looked down at the cadaver, cracking her knuckles.

"Surgical instruments," she said. "Please."

An invisible tap against her right thigh indicated the location of the tools. She pulled the compartment open and found a set of five stainless-steel precision tools set in a leather sheath. She pulled out a scalpel, catching her reflection in the polished metal, and remembered how *he* had held the scalpel next to her skin. She squeezed her eyes, forcing the memory away, before examining the corpse.

"I filled its body with bullets, but nothing happened until I shot its head. This leads me to believe a head wound will terminate these creatures ... again."

She flipped the magnifying lens over her goggles, peeling the flesh away from the face with forceps. A few tugs, and the flesh lifted with a wet, sticky sound.

Thin cracks spread out from small clusters of dark puncture marks embedded deep into the bone. The marks surrounded both eyes and were prominently in the center of the forehead.

She leaned back. They looked like bruises. But bruises didn't shape themselves into perfect lines, they bloomed from burst capillaries. Unless these marks were purposely set there. Is that what had happened? Had someone tapped these marks around the eyes and center of the creature's forehead? What would the purpose be when they were just turned into a creature like this?

Her eyes focused on its face. Its wide mouth was slack and full of jagged teeth. A thread of thick, dark blood bubbled and seeped from its nose and disappeared into the darkness below.

She sighed.

There were so many things she would rather be doing right now. Hot bath. Eating. Sleeping. Lounging on the sofa with a good book and a cat warming her lap.

Alas.

She pulled the torn shirt aside and found more of the curious marks etched across its chest, shoulder joints and wrists. She refrained from pulling away the trousers, but guessed she would find similar marks on his hip and knee joints.

There was something else here, but she wasn't sure what. She slid the most powerful lenses over one eye and returned to the marks on the head. Using her handkerchief, she brushed away seeping blood and other debris. Then she squinted and studied.

"Oh!" she said. Staring at the marks. These were not random wounds caused by an outside source. Rather, they were distinct formations with lines, curves, abrupt angles, similarities, patterns. What was the term?

Ah. Runes.

"This is what the book does," Coyle said. "And here's the end result. The curse, as it were."

She studied more carefully, curious as to what fae inscriptions looked like. Her face was mere inches away from the corpse, and the scent of it was unbearable. But the payoff was worth it. Her lenses magnified the script until it was as large as her hand.

She leaned back and frowned. Why did the fae characters seem familiar but at the same time… not? There was something there, but she couldn't quite place her finger on it. And then…

"Oh!" she said again. She started searching her suit. "You can't be serious. This can't be happening. It just can't! Wait. What do I ask for? A pad of paper and pencil?" A brief vibration pulsed against her abdomen, near the left side. She reached down and pulled out a pencil and pad of paper.

She wiped away all the moisture she could from the creature's forehead before she placed the paper over the runes and with the pencil at an angle, she rubbed until all the runes were transferred to the paper. She peeled the paper away and inspected her work.

A small dark smudge of graphite surrounded the empty spaces of the inscription. She was looking at a reverse image of what she'd found on the corpse.

Her hands trembled, but this time from excitement. If this worked the way she thought it might… She turned the paper over and shone a light behind it.

"Oh!" She covered her mouth with her hand, her mind refusing to believe what she was seeing. But it was there. Plain as day. The runes were written in backward English. The message read,

Reverse the darkest deed,

In ageless artifacts dwell,

Repeat the faithful creed,

Mirror cast the spell

She leaned against the wall, her mind racing through different emotions: relief, exhaustion, disbelief, exultation. All coursing through her head all at once.

But despite the joy of finding such a clue, of course, the more difficult questions loomed: who crafted the message? And what exactly did it mean? Was it designed for anyone to find … or only her?

She looked at the creature. This was all Moreci's doing, she was sure of it. This poor soul was turned into a monster when Moreci used the book. But the translation was in direct contrast to the book's effect. 'Reverse' and 'mirror' meant the opposite of what had transpired. And why, and how, was this written in backward English?

She bit her lip, staring at the darkness, tapping the back of her head against the metal railing. It was Moreci who used the book, but this message couldn't be from him. Who, then? She frowned. Mumbled. Tapped her foot. Tapped her head.

She froze.

This message was created for me.

She stood and paced. This message was for her. She was supposed to stop Moreci, and she didn't know how. She looked down at the corpse. Her mind became a mixture of excitement and confusion. She clapped hands and smiled.

"Like Christmas!" she said. "Except this time I'm getting something I wanted." She hopped on the metal floor. "Like Christmas!" She stopped and covered her mouth. Her hands curled into fists.

She let her mind race along the new path she'd uncovered. The message was for her. From…? Who would make sense? Treece? But how would he have—

No. Not Treece. Dame Graethe?

She slapped her forehead. Of course. She was fae. She would know the language. It had to be her! But why was Dame Graethe involved with this? She chewed her lip more. Paced more. She cracked her knuckles. Dame Graethe was dead. It couldn't be her. Then who? Fang? She was definitely helping, but this wasn't the type of work Fang would be involved with.

She looked at the paper again, even though she had memorized the verse.

Reverse the darkest deed,

In ageless artifacts dwell,

Repeat the faithful creed,

Mirror cast the spell

The ship groaned. She had to find the others, get them involved, and share her knowledge. More brains were better than one, she had heard somewhere. She would need help figuring out how to use this vital information.

She slipped the tools back inside the pouch and stepped lively down to the next landing, the new light revealing her gun. She reloaded the weapon, took one last look above and moved deeper into the ship.

CHAPTER 22

Main hangar bay

Dawn's Edge

The sharp odor of antiseptic floated through the empty space. Survivors lay in groups throughout the cargo bay. The wounded were being treated with the few medical supplies they had. Arms were bandaged, legs sutured, faces gauzed.

The unfortunate dead lay in rows, their bodies under emergency blankets. Quolo kneeled beside a victim and pulled the corner of the blanket away. He stifled a cough. The man's flesh was peeled away from the bone in ragged strips. An eyeball had been gouged out. Gaping bite wounds on his shoulders and neck had been bandaged, but to no avail.

"We tried," a soldier said. "They bled too quickly."

"This is a nightmare," Quolo said. "A bloody, living nightmare. What did we get dragged into?" Some of the soldiers glanced over.

"We came here together, and we'll leave together," Chief Sykes said.

"We need to stay here, where there's safety," Quolo said. "We need to regroup a-a-and get a hold of more people. We need more men, more firepower."

"Calm down. Someone get bandages and antibacterial ointments for him." Chief Sykes pointed at Quolo. "Now, we suffered some casualties—"

"Some? We lost a lot of men just now, and I'm not sure we're appropriately equipped for this excursion. We need more men, Chief Sykes. We need more men a-a-and more guns and more bullets!" His eyes were wide open, his expression chaotic. Spittle flew from his dry lips.

"You're in shock. You need to get bandaged up or you'll get worse." Sykes glanced at one of his soldiers. "Have a look at his wounds."

Quolo's bottom lip quivered as he stared into the sky.

CHAPTER 23

Mid-level maintenance decks

Dawn's Edge

Coyle stepped deeper into the chasm. The opening she'd used far above was barely a pinprick now. Her steps quickened when she heard a scrape against metal. She swore there were more creatures stalking her, but all of it was in her head and she knew it.

Ever since that night with Ronan, she struggled to distinguish between reality and her dark fears. Would it ever end? Could it? The doctors and nuns assured her there was peace to be found. Strength. Courage. But, right now, it was so far away, and she was almost certain she would never reach it. Besides, she certainly didn't deserve it.

But she was here for a purpose much larger and more important than her fears. Her only hope at this point was to continue down through the ship and find the hangar bay where her friends were. She hoped they were waiting. She hoped there was a way to use the secret message left for her to find. She hoped they could leave this airship.

The ladder led into a much wider space built more like a floor than a simple landing. She gazed at her new surroundings. Machinery twice as tall as her lined the area. Clicking gears, whines and other strange sounds filled with the air.

A flashing light caught her attention and she pulled out her pistol. A pair of offices were just in front, and as she drew near, there were new sounds: paper shuffling, someone mumbling. She raised her weapon. The bold, broad glare of someone's light flashed inside. This wasn't a creature, but she kept the gun trained on the open door just in case. She eased around to the front of the office and peered inside.

"Stop!" she commanded. "Put your hands in the air where I can see them."

"Don't shoot!" a short man said, stepping out. His uniform was filthy. His face, arms and hands were covered in grime.

"Who are you?" Coyle asked.

"Name's Conroy," he said. "I'm one of the engineers."

"What are you doing here, Conroy?" Coyle lowered her weapon. She could tell he was no threat. She didn't fully trust him, but there was sincerity in his voice. And she was quietly glad she wasn't alone anymore.

"Depends. Are you with them or someone else?" he asked, lowering his hands.

"Keep your hands up," Coyle said. "I'm with Treece, and I'm looking for my team. Who else would I be?"

"I know Treece. He's a good man, but I don't know the others that took over the ship," he said, wiping the sweat from his balding head. "I set off an emergency beacon that only Treece would receive. I guess it worked." His thick mustache lifted in a smile.

"It did." Coyle put her weapon away. "Is anyone else with you?"

"They're all gone," Conroy said, and leaned against the wall. "We heard some distress, and the others went to check. I... I'm a coward. I hid. Strange men in uniforms started going through the offices, searching for more people, I guess. After a while, I snuck down as far as my courage would let me. That's when I heard the screams, the shouting. I figured that had to be trouble, and my crew never returned. I came back here and activated the beacon."

"It looks like you made the right choice," she said. "Which way to the main hangar? We should get to my group."

Conroy shook his head. "I don't think that's the way to go. Too many possibilities of dying that way. Especially with that man and his book."

"What do you know about the man and his book?" Coyle asked.

"Well, I thought it was my imagination, you know? I heard him talking to a group of people. He said they would be shot unless they listened to something he read out of a book. He told them they were to be Turned. So they got real quiet and listened. I couldn't hear because I was on the other side of the steel plate. Then I heard… all kinds of voices. Things I've never heard in my life."

"Turned? And? What else happened?"

"Well, the man and someone else, I thought it was a lady, walked out. And then these people became something else. The way they sounded and moved, it was horrible!"

A lady? "Did you see any of these people?" Coyle asked.

"The man with the book called them the Turned, and I wish… I wish I hadn't seen them."

"These Turned are between us and the main hanger?"

He nodded. "Yes. I shut the power off, thinking it would slow everything down. But I had another idea."

"Yes?"

"I don't know what the man with the book is up to, but if we shut the engines down, then we could stay up here until we're rescued."

Coyle chewed on her lip for a few minutes. "That's an excellent idea, Conroy. If we shut the engines down, we won't land in Chicago." She paced a few steps away before facing him. "And we could do this by ourselves?"

"We could try," he said.

"It sounds like a good plan, but it also sounds like we'll need my people," she said. "We're going to have to get to the main hanger."

"I don't know. I don't know about that," he said, staring at a set of stairs.

"We have to try," she said. "Do you have any weapons?"

He shook his head. "No, but I found this iron rod."

"I think that'll work just fine," she said.

"You never told me your name," he said.

"My name is Coyle," she said, walking toward the stairs.

"It's none of my business, but where's your husband?" he asked.

She shot him a glare before pushing her communications tab.

"This is Coyle on the grand airship *Dawn's Edge*. Can anyone hear me?"

Silence.

"This is Coyle. Can anyone hear me? GEM? Detectives? Poes? Bolt? Quolo? Chief Sykes? Anyone?"

Hard static blurred through and then, "Can-fzzzsst-me-ssszzt-whe-fssst." Static took over for a scant few seconds until the radio went completely silent.

"This is Coyle. Can anyone hear me?"

She shut the static off. "We need to find my team before things get worse."

CHAPTER 24

Starboard ballroom

Dawn's Edge

A knock on the door interrupted Moreci's thoughts, but he allowed the distraction.

"Sir." Cavin stepped inside.

"Go ahead, Cavin."

"We've picked up a radio communication from somewhere inside the ship. She was trying to reach members of Treece's team," Cavin said.

"*She?*" Moreci said, glancing at Veiul.

"She identified herself as Coyle, sir. Her attempts were unsuccessful, however, and we believe someone from the train was able to send her communications on a coded radio channel," he said.

"And we haven't been picking up these signals?" Moreci stood.

"No, sir. But we were able to jam the transmissions, preventing further communications. Shall I send a unit to investigate?" he asked.

"For one person? No, of course not," Moreci said.

"Then let me go out there," Veiul said. "I'll make sure she gets fed to the wolves."

"She's just a simple, washed-out constable, Veiul." Moreci shook his head. "She's not a threat."

"I'll make sure she isn't," Veiul said. "You didn't let me kill her in Fort Alcatraz. This time, I'll do her right."

"Make it quick," Moreci said. He knew Veiul was a perfectionist, and the past few days weren't her best.

"How are things in the hangar?" he asked Cavin.

"No word yet, but the effects of the curse should be showing themselves soon," he answered.

"And the emergency skiff is ready to deploy?" Moreci asked.

"It will be, sir," Cavin said. "We're trying to locate the pilots."

"Thank you. You're dismissed," he said, smiling as his plans bloomed into existence.

***

Main hangar bay

How do you feel, Quolo?" Bolt asked. "Need some water?"

"No, thank you," he said. "I'd like to know when the radio transmissions will be back. Any word on that?" He unstrapped the buckles from his leathers and wiped his sweaty face.

"Chief Sykes and I will be heading to another part of the ship to fix what's broken." Bolt glanced around at the others. Men were rubbing their hands for warmth. The wounded were wrapped in blankets. "You sure you're well?" Bolt asked again. "You look like you have a fever."

"No, I'm fine. Don't worry about me," Quolo said. He pulled open his leather top. "I just need some air is all."

"Good man," Bolt said. "We'll get the radio service up and be back in a jiffy." He patted Quolo's shoulder and walked off to talk with the others.

Quolo looked out past the edge of the landing, where peaceful, fluffy clouds touched the peaceful, blue sky. Before they left, the men give brief instructions to those staying behind. Quolo's eyes grew heavy, but he watched them fade away into the dark before wiping drool from his wet mouth.

CHAPTER 25

Upper passenger decks

Dawn's Edge

Conroy knew his way around the ship, and the journey to the lower holds was short. Coyle's fears were dampened by his company and the knowledge that they would be at the main hangar in a few minutes. The prospect of rejoining her team gave her strength and a hope that things were coming together.

She remembered the two flaming, spinning pods flying through the air, both carrying living people. For the briefest of moments, she allowed herself hope Poes hadn't been in one of those pods.

"Thank you so much," Coyle said. "I would have been lost up there."

"My pleasure, miss," he said. "I'm sure you would have found the hangar eventually."

"I'm afraid not," she said. "Not in the dark, anyway."

"Looks like you found your way through a lot already, didn't you?"

She smiled. "I guess I did."

"What do you do for a living?"

"I was a constable in San Francisco."

"That sounds tough. You know, my Aunt Rebecca cut her hair and joined the front lines at Gettysburg," he said. "That's what I heard, anyway."

"And how's your aunt?" she asked.

"She did fine until she was on the wrong side of Pickett's Charge."

"I'm sorry to hear that," Coyle said.

"Thank you. Just because you were born differently doesn't mean you can't get what you want," he said with a tight smile. "You made it this far. I hope you get whatever it is you're after."

She nodded. She hoped for the same thing, of course. This mission in the sky wasn't what she wanted. It was only a stepping-stone toward becoming a detective—and even that was just another stepping-stone on her path to bringing Ronan to justice.

They had just stepped into the lush, familiar passenger decks when she heard noises.

"Stop," Conroy said. "Do you hear that?"

"Sounds like a loud party." Coyle squinted.

"Only there's no laughter." Conroy stepped forward into the wide hallway. Long, thin windows lined the wall, and sunlight poured into the dark. "Are they dancing?"

Coyle listened. Sounds of movement were in the rooms beyond. She couldn't tell if they were dancing or marching or...

"Running," Coyle said. "They're running."

"It's getting closer," Conroy said. They stood together and stared down the hallway.

Doors slammed open. The shouts and screams made her blood go cold.

"They're... they're covered in blood!" Conroy pointed.

Coyle pulled out her sidearm. The weapon gave her small comfort as the crowd ran toward them.

"Shouldn't we run as well?" Conroy asked.

"Not yet," she shouted. "We need to know who our adversaries are and hopefully stop them."

Men, women, and children rushed past them up the stairs, through open doors, down hallways, anywhere there was an opening. One woman grabbed Coyle, screaming for help, before she ran away with terror in her eyes. The woman had deep, bleeding gouges across her back.

Someone shouted for her gun. She pulled away. Chaos ensued. People swarmed around her, knocking her down. Conroy shouted. Hands grabbed at her from every direction, but she held on to the weapon. And then other noises filled her with dread: shrieking, snarling, *howling*.

The crowd shrieked. Coyle's arm was punched and her fingers pried apart until the gun was yanked out of her grip. She pulled herself away. Screams filled the air.

Six shots were fired in rapid succession before the gun was made useless. But the screams, the snarling, and the growling only grew louder. Fear took hold of her mind, and ice water flashed through her nerves. She was weaponless and next to useless now. And, for the hundredth time that day, it seemed she wouldn't make it out of this alive.

CHAPTER 26

Upper passenger decks

Dawn's Edge

The crowd swarmed through halls like a school of fish, running upstairs, downstairs, through ballrooms and kitchens. They had no certain direction; they wandered for mere survival. And Poes ran with them.

The Turned were biting at their heels, and no amount of running seemed to matter. Poes kept his hands on the back of an older woman, guiding and persuading her to keep moving, not daring to glance behind at the snarls and howling.

They were less than a hundred strong, and the ghouls had no trouble thinning them out. People lost their footing, or turned down a seemingly empty passage only to find the Turned waiting to devour them.

A new commotion erupted from somewhere near the front. He happened to eye a large ballroom nearby when he heard shouts of a gun. His hand quickly shot to his hip and made sure it wasn't his. Within moments, gunfire echoed through the huge hall, making everyone duck. Bullets raced over their heads and into the Turned.

And just as quickly, the firing stopped. People poured themselves into adjoining doorways and stairwells when his arm was grabbed. He turned.

"Coyle!" he shouted.

"Poes! We need to get out of here!" she said.

"I thought you were gone forever," he said.

"The pods? I feared you were gone too," she said. Poes noticed a rush of color in her cheeks.

He looked around and shoved her into the main ballroom. "Through here. We have to find a way back to the hangar. Quickly!"

They ran together through the chaos of rushing people. A creature slammed into a woman, howling with evil delight. Poes leapt out of the way as another creature grabbed a young man and sank its teeth into his neck. Coyle was knocked to the side, stumbling until she crashed into a table.

Poes finally looked behind, shrinking back. The Turned were everywhere. The closest one followed after Coyle and leapt. They crashed into a table with the vicious beast on top of her. She grabbed a broken table leg, smashing it across its head. It roared, bleeding from its new wound across its eyes. Its long arms held her down, rearing back its head full of jagged teeth and—

Poes shot it through the skull. Its body fell, and Coyle pushed it aside. Poes helped her up as another Turned bounded closer, swinging its disturbingly long claws.

"Get behind me," Poes said, grabbing her arm and firing a shot directly between the eyes of the creature. They backed away, heading for another doorway.

"I lost my gun," she said.

"I have mine." He flipped a switch and fired. The air filled with blinding particles of light and smoke. The creatures waved at the air, coughing and wailing.

"We have to keep moving," he said, guiding her away from the madness.

The screams and mayhem grew distant, but they ran for their lives, holding hands. With each door that closed behind them, the cries of the nightmare grew dimmer until, finally, they reached the upper balconies of a theater.

Poes led them to a large private balcony and closed the door. The suite was large enough to accommodate at least a dozen guests. Ambient light filtered down from windows along the sides.

"Coyle," Poes said. His breathing was strained. "Are you hurt?"

She shook her head, catching her breath. She leaned over, hands on knees, hair disheveled, scratches covering her leathers.

"What happened to you? Where did you land?" he asked.

"I don't know," she said. "Somewhere up above."

"We all thought you were dead," he said, looking around the room. "The two others, Duone and Vonteg. They died. They died in the air."

"This is all horrible." She wiped sweat from her face. "Simply horrible."

"We tried to take the bridge. But it was a trap. We suffered casualties. Wounds, some too severe to wait until we can get help."

"Nothing aboard this airship is turning out the way we hoped," she panted. "What other resources can we look forward to? Who else is coming?"

Poes leaned against a table, shaking his head.

346

"No one?" she asked. "No one else is coming to stop this ship?"

"Our radio communications were blocked by whoever planned this devilry," he said.

"Then no one else knows? And no one else is coming?" She stepped closer. Her hand resting on his shoulder.

"Unfortunately--no," Poes said.

She looked down and sighed.

"Well, that's the best news I've heard all day." She looked into his eyes, smiled and Coyle's face shifted into the shapeless form of Veiul. She slammed a dagger into Poes chest. She turned it once, before ripping it out.

"That's for shooting me in the carriage," she said. "One less of Treece's team and when I find Coyle and stab her pretty little heart out of her chest, well, that's going to be even better." She stepped away, watching the blood trickle out from his wound. "Coyle unraveled our plans a bit faster than we would have liked. And I can't wait to find her." Her face shifted into Coyle's again, her soft hazel eyes gazing at Poes.

"Do you like puzzles?" She smiled. The end of her blade lifting his chin. The lights reflection played on her face. "Here's another piece of the puzzle for you, Mr. Poes. Fae are not easy to kill."

Grunting, growling, and screams caught her attention. She went to the balcony and looked down. The passengers had found the theater below and were streaming inside, hoping for an escape. The Turned followed them. She watched as the passengers fell, one by one and by the handful. The Turned were mindless, ruthless, hungry. She smiled.

"You understand what's happening down there?" she asked. "The Turned. They're a more honest breed of human. More daring, powerful. And yet, despite the differences, they're the same greedy, selfish, bloated monsters. All reaching out with their fingers, trying to take what doesn't belong to them. Destroying everything in the process. Sound like your people, Poes?"

"Actually, it doesn't," said a woman's voice.

Veiul snapped her head around. Who spoke? Her eyes settled on Poes. Blood streaked his shirt, yet he stood, staring at her. Veiul's eyes shot around the room again. Poes said,

"It took a while to straighten everything out. Especially given my distrust of Treece. I knew he'd helped create us, and I'm not sure exactly why. That's the reason I disguised myself as this investigative attorney and played along with Treece's team for a while. I kept an eye on Coyle, as I was by her side throughout. I knew she would uncover everything needed to stop you and Moreci. And I knew I would end up in a room with you eventually." He grabbed the skin of his neck and pulled away the mask. "And my name isn't Poes."

"*Fang!*" Veil hissed and stepped back.

"I'm not sure who my people are. But you're right, Veiul. Fae are hard to kill. And so are vampires."

Fang lunged with her daggers. Veiul blocked and countered with hers. But she wasn't as fast, wasn't as agile. Veiul did everything she could to make Fang bleed. Both of them smashed their knuckles into their faces, knees into their guts. Furniture smashed apart. Glass shattered. Fang spun and disarmed Veiul, her dagger clattered across the room. But, Vieul was ready, she pulled out a different set of knives and lunged. They fought like two beasts in the gladiator ring, each seeking to expose a weakness in the other. They pushed each other away, each crouching in defensive stances. Each bleeding from wounds. Fang winced and grabbed her arm.

"Aurorium-tipped blades," Veiul spat. "Just in case I ran into you."

"I'm impressed," Fang said.

"At my cunning?"

"You thought of me."

Veiul sneered charged, her blades swinging. She dug her heel into Fang's chest, kicking her away. Fang spun in the air, slicing into Veiul's leg. Metal sang against metal as they struck and blocked attacks. Edged blade against edged blade. Will against will. Fae against vampire.

Fang bluffed to the side and leapt, dragging the tip of her dagger across Veiul's face. She landed her somersault while Veiul shrieked with blood streaked across her hand.

"You remember our creed? *Strength through adversity*," Fang asked. "Whatever comes our way will make us stronger."

"You remember your little cage? You're full of madness. You should have stayed there," Veiul said.

They charged each other, stabbing, swinging, blocking. Fang crouched and spun and slammed her fist into Veiul's chin, knocking the fae backward. Veiul kicked Fang's face.

They both pulled back, Veiul flexing her hands. Fang clenched her jaw, knife wounds burning like fire. The sounds of the deathly feast raged just behind her.

Veiul coughed strings of blood. "You're an animal, cross-bred from the worst of two weaker species. You don't belong with humans, fae or the vamperion. You're a traitor to all the people you ever knew. At least I know where I belong. I know who I am. I am a perfect, created being. And I'll take pride knowing that."

"Come, then," Fang said. "Show me this pride you speak of." She threw her daggers into the floor. Veiul did the same and rushed, her eyes blazing with murderous fury. They tore at each other with fists, elbows and knee-strikes. Veiul grabbed a chair leg and swung. Fang blocked with one kick and sent Veiul backward with another.

Veiul landed in a heap of splintered wood, wiping blood off her face. "You think you're going to win," she said, panting. "But Moreci gave me assurance that you wouldn't, Charlotte. That's your name, isn't it?"

Fang flinched as if she'd been struck. Her dark past crept through her mind, and she fought against the hazy memories threatening to pull her down. Veiul was weak, too. Barely able to move. Yet, Fang had to finish this.

"You thought no one would remember the little incident aboard that ship oh, so long ago," Veiul said. "Speaking of memories, here's a little something made especially for you, *Charlotte*."

She flung a vial at Fang, and the glass exploded before she could block it. Gold and purple dust filled the air. Fang coughed violently, her chest cramping, her eyes burning. She backed away, swinging her hands, trying to see her adversary. She bumped into the wall, crashing over furniture, coughing again—and opened her eyes to the nightmare she'd buried so well.

***

"Charlotte!"

She gasped and backed away, coughing. She wiped her face, catching her breath, her eyes taking in the room. The floor tilted over the roaring seas. Empty chairs scooted to the side and back again. Wood creaked under the strain of the waves. Hurricane lanterns swayed from their posts along the ceiling and walls, casting shadows and fears throughout the galley. Thunder rolled over their heads, and she blinked, flexing her hands—wasn't she holding something? Cutlery or… knives? Her eyes focused on the table. A plate of half-eaten hardtack sat next to a spoonful of jam.

"Charlotte! Are you listening?" Embeth asked.

"What? Of course I am," she said. "I just swallowed my food wrong."

"Mommy says you need a doctor for that head of yours." Embeth squinted, her lips pursed.

"I told her I don't need a doctor," she said. "I have a bit of fuzziness when we travel is all."

"Oh, really? Then how come you didn't hear me—*again*? It's like you're in a different world altogether." Embeth took another bite of her biscuit, and crumbs dropped onto her favorite green dress.

"I'm obviously not in another world, dingbat. Can't you see I'm right in front of you?" She grabbed the cup of water, swallowed, plopped the empty cup on the table and wiped her mouth.

"I just want to eat and go back to our room, please," Embeth said. "Mommy said to stay in our rooms if it got stormy."

"Mommy's too busy playing Countess back home," she said. "Besides, she left me in charge. I'm the older sister, aren't I?"

"Just by five years. You're not that much older." Embeth stuck her tongue out and squinted. "What are you looking at?" Embeth turned around.

"Hmm? Nothing," she said. "I thought I saw someone back there."

Embeth turned in her chair, eyeing the dark corner, her dark-brown locks swinging back and forth. She turned back and squinted. "You *always* think someone's hiding in the dark. You always wake up screaming. You're always in another world. Mommy's right, you know."

"I don't need a doctor." She squinted back and shook her head. "Want another biscuit? I'm still hungry."

"I just want to go to our bunk before you start seeing shadows again."

"That's it." She grabbed Embeth by the collar. "Let's go outside for a bit, shall we? Maybe some fresh air will do you good."

Embeth screeched and kicked her heels as Charlotte dragged her to the cabin door, begging to be released, but her older sister refused to listen. She turned the handle, and the storm ripped the door out of her hand.

Strobes of light flashed across the rolling deck. White water sprayed from all directions at once. Wind howled through their ears. Freezing rain shocked their senses.

"Never mind," Charlotte said. "Let's get back inside."

She pulled herself out of Embeth's grip and reached for the door. A gust of wind slammed the door in her face and knocked her down. She slid across the wet surface of the deck and into the railing. Crashing waves soaked through her nightgown. She reached up to the sharp sting on her head and pulled back her hand. Red streaked across her palm before it was washed away.

She screamed.

"Charlotte!" Embeth screamed from the doorway.

"Stay—"

A wave crashed over Charlotte, and she slid and tumbled and flopped across the deck. She reached out, grabbing at anything, until her fingers wrapped around a thick line. She pulled herself up, coughing violently.

"Embeth, stay there!" she finally said, peering through the white spray, trying to find Embeth. The salt water burned her mouth and eyes, but she had to find her little sister. She spotted a small shape along the deck.

"*No!*" she screamed as Embeth crawled out to her. "*Stop!*"

Another wave crashed over the ship, and the rope bit into her skin. Embeth was on her knees, sliding across the deck. Something crashed into Charlotte, the pain of it jarring her bones.

***

Fang opened her eyes, reeling into a table. She back flipped, set her feet against the wall, and vaulted forward. She crashed into Veiul and rolled away, but not before the aurorium-tipped blades bit into her skin. Searing pain tore through her bones, weakening her muscles, slowing her reaction time.

Veiul spun in the air, kicking her in the face. She slammed into the wall, recovered and blinked, wiping blood out of her eyes. Fang rolled out of the way as Veiul's boot smashed into the floor. She grabbed Veiul's leg, picked her up, and slammed her into the far wall.

Pain wracked her chest. She shook her head, bending over with another coughing fit. The strange powders altered her mind, displacing reality, forcing her back in time.

***

She raised her head and wiped her burning eyes. Her body shook from adrenaline, the North Atlantic waters or… something else. A quick glance around the room—or *the ship*?

"*Embeth!*"

Her sister's little fingers clung to a loose board as the ship lolled. Embeth spat and coughed and cried out. Her feet dug into the old wood as best as they could.

"*I'm coming to you! Hold on!*" she screamed at her little sister.

Lightning strobed across the sky, highlighting the ship as it rose higher. Charlotte loosened her grip from the line and climbed forward, but the pitch made it difficult.

Embeth's body slid sideways and down until her feet were within Charlotte's reach. She stretched out to her little sister and grabbed her foot.

The ship crashed down, and they both slammed into the deck. Water splattered around them, but Embeth let go of her hold and reached out.

They embraced.

She wanted to hug her little sister so badly, wanted to feel the warmth of her cheek against her own, wanted to feel their hearts beating together. Embeth's soaked body trembled in her arms. She sobbed and held Charlotte's neck so tight, but it was all perfectly wonderful. Because she had almost been lost, and now she was here, right in her arms.

"Don't leave me!"

"I'm not going anywhere, Embeth."

She opened her eyes. Eruptions of blue-white light pulsed through the darkness, enough to create a false sense of daylight, enough to see a massive wall of water rising in front of the ship.

***

A glass cabinet crashed on her head. Shards bit into her back and shoulders. She pushed herself from the floor, and pieces fell to the side. She looked up at Veiul, whose own body was bleeding and broken.

They were both fighters, sharing the same deadly training and unbending will to finish their objective. And now who was going to finish this?

"How was your trip down memory lane?" Veiul asked, panting. "Moreci said you had weak points, deep inside. I could have killed you much earlier, but you know me. I like to make things as painful as possible. Even if I can't see the damage being done."

Fang spat blood and raised herself to her hands and knees until she crouched. Her head was dizzy, her gut nauseated. She stuck a dagger into the wood, pushing herself up.

"That was a lot of work," Fang said. "A big effort. Just for me?" She sidestepped into the hall. "And here we are, not really any different from when we were kids fighting in the combat ring. Making Papa Moreci proud with our bloodied fisticuffs, making him wipe away your tears when you lost, again and again." She smiled.

Veiul sneered, lunging, tackling Fang. Pain exploded in her ribs, and air rushed out of her lungs. They tumbled across the floor, closer to the balcony. Veiul pulled herself on top, landing blow after blow, slamming her fists into Fang's face and head. Relentless.

Unmerciful. She grabbed Fang by the collar, yanking her up so they were face to face.

"Nothing," Veiul hissed. "You. Are. Nothing. And what would Embeth say? Huh? Knowing her death was just—"

With a grunt, Fang launched Veiul in the air and over the balcony. The fae fell over the edge without a sound. Fang heaved herself up and walked to the balcony, looking over the edge.

Veiul gripped the bottom ledge with white knuckles. They stared at each other with their bloodied faces. The roar of the melee below filled their ears. The Turned were bathed in blood, roaring, howling, their greedy hands stretching up for new flesh.

"You said I don't belong with humans or vampires or the nether-realm. But I know where you belong, and it looks like your people are ready to take you," Fang said.

Veiul smirked. "And who will you be joining? Do you think anyone will let you in their little club? Maybe that pretentious detective Coyle? How long before you end up killing her? How long before she cries out while you watch helplessly?" Veiul's face shifted and changed into Embeth's.

"Help! Help! Help me!"

Fang stiffened, staring back into Embeth's bloodied face. Her mind reeled. The thrashing crowd below melted into rolling, white-capped waves, the balcony under her hands turned into the ship's railing, and her feet shifted under the sway of the deck.

"No." Fang shook her head. "No, this… this isn't real." But that was a lie. The crashing waves were just underneath Embeth's feet as she held on to the railing. Freezing salt water drenched her face, the shock of it stealing away the breath in her lungs.

"Sister! Help! Help!" Embeth cried out.

"I'm trying." Fang's heart hammered louder than the crashing waves. But something wasn't right, and she hesitated. Why wasn't she trying harder? What was wrong with her?

"You don't love me!"

"That's not true."

"Then prove it."

The little girl reached up and Fang's hand shot down to grab it. They held each other, arm and arm, hand to hand. Fang smiled. She'd done it. She'd saved her sister. This was all so different from her memories, but she didn't care what was real anymore. She had her sister now, they were together—

Veiul slammed her knife into Fang's arm, tearing through skin and bone and out the other side. Fang screamed and yanked her grip away.

Veiul held on to the knife with both hands, grinning with bloodied teeth, cackling like a maniac. Fang yanked her arm away and ripped out the blade. The shape-shifting woman fell, her face melting, shifting from Embeth, to Fang, to Coyle and back to a grinning, giggling Embeth before she plunged into the melee of hands and claws and death. The Turned tore her to pieces.

Fang sank to the floor, melting under the horrible strain of seeing Embeth dying—again. Her ears rang with every one of her sister's cries for help. She stared at her trembling hands, her numb fingers, too slippery, too weak to hold on.

And then the waves took her.

Her head tapped against the balcony, deep wounds in her soul stealing her strength away. She squinted, remembering her voice stretched thin from crying out. Her body shaking as the men grabbed her and hauled her inside the ship. She didn't speak again for months. Her mother disowned her almost immediately after the news broke. Everything was a blur after that.

Something stirred, and Fang looked up. Embeth stood at her feet, staring.

"She wasn't telling the truth," Embeth said

Fang said nothing.

"Are you hurt?" Embeth asked.

"I'm fine," she said. The aurorium burned like fire through her veins.

"What's wrong?" Embeth asked.

Fang pulled a medical kit from a pouch and opened a glass vial. She gritted her teeth and poured a blue-colored potion over the wound before wrapping her arm tight with gauze. Horrible stabs of pain shot through her body, blurring her vision. Aurorium coursed through her veins, eating away at her healing factor, exposing the nerves to unbridled torment. She tightened her fists and squinted her eyes, willing the pain to ebb away. But it didn't.

"What's wrong?" Embeth repeated.

"I didn't try hard enough for you. I'm so sorry. I never should have opened that door. And then mother abandoned me. And now look at me. Look at us. I don't know what I am, and I don't belong... anywhere or with anyone."

"You have me." Embeth smiled. "We have each other."

Fang's smile was weak, and her eyes stung. She wiped away the tears. She said nothing because… what was there to say? How could you possibly top the wisdom of a child? Of someone washed away into the sea of darkness?

"The one who's helping you. What was her name?" Embeth asked.

"Coyle."

"She's smart. Friendly."

She looked into Embeth's eyes. "I think she's just like you, little one."

Embeth shook her head. "No. I'm smart, but I'm not *her* kind of smart. Where is she?"

Fang stood and searched the ceiling. The sounds of the Turned echoed throughout the cavernous theater. "I'm not sure."

"I guess we can go looking for her, then," Embeth said. "I think if we help her, maybe she can help you."

"Help me with what?"

Embeth beckoned her to kneel down. They looked into each other's eyes and leaned their heads together. Warmth rushed through

Fang's body. Her lip quivered as Embeth held Fang's face with gentle hands.

Embeth patted her big sister's head. "It's foggy here, and I think Coyle can help brush the fog away."

Fang stared into her sister's eyes with tears streaming down her cheeks.

"Why do you love me?"

"Why do *you* love *me*?"

"Because you're more valuable than all the stars in the sky. You're all I have."

Embeth grinned. "You're my big sister, remember? And nothing will change that."

They held each other tightly, uncaring that all the monsters in the world were trying to get them. Fang wished she could bottle this moment and open it whenever she was blue. But she knew there was still work to do, a job to finish. Embeth pulled away first.

"Besides, somebody has to love you. May as well be me."

"You little brat." Fang stood and tousled Embeth's hair. "But you're right. As always. I need to find Coyle."

Embeth smiled.

CHAPTER 27

Mid-level passenger decks

Dawn's Edge

"Conroy!" Coyle shouted. "Conroy, we need to get to the engine rooms. We need to shut them down." She turned and yelped as the Turned pulled down a man running beside her.

"We can get there," he huffed. "But that means we have to go back that way." He thumbed behind him.

"There must be another way!"

He was silent for a few moments before he answered. "There is. Up ahead on the right."

Coyle spotted a doorway. "This one?"

Without answering, Conroy shoved her through the doorway. Other passengers followed. So did the Turned. The small hallway echoed with fear and hunger. Heat poured into her legs. Exhaustion was setting in. But she had to find a way to live, had to find a way to stop the engines from running, before she could stop Moreci.

"Doorway on the left!" Conroy shouted.

Her heart wanted to burst. Her muscles ached. But it was the victims who urged her onward without stops, their panicked screams long since burned into her mind. A doorway waited at the end. Just one door with a small window. She prayed it wasn't locked.

"Go up two flights," he rushed. "Turn right, go down the hall and up again twice. You'll find the engine rooms!"

Conroy opened the door for her and she dared a glance behind. The Turned were steps away. Conroy grabbed her shoulders and shoved her inside.

"Go!" He shouted his last.

The door slammed. She pulled herself up in time to see Conrad's last moments before the Turned were on him.

She ran.

CHAPTER 28

Maintenance deck

Dawn's Edge

Electric lamps blinked incessantly, scattering light through the dark halls and rooms. The light show was just another distraction, because the lights from Coyle's suit worked perfectly, illuminating the space in front of her.

Conroy's efforts had limited the power, but the massive ship was still moving toward its final destination. Without additional help, the fate of the engines was left to Coyle. Though she was unsure how exactly all this was to take place, she knew there would be means.

Everything around her was unfamiliar, but she followed Conroy's directions. A door led to another passageway, which led to another door and on and on. She finally reached a series of open spaces with stacks of heavy machinery. The outer edges were lined with railing to keep the workers safe. She picked a route and pressed on to where the engines were.

The screams of the living had long since faded away—whether from distance or death, she would never know. She stopped. Something wasn't right. Stench filled the air.

And then she saw them.

The lights flickered over their ghastly forms, making their movements jittery, convulsive. Pale, yellow eyes shone from deformed skulls. Long, bony hands stretched, reaching for her soft skin.

Her legs pivoted without command, every fiber of her being begging to escape. The fringes of her mind pushed close to unbridled madness. She had to leave, had to run, had to get out.

Stay alive!

She took a step—just one. The hesitation was enough to make her reconsider. She couldn't. Running away wasn't an option anymore. She had a job to do. If she didn't fight now, they would lose everything. Coyle pulled out her knife and braced herself. She had time for one quick prayer under her breath before her knife flashed like a hammer, stabbing and slashing anything close. Some fell and crawled toward her, grabbing at her legs. She kicked them away, slashing at the others, and still they crammed forward to grab and pull and bite.

Something grabbed her shoulder. She pulled to the side, stabbed the ghoul in the temple, and sent another over the railing. She was pulled backward, but she leaned forward and spun away, jabbing the end of the blade into each of their heads. The last fell away with her knife wedged in its eye. She grabbed for it but wasn't fast enough. One of them slammed into her, knocking her down. She pushed away from the floor, but the ghouls heaped on top of her. Claws scraped at her back and legs and head, desperate to dig through the leather armor. She squirmed away and twisted around on her back, kicking at everything close. She crawled backward and got lucky; the Turned tripped and tangled over one another. Their long arms crossing over each other until they were locked in the struggle of pursuit. She used the moment to push herself up, hobbling away as quickly as she could. She reached a wall of machinery and looked over her shoulder.

Her eyes bulged.

A small horde followed behind the initial rush. Echoing howls chilled her blood. There were too many now. Far too many. But a thought flashed through her mind. She flipped open the tab on her forearm and pushed the button marked *Tesla Mode*. And then she heard the mechanical voice of her suit.

"Power at full capacity. Tesla Fist activated. Point weapon toward threat."

Tesla Fist?

Sparks hopped between the metal studs on her left fist. Warm energy tingled through her arm.

What am I wearing?

"Point weapon toward threat," the voice repeated.

A high-pitched whine grew, and her arm hummed. She squeezed her fist at the horde. Chain lightning erupted from the metal studs of her gloved hand. White ribbons of electricity jumped to each of them, spraying the air with blood, flesh, and bone. All at once, they fell in a heap of sizzling ruin. She took a few steps back, wiped the mess from her goggles, and observed. Nothing moved. She wrinkled her nose at the acrid stench of charred flesh and ozone.

She shook her hands of gore and sighed.

"So that's what Tesla Mode is," she said, shaking spattered gore from her hands. She inspected the smoking metal knobs on her fist and, remembering her knife, stepped through the mess to find it. She grabbed the hilt and felt someone staring at her.

"All done, then?" Fang asked.

Coyle spun around. "All done being disguised as Poes?" Coyle pointed her knife at her.

Fang cocked her head. "Took you long enough. Points for being the sharp one."

"On this ship? In these circumstances? Yes, I am going to be as sharp as I can. It's kept me alive this long."

"I thought I was careful." Fang smirked. "How did you know?"

"There was something off about you, about Poes. I couldn't be certain, but I had my suspicions you weren't who you said you were. Your eyes held the same gaze they did when we met in the jail cell. I let you hold my arm twice and used the opportunity to test your pulse. It wasn't as strong as a man's, yet certainly not a woman's. Your natural scent was fully covered by the cologne you wore. And then I passed out on your lap. You definitely weren't a man."

"That doesn't sound very ladylike."

"Does any of this look as though I'm trying to be a lady?"

"Touché."

"Why did you disguise yourself as Poes?"

"I had to find out who I was, where I came from."

"So none of the others know?"

Fang shook her head

"And then Veiul showed up in Fort Alcatraz. She could have killed me."

"But she didn't, oddly enough, and that brought more questions. Why not? And more importantly, who told her not to?"

"Couldn't it be Moreci?"

"Why does he want you alive?"

Coyle shrugged. "I haven't the faintest."

"I normally don't say this, but the thought that *someone* wants you alive makes my skin crawl. Someone else is in this game, besides Moreci, besides Veiul."

"So who's the inside threat?"

"I had to leave the main group to find you, but I'm sure we'll find out who it is soon enough. Have you found anything useful?"

"Yes, actually. I discovered a hidden message etched into the ghouls. Someone left it for me."

"And?"

"I think it tells me—*us*—how to stop Moreci."

"Well, how does it go?"

"Reverse the darkest deed / in ageless artifacts dwell / Repeat the faithful creed / Mirror cast the spell."

Fang clenched her jaw. "*Ageless artifacts dwell.* Sounds like the book to me."

"You think there's a faithful creed in there somewhere?"

"I don't know. But we'll sort this out. Who would leave a message for you to find?"

"It must be Treece."

Fang nodded. "That's the only thing that makes sense. He doesn't tell us everything." She turned behind and looked back at Coyle. "We need to stop the engines."

Coyle nodded but didn't move.

"What? What's wrong?" Fang asked.

Coyle paused. She had to ask. It was in her nature to ask. Just like it was in Fang's to kill.

"You're a murderer. Why should I trust you?" Coyle wasn't sure if her voice was trembling.

Fang shook her head. "No answer is going to satisfy you," Fang said. "If we stray to this topic, the point of trust will be moot. I

374

suggest we continue to work together until we find a decent solution to your morality issues."

"Morality issues? My beliefs are central to my motivations, and I have to know whether or not I can trust... someone like you."

"We wake up with choices every day, don't we? I'm not sure what brought you all the way up here, yet here you are. And please correct me if I'm wrong, but how many times have we been in the same room without you receiving so much as a threatening glance from me?"

"You didn't stop Veiul from knocking me senseless. You almost let me get slaughtered by these creatures just now."

Fang crossed her arms. "And you're still alive. You know what? You're far more capable than you think you are. Maybe you just need a few more opportunities to unearth the real you."

They faced each other. The heat from Coyle's cheeks matched the fire in Fang's eyes. But Coyle realized Fang was right. No answer was going to satisfy her question, and they still had a city to save. Coyle let out a deep sigh and shifted her feet.

"I guess we'll find out," Coyle said.

"Perfect," Fang said.

"On one condition." Coyle grabbed Fang's shoulder before quickly letting go. "We don't kill anyone we don't need to. Especially Moreci. Agreed?"

Fang tilted her head. "No promises."

The same sharp static filled their ears. The metal floor pulsed with chaos. Howls filled the air. The Turned were coming.

"You have your knife? Good," Fang growled. "Remember: eyes, temple, *basis cranii.*"

"What was that last one?"

"Base of the skull," Fang said, and she leapt over the tide of rot. She landed a kick to one Turned and stabbed the other's head. Both dropped. Her blades flew into the eyes and temples of the next two, sending them to the floor. Her body twisted in the air, daggers flashing, skulls cracking, blood spurting.

Coyle turned. More ghouls were shambling along the walkway behind them.

"I'll take these back here," she said.

"Forever grateful, Coyle," Fang replied. "This time, get a better grip on the knife."

Coyle rolled her eyes, swung into the ghoul's forehead and yanked it out. Then she stabbed another, and another, and another. Her arms burned, but she found her rhythm, and soon the small squad was silent at her feet. She turned to see Fang walking away from a fresh pile of dead.

"There are four engines. Two above and two below. I'll take the upper section first. That means you need you to keep an eye out for more of those ghouls while I work, understand?"

"Well, yes, but—"

"Good." Fang snapped out a rod and pointed it above. A cable shot out from its end and pulled her high into the dark. She was gone.

"I knew something like this would happen," Coyle growled. "Sherlyn, remind me not to work with vampires anymore."

She jogged toward the lower engine room, but not before another wave of ghouls came around the corner. She sighed.

"Oh, come on, then. How many of you things did he make?"

CHAPTER 29

Starboard ballroom

Dawn's Edge

"Where are they?" Moreci asked, slipping his pocket watch inside his waistcoat.

Cavin turned aside and spoke into his radio headset for a brief moment before answering. "Coyle was last seen heading aft, away from her team. None of us know why."

"She's headed to the engine rooms," Moreci said. "She's planning on shutting the engines down, though there's no way she could do that by herself." Moreci paced around the ballroom. His mind searched for answers to the new questions forming in his mind.

"And Veiul?" Moreci asked.

"She's hasn't been seen yet," Cavin said. "Reports are she mixed in with the passengers, presumably on her way to stop Coyle." His shoulders slouched and his chin dropped.

"What else? Out with it," Moreci said, and looked at his pocket watch again.

"One of the reports—unconfirmed reports, sir—is that Fang was seen leaving the theater," Cavin said. "Possibly."

Moreci blinked. "Fang?"

"Yes, sir."

"How in…" Moreci looked out the window, unsure of this new information. Finally, he shook his head. "Coyle and Fang. Coyle and Fang. I shouldn't be worried. Two women against all of us. I won't worry. When do we land?" Moreci asked.

"Within hours, sir."

"How is Quolo?"

"Oh, splendid! The remaining crew in the cargo hold have either been destroyed or Turned." His smile was wide.

"Excellent! Now—"

There was a sudden lurch, and the ship leaned gently.

"What?" Cavin said and looked outside at the tilting horizon.

"The engines," Moreci said. "One of them has been disabled. Get our other operative on that immediately."

Cavin nodded and adjusted his radio.

***

The stench of hot metal and ozone filled the communications room. Sparks shot out sporadically from the jumble of wires and machinery. The massive radio antenna array had not been just disabled but completely destroyed.

"How on earth did this happen?" Chief Sykes said.

Bolt shrugged. "I'm not sure, but as I said earlier, I can fix anything."

The floor shuddered and tilted enough that the men had to adjust their stance.

"What was that? Were we hit?" Bolt frowned.

"No. It feels as though one of the engines died." Sykes squinted at Bolt. "What in blazes have we gotten ourselves into?"

Bolt held a finger up and pressed the radio receiver against his ear.

"How are you getting communications? Who's talking to you?" Chief Sykes asked.

Bolt looked at the tangled mess. "This won't be fixed for a while. I have other business to attend to."

Chief Sykes turned around. "What business? What are you talking about?"

Bolt slammed his fist into the back of the Chief's neck, sending him to the floor with a clatter. Another punch to the older man's head, and he was still.

"Chief's out," Bolt said into the radio. "What's the next objective, sir?" After listening for a short time, he reconnected wires, and the lights flickered back on. Then he turned and headed off to the engine rooms.

CHAPTER 30

Lower engine platforms

Dawn's Edge

Crimson rivulets dripped down Coyle's arms. Her gloved hands were soaked with chunks of flesh, bits of bone and blood. The grip on the knife was slick as she limped on one boot until she arrived onto a wide open platform where the engines thrummed with life. They were massive, the size of train cars stacked side by side and on top of each other. Flames burst from the opening, and shimmering waves of heat emanated from the dark iron. She stepped back a few paces and studied the moving parts. Automated metal scoops on a conveyor belt made their way from the coal bunker and dropped their loads into the firebox opening. Her knowledge of steam engines was sparse, but she knew moving parts had to move if the engine was to function. Rods were connected to other rods, which were connected to more rods, which were connected to pistons.

She spotted something. *There*. Something needed to get jammed into the spot where the pistons were if this engine was to be stopped. Though she was wearing a helmet and face mask, the heat was too intense. She shielded her face and searched the floor for a tool, a spare rod, a box of tools. Something heavy. A collection of shovels was near the belt. She grabbed one and, using careful aim, threw it where the pistons slammed up and down. The wood splintered into a hundred pieces and she ducked as the metal spade flew past.

The pistons continued their violent cadence. She looked for something heavier. An ax lay nearby, but she thought better of it after the results with the shovel. She walked a few paces away and found an iron rod the length of her body. The weight of it almost pulled her over. She pulled off her mask, helmet and goggles and tried again. With a grunt, she lifted the rod up to her knees before stepping backward. She took another step and another, the other end dragging a long, thin line into the metal floor. Smoke and hot air burned her throat, and she coughed. A quick glance behind showed the fiery engine was only a few paces away. Damp hair was pasted across her face. Sweat stung her eyes. Her hands, legs and back ached, but she refused to let go. She squinted and heaved the rod closer to the engine. She looked over her shoulder, waves of heat slamming into her face. She squeezed her eyes shut and turned away. This was it. She had to find the strength to lift and throw the rod. Gritting her teeth, she lifted the rod. Her back and legs and arms taut with as much strength as she could put together.

With a shout, she swung the rod with all her might and felt it slam into something. She opened her eyes and stumbled backward.

Bolt was standing between her and the engine. His eyes were slits of anger, and his lips tightened into an ugly smile.

He held the iron rod with one hand.

CHAPTER 31

Lower engine platforms

Dawn's Edge

Bolt's eyes flickered. The glowing flames framed his silhouette, and he resembled a massive demon coming to collect his due. He pointed his chin at her and swung the rod over his shoulder as if it were an umbrella. Coyle fell on her backside.

"I say," she said. "It's so good to see you, Bolt. Where... are the others?"

He stepped closer. "There are no others. The detectives are dead. I set small charges in each of your pods, but obviously you're still alive. Everyone in the hangar is dead. And everyone believed you to be dead until recently."

"You're working for Moreci."

"He pays better."

"Why would you work for a madman?"

"Because I'm smart, and you're not. I didn't like what I saw the first time I laid eyes on you. Not one bit. You're too progressive. You want things for yourself that are only meant for a man's world. Look where it got ya. Lying on the floor, helpless. Typical."

Her hand shot up into a fist. The metal studs covering her wrist and glove popped and snapped before a small puff of smoke coughed from her knuckles. But there were no threads of deadly electricity.

"Power at minimal level. Please wait until fully charged to use again," the mechanical voice chimed.

His head tilted. "Trick of some kind? You trying to outsmart me?"

She pulled herself up. There was no talking herself out of this situation. Adrenaline rushed into her hands and feet, dulling the pain. Her hands balled into fists, and her feet spread apart in a boxer's stance.

"Bolt, I will not let you circumvent my investigation with wild guesses and chauvinistic insinuations. I'm investigating multiple crimes aboard this ship. Either you assist me or stay out of my way."

"Ah! There's what I was looking for." He grinned and held the rod across his body. "Now I get the fight from the little girl."

He shifted his weight and swung. The rod blurred through the air. Coyle lunged. Air rushed past, and sparks flew as the rod slammed into the floor. She pulled herself into a crouch. He swung again, and the bar zipped over her head. She charged and used his knee to launch into him, grabbed hold of his ears and smashed her knee into his face. His body shuddered and she leapt off his wide chest, landed on her side, and rolled like a block of wood.

A trail of blood ran down his grease-stained shirt. The rod banged onto the floor. She lowered her shoulders and charged again. This time, he caught her around the waist and threw her aside. She crashed into a pile of tools.

He smeared the blood off his proud face. She turned and reached for something, anything. Her hand wrapped around a wooden handle. *The axe!* Bolt roared and slammed his foot down. The handle snapped, leaving her with a club. She swung, but he caught her wrist. He leaned into her, rage and sweat dripping from his skin.

"You're a whole bit of trouble, hey?" He swung his fist into her body. Air exploded from her lungs. She gasped, trying to catch her breath. Bile filled her mouth. She was dizzy, her eyes watery. She didn't want to be here anymore.

Bolt punched her again. She couldn't move. She retched, coughing blood. He picked her up and tossed her to the side. She curled herself into a ball, trying to breathe. *Trying to live.*

"I tell you what, lass," he panted. "You gave me a good round there, but it looks like you may be down for the count. Now I have to decide what to do with the body."

Every bone and muscle screamed, but finally, her lungs filled with air. She glanced at him. He was bent over with his hands on his knees, trying to catch his breath. Blood streamed from his nose.

I did that much, at least.

The thought of running away was still in her mind. Then again, it wasn't. She was past all that now. She wanted to change things. *For her.* She stood on wobbly knees and clenched her fists. Her hand-to-hand combat training breathing life into her weak muscles.

He stood, flexed his hands, and spat blood on the floor. So did she. He swung first. She dropped to a crouch and swung hard into his groin. He yelped. She pulled and swung at his face. The metal knuckles dug troughs through his skin. Blood gushed across his face. She swung again, connected, and he tripped backward, landing with a thud. His eyes went wide. He muttered something, rolled himself up and charged. She crumpled under his power, and they crashed to the floor. He pushed himself up and swung into her. Her arms came up, guarding her face. His fists hammered into her arms and head, every blow making her weaker.

Her hands and arms softened until they were useless. He stopped and stood over her. The world blurred in front of her eyes. He stepped away and turned his head to the firebox. He spat and pulled on her leg. Words dribbled from her lips, her head bouncing along the rough metal floor.

He yanked, and heat rushed over her. She covered her face. He grabbed her, lifted her up. He shouted something. Heat flared. She mumbled and squeezed her eyes shut.

And then she fell. Flames tangled in the air. Her body melted. Strong hands grabbed her, but different this time. Careful, gentle, powerful.

Blood bubbled from her lips as she was carried away from the flames. Bolt's body lay face down, the back of his head torn apart. She looked up.

It was her.

"You'll thank me later," Fang said.

CHAPTER 32

Lower engine platforms

Dawn's Edge

Fang carried Coyle down a hallway and into a large office. She lay Coyle on the floor and fashioned a coat for a pillow. Then she closed the blinds and peeked outside.

Coyle's breathing was loose and shallow. Fang pressed two fingers into the hollow beside the trachea. Her vitals were very good considering the trauma she had fought through. But at a glance, Coyle was also an absolute mess. Her left eye was bruised, almost swollen shut. There were small cuts to her upper lip. Drying blood streaked one side of her face.

Fang had arrived just as Bolt was about to toss her into the fires. She used her cable baton, pierced the back of his head, and pulled his brains out. She had no qualms taking a life, especially when necessary. Coyle, on the other hand…

A dark bruise ran down Coyle's neck. Fang debated cutting through Coyle's leathers. It would be quicker, of course, but the material was made by Treece and would most likely deflect the edge of a blade. As it was, her uniform was covered in scratches. It had held together despite the bony claws of the Turned.

She pulled the straps apart and found smaller, less threatening contusions. She also noticed the long, jagged, pink scar near her collarbones. She pulled away the leathers and followed the scar down to just below her navel. It was old.

She tilted her head back and thought. The injury was precise, straight—a scalpel's blade. Typically incised for the purpose of forensic science, something Fang had learned through her training with combat medicine. Had someone mistaken Coyle for dead, and then she'd come back to life? No, she had been *left for dead*. That meant someone had done this purposely. Someone had cut her open. But who?

Her eyes were studying the ceiling when the idea flashed into her mind. She'd seen wounds like this before. She'd read the reports, in fact, and was just about to be put on a mission to find him.

The Ripper.

So this was why Coyle wanted to become a detective. She'd been attacked by him. But that didn't make sense either. He never left his victims alive. What motive would he have to not kill Coyle? Did they know each other?

"What is it?"

"Not now, Embeth."

"But what's wrong?"

"It's nothing, Embeth. Just trying to think."

Embeth gasped.

"What happened to her?"

"She'll be fine. It's just some bruises. A few cuts…"

"Is she hurt?"

"Yes, but not bad. She'll be fine." Fang pulled out her medical kit and retrieved gauze and alcohol.

"It looks like someone sewed her all up. Was she broken?"

"Some of us are, Embeth," Fang answered without thinking.

Embeth frowned. "Am I too?"

Fang brushed Embeth's bangs out of her eyes.

"No. Not you. You're perfect."

"How about her?"

392

They looked down at Coyle. Her chest rose and fell. Gloved hands rested by her hips. Pink, bleeding lips mumbled incoherent words.

"Where did she get that…" Embeth's finger dragged down her own chest.

"Scar. She has a scar."

"Where did she get that scar? "

"Someone hurt her. A long time ago."

"Who? Who hurt her?"

"Someone… stronger. More dangerous."

"Do you know who did it?"

"I think so."

"Maybe your friend needs help finding them."

"Yes. I think she does."

"She's waking up."

CHAPTER 33

Lower engine platforms

Manager's office

Dawn's Edge

Coyle moaned and shifted on the floor. With a start, she cried out and grabbed her chest, panting. Pain tore through her body. Her insides were on fire. She groaned and held her belly. Fang handed her a rag to spit into. Coyle rubbed her eyes and looked up into the blurry face kneeling beside her.

"We don't have much time," Fang said. "Are you with me?"

Coyle tried to sit up, but her abdomen resisted with flares of shooting pain. She winced and lay back down, and her mind spun. She had heard another name mentioned. *Embeth?* It sounded familiar.

"You may have a couple of fractured ribs, strained muscles and ligaments, a mild concussion, numerous lacerations and contusions. Nothing life-threatening."

"Are you a doctor as well as a vampire?" Coyle asked.

Fang tilted her head. "I was trained in combat medicine. It does come in handy from time to time." She stretched pieces of gauze across her lap and reached for scissors.

Coyle rested her head. Soft light from a small lamp allowed her to see what was necessary. They were in a small room with rough, used furnishings. Almost everything was made out of metal. Desk. Chairs. File cabinets. The slightest odor of old rust and cigar smoke lingered. This was an engineer's office, and she was lying on the floor. Cool air brushed over her skin.

Her bare skin.

Her hand went up to her chest, and she squinted at Fang.

"Your suit got in the way of my assessment. Not to worry, though. I didn't bite, and after I'm done wrapping your wounds, you can re-dress and be ready for the rest of our short adventure."

Coyle closed her eyes as she let the trained killer sew a cut on the back of her head. She winced at the pain. "Thank you."

"Been a while since I sutured someone beside myself. My business is wounding, not healing," Fang said. "But I need you in tip-top shape."

"Again, thank you for… Why," Coyle asked, "Why are you helping me? You could take out Moreci by yourself."

"I've been asking myself the same question." Fang bit the thread and pulled it tight. Then she picked up a long strip of gauze and measured it before using the scissors. "Roll toward me. There, now roll away. Perfect. Yes, yours is a complicated question."

"I love complicated questions and answers. They're my bread and butter, as the saying goes." Fang tightened the bandage and Coyle grunted. She reached up and tapped her side where it hurt. She was going to look like damaged goods when she got hold of a looking glass.

"I've noticed. And in a small way, my appreciation of you and your work has increased. Tenacity. Attention to detail. Patience."

"Agency."

"Agency." Fang nodded. "And while we may live and work on opposite sides of the proverbial railroad tracks, I see myself in your personality and habits."

"You're helping me because you see some of me in you?"

Fang stopped and looked at her. "I'm helping you because there is no one else on this ship I'd rather have at my side than someone like myself."

They remained silent, Fang on wound care, Coyle wondered if Fang wanted companionship. Or maybe just a one-time joining of abilities to solve the last few bits of this riddle. Working side by side with Fang seemed altogether beneficial and frightening at the same time. According to Fang, Coyle was someone worth rescuing.

What was going to happen when Treece was finished with her? What was going to happen when Fang was finished with her? She shook her head. All of it had been a huge nightmare, and it all led to death.

"I feel as though the world has been against me since the very beginning," Coyle said.

"Go on."

"My parents were never interested in me, mostly because of my inclination toward subjects that had nothing to do with being a lady. And then I fell in love—and that didn't work out. And then I tried to become a detective. Now I'm working under Treece, and I'm still not sure how things will turn out. It's obvious he's using me to find and stop Moreci, but he doesn't need me."

"You're afraid Treece may eliminate you."

"Should I be concerned?"

"No, I don't believe so. He's made mistakes, but he actually is a decent person trying to do his best to fix his wrongs."

Fang wrapped and tightened the bandage and stretched out another piece. Coyle watched her measure the cloth and hold the scissors. With a quick motion, the blades separated the cloth, and she pulled it taut around her left elbow. Coyle's mind flashed to the still form of Bolt as Fang dragged her away from the firebox.

"I'm not a killer, though," Coyle said.

"Not yet."

"I would never."

"Don't be modest. Of course you would. Apparently, you and Bolt jumped into fisticuffs. Something made you fight, gave you the extra edge you needed to overcome the obstacle you faced. A modern twist on David and Goliath. You may have had him, but you obviously got too close. What was your intention in facing off against a man at least twice your size and obviously more skilled at brawling?"

"He had to pay for what he did to our team. I intended to place him in custody," Coyle said. "He was a criminal, and as the ship's only law enforcement, it's my duty." Heat brushed through her face and chest.

"Ah! There, you see? Feel that?" She tapped her fingers against Coyle's chest. "Anger. Focused, unbent will. Do you think I'm any different? The only difference between us is I used lethal force. I stepped forward and pulled the trigger. I used my anger, focus and unbent will to save your life. We have the same qualities when it comes to our work. That's what I admire about you. Now lie back down while I finish mending your pious frame."

"My unbent will is for the enforcement of the law, not vigilantism."

"Our wills are not so different, Coyle. We actually share the same occupation."

"And what would that be?"

"Rubbish collection. You remove the rubbish from the street to make things safer. Cleaner. Your work involved a lot of rules and the inevitability the trash would be released back onto the street. I do the same. But when I take out the rubbish, it's gone for good. Into the incinerator. Pun intended."

"Only to be replaced by another."

"And that's job security," Fang said. "I end rubbish. Your survival alone should be enough evidence that my job is necessary."

"These are people, not rubbish. Human beings make mistakes, Fang. We can't go around killing people just for the choices they make."

"They make the choice to be rubbish, to act like rubbish. To be thrown away like rubbish."

"Redemption, Fang. We have the courts and the law, which summon them to face the consequences of their actions. People can come back from their mistakes," Coyle said.

"Those meaty fists of that piece of trash back there would have erased you if I didn't pull the trigger," Fang said. "Redemption for the wicked serves up an empty plate for the righteous dead. Maybe his heart could have turned into a pile of gold while the hangman's noose slipped over his eyes, but really, what would that matter if pennies are covering yours? Doesn't the good book say God slays the wicked with the word of his mouth? Is it true his vessels of clay are smashed against the rocks of injustice on a regular basis? Good things happen to bad people, and bad things happen to good people. All without any input from us lowly jars of clay. But some of us"—she pointed to her own chest—"were created to make sure bad things happen to bad people."

"Is it always your first inclination to kill?"

"Just the bad ones, remember?" Fang packed away her supplies, stood and offered a hand.

Coyle grabbed Fang's hand, and the vampire pulled her up. She grunted, tightening her straps together. "I suppose we're always going to have this issue, aren't we?"

"What, bleeding and bandaged?"

"Justification for our actions," Coyle said.

"It can't be easy being a constable, surrounded by men who don't appreciate you. Why do you help those who don't like you?"

"Because it's the right thing to do and it's what I do best. Nothing's going to stop me from achieving my goals."

"I know what I'm trained for and what I can do. And I do it very well," Fang said. "But it doesn't mean I don't care about people—or you, for that matter. I'm not all bad." Fang moved her attention to a corner of the room and gave the slightest smile.

Coyle followed Fang's curious smile and glanced at the empty space in the corner. She was smiling at nothing.

Or was she?

Coyle thought for a moment and was struck again by memories of Treece's journal. There was a name that appeared on page after page. It was the name she had just heard upon waking: *Embeth*. Part of her wanted to know more, if just to understand or possibly help Fang. But, Coyle opted to keep quiet about the dead girl. But she did want to touch on their past.

"I suppose we all have things, or people, that have shaped us into who we are today," Coyle said. "Forged in the fires of passion or malevolence."

Fang said nothing.

"Our experiences of youth prevent or protect us from discovering the answers we seek," Coyle said. "The answers we deserve."

Fang nodded. "And that's how we take our first step along the path we find ourselves on."

"And we don't know how to get back," Coyle said.

"Maybe some of us choose not to go back," Fang said.

Coyle nodded, reflecting on Fang's words. The moving pictures replayed in her mind. The haunting dark eyes staring at the camera. The madness etched into the expressions of a young woman who was experimented and tortured and sent around the world to kill.

"Some of us choose not to go back."

Coyle had spent hours poring through the journal. All the words and plans Treece had written about were manifested in the woman next to her. Tragedy and accomplishment. Fears and failures. Madness and betrayal.

"I could help you," Coyle said. "When the time is right."

"And I could help you find him," Fang said.

"Who?"

"The one who let you live."

Coyle raised her hand to her chest, fingers tracing the bumpy path that would remain with her until she died.

"How's your balance?" Fang asked.

Coyle shifted her feet and flexed her knees and arms and hands.

"Lots of pain." Coyle glanced at Fang's bandaged arm. "What happened to you?"

Fang smiled. "I'm dying is all. Been through this a thousand times, only this time it just may happen. Here, take this." She handed her a small vial of opaque, golden liquid.

"What is it?"

"It makes you good as new for about an hour, but the side effects will put you in bed for a couple of weeks. We used it when we were almost at death's door and needed to finish a mission."

"Why don't you take it?"

"You're more important, and I'm expendable. Besides, I have aurorium running through me. Most of my strength is gone, and I feel as if I'm existing on vapors. But I can manage the simple things."

Coyle glanced at Fang before downing the contents. A bizarre combination of heat and ice rushed through her veins, followed by tingling warmth. The swelling of her wounds subsided rapidly, strength returned to her joints and the pain in her aching ribs melted to nothing.

"Better?" Fang asked.

"Packs quite the punch," Coyle answered, flexing her hands. She took a couple of deep breaths without pain.

"You look miles better, but it's just for an hour. That means we need to get this finished. Now, Moreci sent Veiul to kill me—"

"How do I know you're not Veiul?"

"Don't start— Wait. That's an excellent point. Maybe you should confront Moreci and let me take care of the remaining passengers and crew. He's infused with aurorium. I would die within a few feet of him."

"Or else you'd shoot him on sight."

"Oh, I would, yes, right. And you don't want him dead, so that's out. You'll have to pretend you're Veiul and get close to Moreci by yourself. Think you can handle that?"

"The man who already threatened to end my life?"

"Not like you haven't been in the position before." Fang smirked.

"I do have the coded message on how to stop him."

"Then it's settled. You handle Moreci, and I'll get the remaining innocents on board the emergency ship. I have every confidence you can accomplish your objective. And, if everything goes right, we can have a tea at the end of this. Here, take my gun."

Coyle strapped on her utility belt and checked her weapons. "Why don't we go over what we're facing?"

"We're facing a horde of ghouls who want to tear us apart," Fang said.

"Check."

"There are just under two hundred passengers to rescue."

"Check."

"We have a madman who's going to use an ancient book to erase a major city."

"Check."

"This same madman is infused with aurorium, making me completely useless."

"Check."

"We're stuck a thousand feet in the air."

"Check."

"And just about everyone else wants us dead."

"And check." Coyle added, "Anything else?"

"That should do it for now."

Fang opened the door, and they stepped into the cavernous space of the engineering bay, walking side by side. Flames and smoke poured out of the destroyed engines behind and above them. Iron scraped against iron, littering the metal floors with sparks.

Fang inspected her daggers and slammed them into her sheaths. Coyle filled the gun with fresh ammunition and slipped it into a side holster.

They stopped for a moment and looked at each other.

"Ready to save a world that hates us?" Fang asked.

"What else is new?" Coyle answered.

CHAPTER 34

Starboard ballroom

Dawn's Edge

> *May I speak each word as if my last word, and walk each step as my final one. If my life should end today, let this be my best day.*
>
> *Amen.*

Coyle turned the corner. Two guards stood outside Moreci's door, their weapons at the down-ready position, ready to kill anyone who was a threat. Was she a threat? Absolutely, but they wouldn't know until too late. Just like Moreci.

The two guards nodded to her. She ignored them and, before stepping through the door, caught the last bits of the conversation inside.

"What's the word?" Moreci asked.

"All four engines have been ruined or close to it," another man answered. "Bolt is dead. Veiul just reported Coyle and Fang are dead, and she's on her way back."

"Well, that's not terrible news. When can we get the engines working?"

"As soon as we gather the engineers. Ah, she's returned," said a tall, older man.

She caught Moreci's gaze and smirked.

"Veiul," Moreci said. "I take it you ended your quarrel with Fang?"

"She died in the most horrible fashion," Coyle said.

"Oh?"

"Aurorium-tipped daggers." Coyle darted a glance through the room and spotted what she was looking for.

"How unfortunate," Moreci said. "And you kept your disguise as Coyle? Marvelous." He looked at his pocket watch and nodded to the other man. "Cavin, get the men working on the engines." He turned and looked outside.

Coyle stepped closer to the book. It rested on a shelf in front of the wide, tilted windows. She opened it and casually flipped through the pages. Every one of them was marked with what appeared to be nonsensical writing, but it was authentic fae script in different sizes and colors. She knew the message she was given had to do with the book.

In ageless artifacts dwell.

Repeat the faithful creed,

Mirror cast the spell

Something about a mirror casting a faithful creed. Or was she to use a faithful creed for something? She flipped through the pages, one after another. Moreci didn't bother her, but she wasn't in a library. She couldn't sit here all day until she found what she was looking for.

"Bolt didn't make it," she said. "He went quickly."

"Good enough."

"At least he carried out the last of the plans. And now we'll have to wait until our engines are fixed."

"It's too bad about her, though. Coyle would have made some excellent company."

She turned to him and crossed her arms. "How so?"

"Intelligent, gifted in knowledge, a hunger for things unknown. She reminded me of myself."

"I'm all those things and more."

"Are you?"

She lowered her chin and glared.

"Show me, then. We've time for an interlude up here in the clouds. The people of Chicago will be the first of a long line of alternate creations on our schedule, but they can wait."

She looked outside. Clusters of homes pocked the landscape. People going about their business, living their lives. People who should be protected against Moreci. She side-glanced him. The devil was so close he made her skin crawl. But she couldn't be fearful, couldn't fail all these people. This was it.

Time's up.

She pulled her pistol out and pointed it at him. His eyes widened in shock as he realized what was happening.

"Coyle!" he spat. Then his eyes narrowed into slits. "This means Fang is alive, then. And the both of you are working in tandem." He slammed his fist on the shelf next to him. The two guards threw the door open and pointed their weapons at her. "Step away from the book, young lady. You don't know the power."

The guards stared, ready, waiting for the order to drop her.

She looked him over. He was a dangerous boy with a bad temper. He had destroyed scores of people on the ship and intended to destroy more. Fang was right. Sometimes the trash needed the incinerator. Her finger tightened on the trigger.

"Fang wants me dead," he said, and motioned to the guards. They lowered their rifles. His shoulders relaxed. "She can't kill me, so she sent you. But you can't kill me, either. You're not that type of person. I know you all too well, Coyle."

"No, you don't," she said.

"Sherlyn Coyle. You have a nose for evidence and an admirable way of presenting it," Moreci said. His tone was cheerful, given the circumstances.

Coyle's shoulders hunched. Butterflies crowded her gut. She wanted to shoot. And yet her finger remained frozen.

"I've been studying you ever since you solved Trevin's murder. And when I first laid my eyes on you, I thought you were pretty in the right light. Not in a radiant, beautiful sort of way, but there was this inner glow, this deeply embedded passion I recognized. It seeped out from your soul and bathed you with an effervescent sheen of respectable substance. Relentless pursuit. Unbending will," he said, rubbing his hands together.

"You got all that from one look at me?" she asked. "Yet you can't see the delusion of grandeur being played out from your fingertips?"

He cocked his head, squinting. "Ambition is the fruit from the seed of neglect. You understand?"

She grew uncomfortable under his steady, prying gaze.

"I know your father, Coyle. Good man. Earned a decent living. Provided for little Sherlyn and her sisters. Kept food in your little belly and coals in the hearth. Yes, Denny is a good man." He walked, waving his hand in the air.

"But are you satisfied with what you have? Did father Denny support your interest in becoming a constable or detective? Or in anything, for that matter? No? What a shame. You know, you're good at guessing games. Let's see how well I do, shall we?"

She glanced behind her. The door seemed so close, yet it wasn't.

"You're the youngest of three daughters." He counted his fingertips. "Ellory, Maycroft, Sherlyn. He probably wanted a boy somewhere in there, am I right? After all, we know what kind of brute the man is, what with his dog-fighting ring and the barrels of whiskey he has hidden away in…" He counted silently to himself. "Six different ports. And a lovely arm tucked away at his side in each of those disreputable firms he thinks he hid so well under shell companies. *Tsk, tsk.* No, a man like Denny would definitely hope to have a boy. He needed someone to take over the business when it came time.

"The way I see it—and do tell me if I am wrong—firstborn Ellory's blonde curls were for Momma. That should have kept her busy until the second, but then Maycroft pushed her big head into the world. She was probably shooed in under Mommy's dress. Then Denny had a third and final chance for a little boy, someone to call his own. But you came out, and that was that. Tell me, what did his eyes say to you when he looked down at little Sherlyn? You could remember with that sharp mind of yours."

She blinked, tears threatening to spill down her hot cheeks. Her jaw set on edge. And her face expressed everything she wanted kept hidden.

"Yes. Yes, I know this voice that carries words further and deeper than any song imagined," he said. "But this is the voice that gave us strength to rise above what we didn't want to become. This indomitable will wrapped us in armor no steel blade could sunder. And the void of our want became seed in the field of our destiny. That which we never received became an opportunity we were born to create. Like it or not, Sherlyn, we are presently who we are, where we are, and how we are because we can be nothing else. And you are not a murderer."

Fang's voice echoed in her mind.

Some of us choose not to go back.

Coyle wiped her eyes. "Our past can't be the influencer of our present decisions. We can only learn from those terrible experiences and make adjustments for the course of the future."

"You sound like you almost believe yourself, Sherlyn," he said. "Reach down further, past the self-aggrandizing wretch you expect everyone to see." He turned and faced her. His wide eyes stared into her soul. "Grasp hold of authenticity—truth!—with both hands." He shook his fists.

"Who are you, Sherlyn? There are no expectations up here in the clouds. It's just you and me and a bunch of hired conscripts who don't give a rat's ass what comes out of your mouth. This is your chance to speak your mind. Without judgement, Sherlyn. Without expectations. Is it true there's strength through adversity? Say it! Shout it! What are you made of, deep inside?"

Her fears were fully realized, not because she was going to die, but because she was exposed. She tried so hard to believe in her motives for justice, but really was just grasping at straws all along. All this time she was just buying another step on an unsure journey.

She stared at her feet, her hands. She had no strength--what did he just say? Strength through adversity. Wasn't that the creed of the Templars?

Repeat the faithful creed.

But it wasn't written in English, it was written in Latin. She remembered her flirty conversation with Poes—with Fang.

"You know Latin. I like that. Latin's a nice word, isn't it?"

The Templar's creed was written in Latin, what was it? And then it came to her in a flash.

"Virtus per aspera," she said. The letters glowed on the page, shifting, rearranging into a single phrase.

Moreci blinked. "What did you say?"

Her eyes raced over the newly formed phrase. All of it meant nothing to her. Except—she had seen this before. She squinted. Yes, she had seen this before. The words were mirrored. Her eyes shot up to the tilted windows—to the glowing words reflected in the glass—and read the phrase out loud.

Suffer the wrath of your creation

Word-bearer of lies

Walk in torment and damnation

The room exploded in purple lightning, and all of them were thrown back. She flew across a table and into chairs. Fingers of eerie, glowing light creeped along the walls and floors and ceiling. Rifle fire burst through the air. She covered her head and peeked toward the men.

Cavin and the guards fired wildly at her. Their bullets tore through the furniture and shattered the glass, but all missed her. Tendrils of energy flared through the air and wrapped around her assailants. They writhed in coils of lightning and ruptured into burning ash.

She looked at Moreci. His body shook and twisted, crawling with dark energy. His agonized screams deepened, chilling her blood. The mask covering his face ripped apart, and his mouth widened. Huge, jagged teeth burst forth. His back hunched, his legs widened, his arm twisted and swelled. The light around him grew brighter, more intense. She heard the screams of a man turned into something inhuman. Terrifying. *Deadly.*

She grabbed the book and ran out the door. Horrible sounds echoed through the hall. Long coils of purple lightning spread throughout the ship, changing everything it touched. Timber snapped and splintered apart. Metal twisted and groaned. Glass shattered. The ship was being torn apart. She ran. She had to get away before--

"Oh, Sherlyn," a familiar voice said through a radio device.

She froze.

"Sherlyn? Where are you running off to?"

Her blood turned to ice.

"Is that how you treat a loved one?" he asked. "After all I've done for you?"

She turned around. Moreci's twisted, misshapen form pulled itself into the wide hallway. His skin had been turned inside out. His feet were writhing tendrils of flesh, and his powerful hands gripped the walls. He seethed hunger and hatred.

"Oh, there you are! My little cuppy cake. My sweet, adorable Sherlyn. Oh, how I've missed you."

She stepped away. It wasn't the monster talking. The voice was coming through the speaker-box on Moreci's chest. A red light blinked wildly near the black circle. But she recognized the voice. She would always recognize *his* voice.

"Oh my goodness." He laughed hysterically. "I wish… I wish you could see the look on your face." His laughter was manic, uncontrollable. *Diabolical.*

Fear and trembling and anger and wrath coursed through her blood. The voice came from the one she had been searching for all this time.

"*Ronan.*"

CHAPTER 35

Lower passenger deck

Dawn's Edge

Fang had killed the remaining guard, slipped into a servant's dress, and helped evacuate the passengers and crew to the emergency skiff. Less than two hundred remained. She stood at the door and escorted them one by one, keeping an eye out for Moreci's guards, the Turned and, of course, Coyle. The ache in her arm was almost unbearable and her strength waned considerably. She leaned against a doorframe, panting. If she didn't get treatment soon, she would most certainly succumb to its effect. It made her weak, not just in the physical aspect but also in the carnality of her vampiric desires. A deep-rooted hunger grew inside her, one she could barely resist.

Her eyes searched for men and women who had stains of guilt on their conscience. As yet, none of these people were murderers or rapists, but the hunger grew still. She closed her eyes and concentrated, trying to stop the floor from moving underneath her. She had to get these people to safety. She hoped Coyle would make an appearance soon.

The skiff was roughly half the length of the *Dawn's Edge* but only one level. It was equipped with gnomish technology: short, stubby wings would slip out from underneath the craft and, coupled with something the gnomes called a propeller system, bring passengers safely to the ground.

A bell rang. The ship would leave soon. The bridge was full of activity. A few automatons were stationed throughout the bridge, checking on gauges and pressure settings. Men in gray-and-tan uniforms busied themselves with instrument panels. Other servants helped with minor wounds, food and drink, making the passengers as comfortable as possible.

With a dizzy head, Fang kept her eye on the hall. The crowd of passengers was thinning, and she knew they were running out of time. She wondered if this was the best way of doing things. It certainly seemed so. But who leaves a friend—

Were the two of them friends? Embeth certainly thought so. Coyle was brilliant, sharp and brave. Fang felt as though Coyle could handle herself with Moreci. She trusted her to. And yet, Fang knew she was staying away from Moreci because his blood, his very aura, was toxic to her. She wouldn't survive two minutes in his presence.

She almost hadn't when she'd visited Trevin. She shook her head. Coyle should be on her way.

Soon.

The giant airship groaned. Fang used her sharp senses and listened. Cracks of timber. Shattered glass. Tearing metal.

Not good.

The skiff shuddered, and the crew shouted for all doors to be closed. It was leaving. Fang used her Reach. Coyle was terrified, confused, but close enough to make it to the ship. She would make it. Fang leaned against the doorframe and stared at the hall. And then she heard them.

The Turned were coming.

***

Coyle stepped backward. "What's... what's happening?"

The monster took a step forward. "Oh, really now. What kind of a question is that? *What's happening*. A more interesting question would be, what's *been* happening?"

She raised her pistol and fired. A red cloud of blood exploded on the creature's chest.

"*Now* you want to kill him," Ronan said. "A bit late for that, don't you think? I mean, look at him." The creature grunted.

"What do you mean, what's been happening? I don't understand."

"Ah, much better. Let's take a walk down memory lane, shall we? I challenged you to find me, didn't I? Yes, and you became a constable until you tried out for the detective spot. But you were disqualified. Remember *why*?"

"I punched—"

"No, no."

"My pad of paper was—" *Oh, no!*

"Yes."

"You pickpocketed me."

"You were so delicious that day! Your busy mind fixated on the tests—and me, probably. Right? Always thinking of me. And you never noticed your old lover standing *so* very close to you, never noticed me bumping into you and taking your little pad of paper." He laughed. "Oh, it was such a fun game to watch you solve Fang's little murder mystery, and trust me, I was rooting for you the entire time."

"Why—"

"And then little Fang introduced herself to you. Did she tell you how she got locked in the clink?"

"No."

"Me! I was responsible for putting her there. Goodness, I have my hands in a great many things. It keeps me very busy. And here you thought I was only involved in dismemberment and evisceration. Did she tell you how she was broken out?"

"You?"

"Me again. I paid some hooligans to get her out, only I knew Fang would be more than a handful for those putzes. Oh, she's splendid, just splendid. Anyway, let me tell you about my work. Do you know whose idea it was to infuse aurorium into Moreci and Trevin? Do you know who left the moving-picture box and journal in Trevin's cavern? Do you know who's been giving orders to Moreci and Veiul, taking special care not to kill you? Oh! Another big one, and then we'll move on. Do you know who left the wonderful secret messages for you to work out?"

"You."

"Me, me, me, and all me. And here you are, up here in a ship about to be blown to hell."

424

"But why?"

"Easy."

"No. Don't you dare." She pointed the gun at the creature. At *him*.

"Oh, but I will. You know my heart, and I know yours. We will always desire each other's touch. Our ears yearn for the other's voice. And yet we couldn't have each other for so many reasons. Shakespeare said it best: '*the course of true love never did run smooth.*' I love you, dear Sherlyn. Love you to death and back."

Coyle fired, but her aim was thrown off when the floor cracked open. She screamed and slipped through the broken wood into purple lights and steam. She landed in the debris and scurried up. Her hands were empty. The gun wasn't anywhere to be found. The book? Gone.

The sound of the ship being torn apart was pierced by Ronan's cackling. The monster pulled the floors apart and peeked down at her.

"Wait, you're not leaving, are you? Was it something I said?"

She scrambled up and ran. Howls of laughter echoed through the chaos. She followed the stairs, racing down to the escape ship. She turned down a hall, then headed through a large room. All the while hearing the ominous pounding of the creature's feet. She stopped, trying to decide which direction to turn. Debris exploded, showering her with dust and chips of wood. The creature's head burst through a wall, a mouth full of teeth grinning at her. She pushed herself away until her back pushed into a table.

"You know the funny thing, Sherlyn. You actually took my job position. Yes, I was a detective with the Templars. But, you know, they had a few things they didn't like about me. Something, something mad as a hatter, they said. They kicked me out, but I wanted to get even. It took some planning, of course. Lots of planning. But it looks like it's paying off, doesn't it?"

Claws lunged out and scratched at her side, but she barely escaped their grip. She ran down the hall.

"Oh, stop running, Sherlyn," Ronan said. "Come here and give Daddy a hug."

She flew down more steps and into another hall. Unearthly moans filled the air. She glanced behind. The Turned, with their familiar loping, were in the distance. They were after her. She sprinted with renewed energy when a cool wind caught her attention. She turned and followed the stream of cold air. A platform was at the end of the hallway.

The escape ship!

Just a few more yards to safety. But her slight pause gave the Turned the advantage, and they were yards away from tearing her apart. She was above the skiff, on a maintenance bridge, and the small ship's engines were humming. She turned back. The Turned were almost upon her. She didn't have time to run down the stairs. With a cry, she ran, leapt over the railing and crashed onto the glass roof of the skiff. She barely had time to roll aside before the ghouls landed next to her.

***

Passengers and crew looked up as the creatures slammed onto the glass roof, one after another. One of them broke through, then another.

The captain shouted to launch.

Cables and clamps unhooked themselves from the skiff, and the craft shuddered. Chaos erupted as the creatures poured in. Shots were fired.

Fang pulled out her daggers and jammed them into the nearest Turned. More Turned landed amidst groups of passengers and attacked. She leapt into the fray.

***

Brittle wind tore through Coyle's leathers as the skiff dropped nose-first into the sky. She leaned back and glanced up. The *Dawn's Edge* loomed above. Streaks of purple lightning crawled over the skin of the ship. The Turned had come after her. She got up, pulled her knives out, and slammed them into the nearest head.

***

The propeller blared to life. Fang slammed her daggers into another Turned, but they kept pouring through the broken glass overhead. Each of them landed and went in a different direction. Some of the passengers bled from open wounds. Some of them were too wounded to recover. And still she moved and fought with every fiber of her being.

Fang looked up. Coyle was doing what she could. Fang smiled, and then she was tackled by a swarm of writhing claws and sharp teeth. She was strong, but handling multiple assailants at once was tricky. Especially when they were ghouls.

And especially when she was dying.

The room lurched. She strained her neck toward the bridge. The Turned were attacking the pilots. Fang glanced up. Coyle had lost her balance and fallen to one side. The *Dawn's Edge* spun into view. The crew lost control. They were on a collision course with the larger ship.

She pushed away from the floor with all her strength. Claws dug into her skin. Blood spilled from her broken skin. But she stood, killed the remaining ghouls and raced to the bridge.

***

Coyle gasped. The escape ship was on a collision course with the *Dawn's Edge,* heading for the cargo hold. Misshapen ghouls came into view from the open bay. The glass dome skidded just under the cargo hold. The Turned jumped onto the glass surface. Some lost their balance and fell into the spinning propeller's, exploding into torn flesh. Nevertheless, the ghouls leapt and dropped onto the skiff's dome, pushing Coyle further away from safety, closer to the edge. She shoved her knife into one and pushed off. Another set of hands grabbed her legs—another knife to the head. She pulled herself into a ball and backed away. More Turned fell onto the surface of the dome and still more dropped into the empty sky as the skiff pulled away from the airship. She stabbed another and another, but still they came.

The glass beneath her chipped and cracked. She stopped and swung into the nearest ghoul. Then another. Then another. Then another. Blood ran thick down her arms, but her blades found their mark time and time again. The fetid breath of the Turned became a noxious vapor to her. Dead hands searched for her skin. Screeches and hisses filled her ears.

Coyle wasn't thinking anymore. Survival was the only option her body recognized. Her arms pushed and stabbed repeatedly, and still the things came. Her lungs burned. Her arms were stiff. She stumbled back, and they fell on her. Digging. Clawing. Scratching. Howling.

She remembered her Tesla Fist and squeezed her hand. Nothing happened. The hordes came. And then she knew she was going to die.

***

Fang punched a ghoul with her blade and it dropped in a heap. More were tackling the crew and slamming into the controls. The ship leaned to the side and everyone slid and tumbled. She had to get the bridge clear of Turned if they were to make it safely to the ground. She was tackled again, and a horrible stabbing pain burned into her midsection. She ignored the wound and flipped backward, bashing the heads of several ghouls. Fury filled her veins, and she spun in the air with the ferocity of a hurricane. Her bare fists swung into the creatures. Her blades and arms were soaked with gore. Weakness soaked into her muscles.

Doubt clouded her mind.

***

The ship tilted, and ghouls stumbled aside and fell. Coyle balanced as best she could and watched the monsters bounce and slide off the ship. The ship lurched and she fell backward, twisting and crawling away from the mass of writhing arms. She pulled herself up and wiped blood from her nose. She wasn't sure how long she could keep this up. Something had to change for the better.

A massive shape rose from the pile, staring at her with dead, bloodshot eyes. Tubes flailed from a contraption on its back. Glowing orange blood seeped from wounds in its skin, from its jagged mouth, from its misshapen eyes and nose.

"Hello, Sherlyn," Ronan said. "You were probably wondering where I was. Didn't want you to worry— Oh, my goodness, what a view! Here, let me get closer so we can enjoy it together."

Knocking aside Turned, the creature roared and lumbered towards her. She glanced at the edge of the skiff and wondered which death would be better.

The ship lurched again, and she skidded to a stop. Massive waves of air rushed past her. She over her shoulder. The spinning propeller blades were too close. She carefully pushed herself away and glanced up. Ghouls pushed themselves up off the dome and searched for her. The Moreci creature slammed his fist into the glass and raised his arm in the air. Long, razor-sharp shards jutted out from his fist and flashed in the light.

"I have something for you, my pretty little sweet nothing. Where are you? Ah! There you are. And here I thought you were powerful enough. Unless you have an amazing trick up your sleeve? But, no. This is where you die, up here in the sky."

Coyle fought against the tide of panic. Tears blurred away the shapes coming toward her.

***

Fang looked up at the giant horror. His misshapen body. His impossibly long arm and claws. His glowing, aurorium-infused blood splashed and bled and ran all over him. She was unfamiliar with dread, but the sight before her filled her with it.

"Don't go up there," Embeth said.

"If I don't, she'll die," Fang said.

"If you do, *you* will."

"Promise you'll be waiting for me, then."

***

The small ship shifted and plunged. Coyle's insides trembled as the ship dropped from the sky. Her body lifted off the glass and floated before the ship righted itself and pitched to the side. She slammed into the glass and skidded. The edge rushed closer. Open sky waited to swallow her.

A hand reached out from the broken glass and grabbed hers. She held it and looked. Fang looked back from the other side of the glass. The ship pitched on end, but she held onto Fang with all her strength as her legs dangled in the open air. Turned slid past her and screeched as they tumbled off. The ship rolled again, and she was back on top.

With Coyle's help, Fang pulled herself out onto the glass roof. They glanced at each other. Their leathers were sliced open and tattered. Blood ran from open wounds and cuts. Their hair was a tangled mess in the wind. They nodded to each other, before facing the beastly Moreci. He opened his torn mouth and roared. Spittle flew from his mouth in red strings.

"Ah, there you are, Fang! So good to see you again."

"Ronan?"

"You know him?" Coyle asked.

"Long story," Fang answered.

"The three of us can have a nice, long chat sometime in a cabin with a cozy fireplace. An aged brandy. Dim candlelight. Assuming, the two of you make it out alive."

"I'm not going to make it," Fang said. Her body trembled and for the first time, Coyle saw the hopelessness in her eyes. "My head's cloudy. Can't think straight. Usually I'm the one who comes up with the plan, but I'm a mess."

"Stay behind me," Coyle said. "We'll find a way. Together."

Coyle charged and Fang followed, stabbing and slashing anything that got close. Moreci swung at Coyle. She flew back. He grabbed Fang and slammed her into the glass, once, twice and then tossed her aside.

Coyle charged again and leapt on top of him. Her knife slammed into the creature's skull, but he didn't drop. He grabbed her, brought her close to his mouth and squeezed. The air rushed out of her lungs. He roared into her face. She tried to twist away, but he was too strong. She could barely breathe.

Fang leapt onto his back and slammed both daggers into his skull. Glowing, orange blood sprayed her face. Soaked into her skin. Every plunge of her blades became weaker.

He tossed Coyle to the side. Her body tumbled, and she reached out to stop herself from rushing into the propellers. The spinning blades less than yard away. She glanced back. Moreci slammed Fang into the glass. Her arms flailed like a rag doll. She was covered in aurorium blood. He tossed her into Coyle. Fang's broken body slid. Coyle pulled her close, held her tight and looked up.

"Aww, there you are. Such a nice duo. Coyle and Fang has such a nice ring to it, doesn't it? I say, it's better than Coyle and Moriarty, though our love for each other eclipses your friendship with this pitiful vampire," Ronan said.

Coyle glanced down at Fang's still form. The vampire she never wanted to trust or help, let alone be near was now in her arms.

Defenseless, helpless, close to death if not there by now. And yet, despite all that Coyle leaned in and squeezed her friend. If they would die, then they would go together.

And that's when she saw it.

Coyle pulled out Fang's baton and pointed it at the monster. She flicked her wrist, cable spun out and wrapped itself around the misshapen, glass-studded arm. The creature held up its arm, inspecting the tangle of wire.

"Oh my goodness," he said. "Sweet cakes? You must have thought this was a weapon of some sort. And here I thought you were more powerful. All this work, only to end up here in the sky. And now you'll never why I did all this. Ah, then. Time to die."

"You first." With a flick of her wrist, the baton shot a cable out its other end and into the propeller.

"Oh," Ronan's voice crackled.

She let go before the monstrous form zipped by into the spinning blades and exploded. Bones and flesh and glowing blood splashed the glass-domed roof. The propellers shattered. And then the ship lurched, shuddered and fell.

CHAPTER 36

Two weeks later

The Treece mansion

Sausalito

Coyle stirred another cube of sugar into her cup of tea. She stared at the dark liquid spinning inside the white porcelain and caught her purple eye in the reflection. She shrank back and looked outside. Lace curtains curled in the light breeze, but she could see the rise of green hills across the bay. The streets of San Francisco were busy with people going about their day, running errands, gathering their shopping, holding hands or walking alone. All of them carrying on with their lives as if she hadn't helped save thousands from being Turned.

It had been more than two weeks since the *Dawn's Point* fell out of the sky and crashed into the plains of Iowa. The ship was low enough to the earth so that almost all of the two hundred passengers aboard the rescue ship walked away without too much injury. The *Dawn's Edge* turned into a strange twisted ball of steel and purple lightning before it disappeared in a ball of chaos. Newspapers had a field day with the witness reports of strange lightning in the sky, blaming everything on the nether realm.

The corpses of the Turned had been collected and shipped back to San Francisco under the strict control of the Templars where they would studied before being buried in a mass, undisclosed grave.

A quiet knock on the door gave her the opportunity to focus on something else. Gibby, the train attendant, opened the door with her usual demure smile.

<Tea good?> Gibby asked.

<Yes, thank you. News for me?>

Gibby glanced behind her before signing, <Nothing. No one's seen or heard from Fang. No one knows where she is.>

Coyle looked down at her fingers, before signing, <Thank you.>

<I'll keep my ears open.> They both smiled and with that, Gibby left.

Coyle stared at the mirror across the room, catching just the top of her head. It was just as well. She didn't really want to see herself all bandaged up and bruised. Her body felt as though she had been dragged by a carriage. It was lucky she had been covered in bruises instead of having every bone in her body broken. And what of Fang? She had disappeared in midst of the carnage. And now she was gone without a trace.

But, where?

The why was understandable; almost everyone wanted her dead. Everyone except Coyle. They had formed a quick friendship since that jail cell so long ago. Both of them broken in their own way, and yet they complimented each so well bringing the villainous Moreci to an end.

Together.

Another knock on the door. But, this wasn't Gibby's uncertain, sheepish knock.

"Come in," Coyle said.

Treece opened the door. His face fraught with concern, yet doing his best to smile. She sat up.

"No, no. Don't worry. You need to rest as much as you can." He pulled a chair close. "Can we talk?"

"Yes."

"I feel we, or rather I, owe you an explanation. The past month has been quite remarkable, and I'm not sure where to start."

"Why not at the beginning?"

He cleared his throat. "You deserve that. Ronan James Moriarty was one of our own—a top detective, in fact. But Ronan had many issues, and we discovered he had been hiding things. At first we believed he was suffering from mania, which is common in our line of work when dealing with strange phenomena. But then evidence arrived that he was absolutely disturbed. He vanished without a trace before we could bring him in." Treece straightened his tie and smoothed wrinkles from his coat.

"We looked for him for quite some time. There was word he had... fallen in love with a young woman, but we weren't sure who or where she was."

Coyle frowned.

"We heard a rumor she was a sleuth of sorts. And when you successfully completed the detective tryouts—"

"You used me as bait."

Treece studied his fingertips, sparing her only the slightest glance. He sighed and stood, buttoning his coat.

"We had to draw him out, find out anything we could," he said. "And you were stellar." He pulled out a small wooden box and handed it to her.

She held it in her hands, hefted its weight. She knew what it was and set it aside. Her eyes settled on staring at her feet.

"You worked very hard for that. What's more, you deserve it."

"I feel as though I'm being paid off."

"Detective Coyle, you'll need a front if you're going to become a Templar. Working for a local police department is perfect. You'll be a detective for them and for us."

"And why would I want to join the Templars?"

"Because we know where he was hiding. And we want you to find him for us—and for you. It will take some time, but we're confident you can find him."

"I'll join, but only if it's the two of us."

The look in his eye became defiant. "Coyle. She's a loose cannon."

"And yet the pair of us managed to survive against insurmountable odds, and together we defeated the villain."

Treece huffed and crossed his arms.

"Fang's not meant to be controlled, you found that out the hard way. She's meant to be part of a team, meant to be respected the way any other creature in God's green earth deserves."

Treece stepped to the window and pushed aside the curtains.

"We made a deal," Coyle said. "I help her find Moreci and she helps me find Ronan. I can't find him without her. And I won't."

He stepped away from the window and sighed. "A seasoned professional, such as Agent Fang, and a novice, such as yourself did manage to pull off a frightful event. I'll speak to the Templar Committee on your behalf and ensure she won't be harmed. But I do warn you, Coyle, she is quite dangerous and there's no telling how far you can trust her."

He gave her a small nod and left.

She stared at the box before glancing outside the window. The green hills disappeared into plumes of fog. Bells of a passing ship rang in the distance. If she squinted, she would be able to see people milling about through the streets, ogreks working on the docks, gnomes with insane amounts of colored hair, busy as bees. People enjoying what they did best.

She pushed herself up and reached for the box.

THE END

EPILOGUE
May, 1893

The locomotive *Pegasus*, en route to Chicago

Coyle sat in one of the lounge cars, studying a small herd of wild horses as they galloped along the flat scrub of Wyoming, their wild manes flying. Sunlight glimmered off their shoulders. Coyle wondered where they were headed. Did they run out of necessity? Were they pushed away by predators? Or were they running just because they could? God designed them that way of course.

And was she hurtling toward Chicago, the last known location of Ronan because God designed her this way? All this time, she wasn't sure if He was even listening. And yet, she made it out alive and stopped Moreci—with the help of Fang. She couldn't deny the prayers of a righteous person were effective. But, she wasn't righteous. Or was she? Was chasing Ronan out of duty to the Templars, her own sense of justice, or something else?

Her eyes refocused. The window glass reflected the outline of someone behind her. Female, tall, thin. Poised.

"Good afternoon, Fang," Coyle said. "Lovely outside."

There was a pause as if the vampire were considering the truth of the suggestion. "Suppose so," Fang said. "Mind if I join you?"

"Please," Coyle said. "Tea?"

"Coffee for me."

Coyle signed to Gibby, who was seated nearby and the girl went to find a fresh pot. Fang sat without a sound. Both set their eyes to the passing scenery. The train clicked its rhythmic strokes as they sat in comfortable silence.

After a few moments, Gibby arrived with a cup and saucer and poured coffee. Coyle glanced at her and smiled. The young woman smiled back.

<Anything else?> Gibby asked. Coyle shook her head, and Gibby took her seat.

Fang frowned at Coyle.

"She said she wants to stay by my side and be my assistant," Coyle said. "It's very nice of her."

"First it was GEM, and now it's this girl that wants to stay with you."

"No," Coyle smiled. "You were first, remember?"

A ghost of a smile crossed Fang's lips.

"Cream or sugar?" Coyle motioned to the small pots.

"I like my coffee like my dreams," Fang said. "Black and full of bitterness." There was a pause before they both laughed.

"I take it you're fully recovered?" Fang asked.

"Muscles are still quite sore. I take it *you're* fully recovered?"

Fang answered with a slow nod.

"Bodies kept piling up in the streets." Coyle lowered her voice to just above a whisper. "I was worried there was another… of your kind, until we checked their records. All of them were wanted murderers and rapists. The police paid it no mind, but the Templars began to suspect you."

"I'm always a suspect," Fang said. She blew on her coffee and kept her eyes outside. Silence settled between them. The train tracks clicked and clacked.

The vampire turned and met Coyle's eyes. "There is something refreshing about you."

"Trust?" Coyle said.

She nodded. "Trust. Professionalism. The persistence of a bloodhound." They shared a smile. "Admirable qualities."

"I could say the same about you, Fang," Coyle said. "And I could add a few more. I would much rather be working with you than against you."

"Same," Fang said.

"I've never worked with a vampire. Never even known one. You were remarkable through our whole ordeal. You wanted to do the right thing, and you succeeded."

"I know who I am, but I still have a heart, Coyle," Fang said.

"And that was my fault for being judgmental. I find it both a blessing and a curse, my talent for making assumptions within a few seconds of meeting people."

Fang shrugged. "We all have our issues, don't we?"

Coyle nodded and sipped her tea. "You enjoy stabbing people," she said.

Fang nodded. "And you enjoy marking people before you know them."

Coyle shrugged. "I'm right." She took another sip. "Most of the time."

"And I only stab the bad ones." Fang sipped her coffee. "You handle confrontation fairly well," Fang said. Her smile faded, and she stared at Coyle. "How did you survive the man who cut you open?"

Coyle faced the window, but her eyes turned to meet Fang's.

"He was my fiancé," she said. "He cut me open but let me live. Said I was his nemesis and challenged me to catch him. And that's what I intend to do."

They remained silent for a time and sipped their drinks.

"What do you think will happen when we find him?" Fang asked.

"What do you suppose Embeth would want?"

Fang looked outside and shook her head. "She's gone. I haven't seen her since … our time on the ship. There's been nothing. Not even a whisper. And now the whole ordeal has made me wonder; was she there with me or not? Either way, I don't know what I would do without her." Fang bit her lip, her shoulders trembled. She raised a hand to her eyes. Gibby brought her a handkerchief. Coyle got out of her seat and scooted next to Fang, pulling her close, but said nothing.

Coyle was always good with words, but right now there were no words to console Fang. The vampire shook gently and dapped her eyes.

"I'm a wreck," Fang said, sniffling.

"We're both wrecks." Coyle squeezed Fang's hand. "And together, we'll be beautiful wrecks."

Fang dabbed her eyes. "Thank you, Coyle. I know I wouldn't have survived without your help."

"Same."

After a few long minutes, Coyle returned to her seat and smiled. "You know, we've never properly introduced ourselves, so let's do this the right way." She stretched across the table. "My full name is Sherlyn Rebecca Holmes. My sisters called me Sherlock, just because, right? And Coyle is my mother's maiden name."

Fang accepted the handshake. "My Christian name was Charlotte Ann Watson."

"I promised myself I would never use my surname. It reminds me too much of my father, so I'm just Sherlyn R. Coyle."

"And I'm just Fang, for obvious reasons."

They chuckled as bushes and hills and horses passed and the train tracks clicked away. Coyle stared outside, a delightful warmth filled her soul. Fang looked down at her wrist and scratched at the curious dark streaks that had spread from Veiul's auroium-tipped blade.

***

The locomotive *Griffin*, en route to Chicago

On a different train, heading in the same direction, another pair were conspiring. Two men were having a discussion regarding the proper elements of hunting.

"The most important thing you need is prey," said one gentleman. His English accent was mild, though his tone was condescending. The small, round frames of his glasses reflected the light from the window, giving his eyes a strange white light. A white scar ran lengthwise from the top of his head, down past his small chin. He took a puff from his cigar before continuing. "Prey for the hunt is the perfect matter, especially at hand."

The other shook his head and scratched the thin, neatly trimmed beard of his thick jaw. "You don't understand hunting," he said in a thick Dutch accent. "I do. I've been hunting much longer than you. And the hunting we're up to will need the right weapons. Besides, lab coats and Bunsen burners are more your style. Leave the weapons of the hunt to me."

Their discussion continued until finally they were interrupted. A tall, slender woman arrived at their table and cleared her throat.

"Excuse me, may I have this seat?" the woman asked. Her reddish-brown curls lay stacked in perfect mounds on her shoulders and framed a mildly attractive, although sharp features. Her dark eyes darted around and caught everything, much the way a hawk would. Her dress was finely crafted silk from the latest designers in Paris. The shape of her commanded attention and most every eye turned her way.

"But of course," said the one with his English accent.

She sat, and her personal attendant offered her a cigarette from a solid gold case. The woman pulled one out, and the attendant lit the cigarette with a solid gold lighter before taking his place behind her. She took a long drag and exhaled.

"Doctors, you understand we are heading for Chicago during the grand opening of the World's Columbian Exposition. It will be quite the scene, as they say. Do keep in mind we are also heading there, not for sight-seeing, but for the successful apprehension of one Ronan James Moriarty."

Both men nodded, and she smiled. She took a long drag and let the smoke drift lazily from her full, red lips.

"Good to hear. And you also know *she* is on the *Pegasus*. Just made an appearance, as a matter of fact."

"We do," said the one with the Dutch accent. "I tracked her movements and suspected she would contact detective Coyle in due time." He side-eyed his acquaintance. "And, although we have a difference as to the execution of our plan, we believe it work, Miss Maycroft."

"That's what I like to hear," she said, nodding to each. "I don't hire people to give me their best attempt. And my dearest younger sister, Sherlyn is at stake here. Then, Dr. Van Helsing and Dr. Jeckyll, let's go over this plan on how to kill an unkillable vampire. And you know the rules of the Cult of the Damned: no aurorium."

The men smiled and shared their plan.

If you enjoyed this story (or didn't), please leave a review! Thanks so much!

Coming May 28th, 2021

Coyle and Fang: Prey for the Hunt

You can pre-order the second book in the series here.

Sign up for the free novella, Coyle and Fang: The Bride along with the Coyle and Fang Dispatch newsletter for updates and exclusives.

CoyleandFang

Acknowledgements

This book wouldn't be the same without giving proper thanks.

My first thanks go to my wife of 30 years, Katie. My head is full of ideas and I barely make a dent moving forward with them. When I told her I wanted to write a book, she nodded and smiled the way she always did when she heard my crazy ideas. She gave me plenty of space and time to tap away at the keyboard until I was ready to let her read. She became my proof-reader and always gave me positive feedback with a critical eye. Thank you so much for the time you gave me!

A wonderful set of colleagues in the Historical Fiction Writer's Group has been a great help with the small details and questions I hadn't thought of before. Tons of laughs, helpful tips and brutally honest feedback ("*She didn't really think that, did she?*") were key to shaping this story.

My editor, Amanda Bidnall showed me how to make a decent story into a great story. All of her advice was gold and I implemented all the changes she suggested. And besides all that, she was absolutely fun and easy to work with. This book is a product of her wisdom and guidance. http://amandabidnall.com/

A great chap named Daniel Reed helped me in regards to writing deaf characters. I met him on Facebook and he was so helpful answering my questions. Thanks Daniel!

Great book covers aren't easy to come by, but Christian Bentulan knocked it out of the park! He was patient, professional, helpful and super-friendly! If you picked up this book based on the cover, it's because of him! https://coversbychristian.com/

I have a great help in building my website through ModFarm. Rob McClellan and his team provide the ultimate in website design and great customer service.

Writing historical fiction couldn't be done without the proper resources. The late Herbert Asbury wrote the gem, The Barbary Coast-An Informal History of the San Francisco Underworld. Informative, detailed and engaging, this book was kept within reach throughout my drafts.

Most of Coyle's prayers were taken from The Valley of Vision-A collection of Puritan Prayers and Devotions. This book is filled with wonderful and challenging thoughts about God and life.

And of course, this book wouldn't be possible without awesome readers like you!

About the author

Robert Adauto fancies writing action and adventure stories with fascinating characters. He lives with his wife of thirty years in Southern California, where they enjoy taking care of their three cats and blind rescue dog. When he's not writing, he loves to draw, drink coffee and find interesting things in thrift stores.

Author's note

Action and adventure with some supernatural elements are definitely my favorite genre. The stories are quick, engaging and fun to read. And these are exactly what I wanted to write. Curse of Shadows has all of that in spades and I love just about every page.

The ideas for this series began about spring of 2019. I knew I wanted a detective series with a female protagonist and after some thinking, I set the time period as Victorian era, due to the aesthetics, the possibility of new gadgets and contraptions and there were some wonderfully crafted characters I could use. I felt the time period would also serve as an antagonistic background for Coyle's endeavors.

While Coyle was relatively easy to put together, Fang was much more difficult. I knew she was going to be an assassin, but I wasn't happy with any iteration I put together. While perusing through one of my writing groups, I noticed some people were talking about vampires (and not in a positive light, mind you). And yet, a light bulb clicked. At first I was apprehensive writing about a vampire assassin, but I knew this was the direction to go, it was too much fun writing her scenes! And her name was always going to be Fang, I mean it makes sense, doesn't?

As to the last reveal and their introductions. The idea of this story being a retelling of one of my favorite characters, Sherlock Holmes passed through my head a few times. I dreaded what people would say, mostly because I'm nowhere near a fine author as to do Sherlock justice. But, I put it in and said, heck with it. It's my book, so there.

This is the first book in a series. I have so many ideas for this pair and I can't wait to continue sharing these fun stories with you! I'd love to hear your feedback, whatever it may be. Write me at Robert@coyleandfang.com

Until then, stay safe and keep your necks guarded!

CPSIA information can be obtained
at www.ICGtesting.com
Printed in the USA
LVHW050725090421
683977LV00016B/602